A Daring PROPOSAL

JENNIE GOUTET

A Daring PROPOSAL

JENNIE GOUTET

SWEETWATER
BOOKS

AN IMPRINT OF CEDAR FORT, INC.
SPRINGVILLE, UTAH

ISBN 13: 978-1-4621-3958-3

Published by Sweetwater Books, an imprint of Cedar Fort, Inc.
2373 W. 700 S., Springville, UT 84663
Distributed by Cedar Fort, Inc., www.cedarfort.com

Library of Congress Control Number: 2021950624

Cover design by Courtney Proby
Cover design © 2022 Cedar Fort, Inc.

Printed in the United States of America

10 9 8 7 6 5 4 3 2 1

Printed on acid-free paper

Dedicated to my father, Stephen Wayne Lawlis.

From you, I learned that history is far from boring.

Chapter One

*P*hoebe Tunstall stretched a hand out from within the warmth of her fur-trimmed cloak, revealing a glimpse of her white spencer as she waited at the edge of Hyde Park's Round Pond. Two swans shifted course, leaving an arrow of ripples behind them, and swam toward Phoebe as she released a handful of large crumbs. The swans dipped their orange beaks repeatedly into the water to retrieve the feast before turning in one smooth movement and gliding away.

"I am glad they did not see fit to make our closer acquaintance," Anna observed from the path bordering the pond. "I am not sure our fingers would have survived the introduction." Anna was Phoebe's identical twin, distinguished at present by the telltale bump giving form to her redingote and by the accompanying fullness in her features. She pulled her muff closer to her middle and waited for her sister.

Phoebe stepped away from the water and trudged up the incline. The ground was stiff with frozen earth and grass. With a wisp of regret for a world that moved on without her, she glanced over her shoulder at the departing swans before regaining the path. The birds had swallowed up what she had offered, then left to pursue their own purposes and pleasures. Their flight seemed to mimic a certain pattern in Phoebe's life, and the gray, late winter clouds were a fitting parallel to her mood.

"The swans here are not aggressive." Phoebe rejoined the path and linked her arm through Anna's. "Shall we return home? If you are to get the timely start to your journey that Harry hopes for, you had best make haste."

"Nurse is caring for Peter, the trunks are packed, and Harry knows that the word *haste* does not appear in my vocabulary." Anna smiled at Phoebe but picked up her pace. Their breath came out in clouds as they followed the path leading toward the gates of Hyde Park. There was no one else about, which was not surprising, since it was early and cold.

Phoebe's heart was too heavy for her to speak, and in the mystical way of their twinship, Anna put Phoebe's feelings into words. "It is such a misfortune that you must endure the Season without any of your particular friends here to share it with you. What will you do? I cannot think Mrs. Morris an acceptable companion for you." Anna sent her sister a wry, scolding glance. "It was one thing for you to wait hand and foot on Aunt Shea. She was flesh and blood. It is quite another thing for you to endure the conversation of the likes of Mrs. Morris. Wherever did Stratford dredge such a woman up?"

Mrs. Morris, a hired companion, had come recommended by the aunt of Eleanor, their brother's wife. Phoebe knew Anna's rallying tone was meant to lift her mood, but her spirits were so uncommonly low she was not sure anything could. "It is meant to be a temporary solution. I suppose it serves well enough for now."

At age twenty-two, Phoebe had given up the hope of being married. She supposed it was ridiculous that she should, for twenty-two was not so very old in truth. But after being consistently overlooked for four London Seasons, she had begun to wonder if she were simply uninteresting next to her more engaging twin. Or perhaps the gentlemen sensed that Phoebe's heart was not entirely free.

This Season, there had been no one to sponsor her, as Stratford and Eleanor were about to welcome their first child into the world, and their brother and his wife were the only family left to Anna and Phoebe. Anna's life was now with her husband and son in the quiet town of Avebury, and that Anna was content with her lot surprised no one more than she. That left Phoebe, the only one of her siblings or friends yet unmarried. Despite the fact that Stratford had granted Phoebe the use of his house for the upcoming Season, nothing plunged her spirits more than the thought of attending all the ton events with Mrs. Morris as companion. The only silver lining to be found in the past months spent with Mrs. Morris was that she rarely appeared before noon, and Phoebe was an early riser.

Arm in arm, the sisters exited the park and walked along the flagway bordering the busy street that was crowded with hacks and the more humble carriages. The fashionable set would still be abed. Anna refrained from her usual light chatter, which Phoebe knew meant she was about to speak her mind on a weightier issue. At last, she did.

"Phoebe, I am convinced that this is not your destiny." Anna squeezed her arm to emphasize the point. "You have spent enough years seeing to the needs of others. You have had four Seasons, and it is not your lack of beauty—if I may say so myself—nor your conversation that has made you ineligible. It is only that by your reserve you give off the impression you are unavailable. But I cannot see this as your life. To serve as companion to a disagreeable older woman instead of her serving you? For that is what the arrangement will become if you do not take care."

Anna's words were just, and Phoebe knew it. Her relationship with her companion had already begun to shift. Where Mrs. Morris had arrived, eager to please and propose entertainment, she had now begun giving Phoebe suggestions that surmounted to orders designed to curtail Phoebe's fun. *A morning call on Miss Harris is not convenient today; she is not likely to be home. It is too cold to attend the theater tonight; you will fall ill. The Maxwells' dinner party will prove to be insipid; wait until the Season is in full swing before attempting such a thing.* It took more will than Phoebe possessed to argue.

"There is truth to your words, I suppose. But I do not see how I can change anything now." Phoebe knew that deep down she feared missing a Season meant giving up her chance to be married. And she *so* wanted to marry, even if the man she had always loved had never once looked at her in a way that allowed her to hope. But he would be in London this Season, and perhaps at last he would . . .

No. She must give it up. After all, no one had ever guessed. Not even Anna—not even his sister, Lydia. Certainly not him.

Phoebe mustered a smile to reassure her sister and hide the melancholy plunge her thoughts had taken. "I don't suppose you have an eligible bachelor sitting around in the town of Avebury, pining away for a wife?"

"That we do not have, I am sorry to say. Nor are we likely to find one in Avebury when it comes time to securing matches for our children. Harry knows that several London Seasons are in his future when it is time for our daughters to make their come out. He has promised to bear it cheerfully."

"Supposing you have at least one girl," Phoebe said.

Anna rested a hand on her midsection. "I believe we may not have to wait long for that. This one is showing herself to be more capricious than Peter ever was. Demanding oranges every day!"

Phoebe laughed, filling her lungs with cold air and grasping at the flash of joy that came from humor and sisters who were increasing again. It was a short walk to Stratford's townhouse, where they had been staying for the past month. Anna's husband, Harry Aston, had not liked to leave his parish for such a length of time, so after having accompanied his wife and son to London, he left the sisters to their own company. He had returned only yesterday to escort Anna and Peter home.

As they drew near the house, Anna chuckled suddenly. "I had quite forgotten to tell you that I had run into one of your acquaintances upon our arrival in London. A short girl with a profusion of freckles and exclamations. She mistook me for you, so I am assuming she does not know you have an identical twin."

"Yes." Phoebe suppressed a sigh. "You must mean Martha Cummings. She is bent on a more intimate acquaintance, which I've been trying to discourage without much luck. She is most determined in her affection. We were introduced last Season, and for reasons unbeknownst to me, Martha has taken a liking to me."

Anna slipped her arm out of Phoebe's and grasped the railing of the townhouse to climb the steps. "I may have led her to believe you were above her touch."

Her sister's voice was entirely too mischievous, and Phoebe regarded her with misgiving as the footman opened the door to let them in. "Impossible. She will only become more determined. What did you say?"

Anna unbuttoned her redingote and turned smiling eyes upon Phoebe. "Well, she came rushing up to me out of nowhere on the street with exclamations of 'Phoebe!' before stopping short with a shocked glance at my midsection, adding that she'd no idea I'd been married. Since she had mistaken me for you, I merely answered that I had married the son of a *duke* and where had she been? Everyone in the ton knew about it."

A laugh sputtered out of Phoebe, and she turned to Anna, mouth agape. "Now Martha will tell everyone I'm expecting and will set all of London talking. There go my prospects for a match."

"No such thing," Anna countered. "All of London will observe you are *not* with child and see the joke. Or, you need only leave town and come to Avebury with this as your excuse to flee."

At the end of the corridor a door opened, and Harry came toward them in his brisk stride. "Anna, you have returned. Good morning, Phoebe. Let us eat, so we may be on our way." With an imperative gesture to follow, he turned to the breakfast room, giving—to the uninitiated—the semblance of a man possessing limited patience. Anna sent a droll look after his retreating form before trotting after him comically. "You heard the man. I must eat."

Phoebe laughed, but it sounded melancholy even to her own ears. How would she go on without the comfort her sister's presence had brought her these last weeks? And what lure was there to attend social gatherings without anyone comfortable to share them with? Only one hope dangled in front of her, enticing Phoebe and giving her the courage to attempt another Season. But even that hope had begun to fade with the years. If he hadn't noticed her yet, what chance was there, really?

They made quick work of breakfast, and then Harry dropped his napkin beside the plate. "I will go see that the carriage is brought around and Peter is ready to leave." He leaned down and kissed his wife on the cheek, and she reached up to clasp the hand that rested on her shoulder as she ate her remaining bite of bread. He left the room.

Anna eyed Phoebe above her patterned China cup before finishing her tea. "Do you plan to see Lydia again before she and Fitz travel to the Continent?"

They had known Lydia Fitzwilliam from childhood; she was the sister of Stratford's closest friend, Lord Ingram. Lydia was to accompany her husband to Brussels to join the 33rd Regiment of Foot where Lieutenant-Colonel Fitzwilliam had recently been assigned. "Yes. In fact, we have made plans that I should come today, so that I will not feel your departure so keenly." Phoebe met her sister's gaze and gave a soft smile. "But I will be much depressed without you to bear me company all the same."

Anna came around the table and sat next to Phoebe, throwing her arms around her shoulders. "And my spirits will be low without you. Don't keep yourself hidden from those who might otherwise see your worth. Let *this* be the Season where you make a love match and have the happiness that I have. Promise me." She pulled back and fixed Phoebe with her stare. "Promise me that you will take a risk and let others see what a treasure there is in you."

Anna was unusually serious, and Phoebe could only nod, swallowing the lump that threatened to rise in her throat. What her sister could not know was that making any sort of match at all would require giving up hope of the one man she truly loved, and that felt a little like death. But as Phoebe nodded her agreement, a new determination seized her, infused by her twin, who had always been the more outspoken and adventurous one. Anna was right. She must not fall into dejection or throw away her dreams of marriage when all it wanted was a little resolve. She could be as outgoing as Anna if she applied herself to the task, and she could find someone new. "I promise."

Harry returned to the breakfast room and paused, his eyes softening when he saw his wife and sister pulling out of one another's embrace. He came around the table. "Phoebe, I am sorry to tear Anna away from you. Please come to us as soon as you may, and know that you will be welcome for as long as you wish to stay."

Phoebe stood and received her brother-in-law's kiss on her cheek. Harry was naturally of a generous and loving disposition, and that—compounded by the fact that his love for his wife extended to caring for his wife's sister—made him an ideal brother-in-law. She could not begrudge him his wife.

The door opened again, and Peter toddled over the threshold, followed by his nurse. A smile lit Phoebe's face as she went forward and lifted the chubby, blond-haired child into her arms, nestling her cheek next to his and pulling back to look at him. "Are you going with the horses?" she asked him. "You will have an exciting adventure."

Her nephew pulled at a curl that was draped stylishly over Phoebe's shoulder—Anna's influence. Then he put his other thumb in his mouth. Phoebe kissed his head and followed her sister and Harry to the door, where she watched the footman loading the last of the trunks. She went down the stairs to the street and handed Peter over to the nurse, who stepped into the barouche with the child.

Anna threw her arms around Phoebe for one last hug and pulled back to look her in the eyes. "It is a new Season," she said. "But it can be a new season of life, love, and hope, as well. Write faithfully and tell me your news."

Phoebe nodded. Anna was the last one in the carriage before the footman closed the door. She leaned out the window and furrowed her brows at Phoebe's expression, which must have displayed just how forlorn she felt. The footman climbed up next to the coachman, and then they were off.

Chapter Two

The Right Honorable, The Viscount Ingram—Colonel in the British Army, and known as Frederick by only the most intimate of friends—quit the offices of the Secretary at War with his thoughts on anything but the Congress happening in Vienna. He exited into the chill of the outdoors, the sky pale and cloudless, and found his groom standing in front of his carriage, holding the reins.

"Take the carriage home, Joseph. I'm going to walk."

Frederick turned toward home, and frustration propelled his steps into a brisk pace. He should have been thinking about the conference, as he had just received fresh reports of Talleyrand's negotiations for France. The concessions made by England and its allies had been surprisingly lenient to their former enemy. As one who had spent his career as both a soldier and a diplomat, the news concerned him.

Instead, Frederick was thinking about the off-hand remark his friend Rowland had let fall that Georgiana Audley was to be married at last, and had likely already tied the knot. He supposed he should not have been shocked by the news. She was beautiful, vivacious, and most certainly eligible. Nevertheless, when she'd sworn in turning him down that she would never marry, he had believed her. More fool he.

Frederick and Georgiana shared a complicated past. From the moment he'd first set eyes on her on the Peninsula, where she was following the drum beside her Major-General father, he had never loved anyone else. Nothing daunted Georgiana—not the pop of artillery that came of a sudden and sounded too close for comfort, nor the thought of packing up their tent and moving on a forward march, or even a retreat, at a moment's notice. She livened their officers' dinners with her wit and ready laughter, and there was not a soldier or officer who had not fallen head over heels for her.

After he left the Peninsula, Frederick kept up with news of her but not with any regularity. Georgiana had made it clear that she had no interest in attaching herself to anyone at all. On his side, he found he could not let it go. When she returned to London two years later and they rekindled their friendship, he had almost begun to hope. It was not to be. Georgiana shot down his offer quite decisively before accompanying her widowed father to Vienna, where—from the news he had just received—she met a diplomat and agreed to his marriage proposal in weeks.

Weeks! Frederick began to cross the street and had to leap back to avoid being hit by a phaeton pulled by two high-steppers. He became aware of his surroundings and waited until he had a chance to dart across the street without hindrance.

Frederick had been pursuing Georgiana for years. He'd had eyes for no one else. How unfortunate that she had not had eyes for him. He would not be so foolish as to embark on such a fruitless pursuit again. No, he must find a wife in the more traditional manner, even if what he might feel for her would be tame by comparison. For all that, Frederick knew he could never settle for someone with less spirit. It was Georgiana's daring that attracted him—her willingness to go anywhere and brave any adventure. It was like having a companion with all the spirited larks and raillery of a gentleman and the womanly delights of a lady rolled into one. He could not imagine settling for some young miss who had no conversation and did not dare make her way across a ballroom without clinging to the arm of some other foolish young lady.

Frederick entered his townhouse, where he expected to hear the noises of preparation as his sister Lydia and her husband Fitz arranged their departure for Brussels. The house was still, and Frederick paused in the entryway as he divested himself of his cloak and handed it to the footman. The silence still caught him by surprise, though his mother had been gone a year.

The butler exited the library and advanced down the corridor toward him. "My lord, the post came this morning, and some cards were left for you. I have set them on your desk in the library. Mrs. Fitzwilliam said to tell you she is running last-minute errands and that she and Lieutenant-Colonel Fitzwilliam will be at home to dine if you should wish it. Cook also said to let you know she is preparing Mrs. Fitzwilliam's favorite."

"Excellent. Have dinner set for eight o'clock."

Urgent business at Frederick's estate would take him there tomorrow, and he would not miss this last evening together with his sister and her husband. Frederick was happy for both of them and thought that Fitz more than deserved the easy post that awaited him in Brussels. After a year of campaigning together on the Peninsula with his wife, Major Thomas Fitzwilliam had left Lydia in England as he traveled to the Americas to lend assistance to the war. There, he was promoted to the position of lieutenant-colonel for his brave leadership.

Their joyful reunion had occurred only a month earlier, and Lydia had sworn to Fitz she would never allow him to go away without her again. Fitz's upcoming post in the Low Countries, establishing the French and Dutch nobility after Napoleon had been sent off to the Island of Elba as prisoner, promised to be a delightful holiday compared to the horrors of war and separation. These days, the smile did not leave Lydia's face.

Frederick looked up to see Caldwell descending the stairs. "Is my trunk ready?"

His valet was a former soldier, who had served for a time as Frederick's bâtman in the Peninsula, but Caldwell had chosen to stay in active service rather than follow Frederick to London. He had carried on in Spain as servant to Colonel Mardland until his death, and now that the war was over, Frederick had been glad to offer him the post.

"Nearly, milord." Caldwell's appearance was coarse for a valet—and his manners even more so—but Frederick trusted him. "Your coat has not arrived from Schultz's in time."

"Never mind that. I am more likely to need my riding coats. I do not intend to do more than dine with the squire. See that all is ready for our seven o'clock departure tomorrow."

"Very good, milord."

Frederick went into the library, where he rifled through the letters, picking up one that had come from a friend in Vienna who was on Wellington's staff. It was dated two days later than the news Rowland had at the War Office and was more likely to be of an official, rather than gossipy, nature. He broke the seal and smoothed out the paper that had a few lines scrawled across the page.

Ingram—

> *We are having splendid fun. One would hardly know that the treaty is being renegotiated once again (and not to our favor) with the gaiety that surrounds us. You will not be surprised that Talleyrand has spurned his so-called allies, which of course calls into question his royalist intentions. We did not suffer any surprise over that, as you may guess. By George, I almost prefer Napoleon. At least one knew where the man stood on matters.*
>
> *Wellington mentioned you by name. I begin to think he will ask for you if there is anything further to be done to establish the French borders, so prepare yourself. You know how he likes a man who can follow instructions without argument, and Sir Hudson is threatening to send him into a state of apoplexy. Meanwhile, Slender Billy has just left and prepares to return to Ghent. Who knows whether he will be content to stay there with his father, or if he will come and join us in Brussels. If the duke asks for you, I will be the one writing. Look out for my letter, for he may have need of you yet.*

> *Yours—*
> *Wrotham*

Frederick dropped Wrotham's letter on the desk and stared across the room at the fire that danced in the grate, a smile on his lips at the mention of Slender Billy. It was their nickname for the young Prince of Orange, whose father was the Dutch king. Frederick wondered how much help the prince was to the negotiations and how much of his stay was devoted to amusement.

He could not help but be gratified that Lord Wellington would think of him. Frederick had been content to set aside his life as a career soldier if it meant serving as liaison between London and those who were actively campaigning. True, his life was less exciting—apart from the attack by an English spy that had left Frederick with a broken leg and only the slightest limp—but he knew his ability to communicate expertly with allies and foes was of value to his country. And Frederick was not insensible to the honor that England's hero would know who he was.

There was a knock on the front door, and Frederick lifted his head from the stack of remaining correspondence. Hartsmith would come and enlighten him if the visitor was important. With Lydia in residence, there was always a steady stream of morning calls and invitations. Now, as she prepared for her departure, those calls grew fewer and fewer.

His butler slipped inside the door. "Miss Phoebe Tunstall is here to see Mrs. Fitzgerald, but I do not know when the mistress may return. What shall I tell her?"

Phoebe! She was the younger sister of his closest friend Stratford, now Earl of Worthing, and the name drew Frederick to his feet. "I will go and see her."

He went into the corridor, advancing to meet Phoebe, his hands held out to her. She clasped them, smiling up at him, and he was moved to kiss her cheek. He had seen Phoebe only once this winter since they had both been in London, which was surprising, considering how frequently she and Anna had been in Lydia's company.

"Come into the drawing room." Frederick extended his arm, and Phoebe slipped her hand around it as he led her forward. "I will wait with you until Lydia returns. Leave it to my harebrained sister to invite you and not be here in time to receive you."

Still smiling, Phoebe protested with the shake of her head. "No, we had spoken of meeting today, but I did not tell her when I would come. I was not sure what time Anna would leave, and I suppose I am on the early side."

They entered the drawing room, and Frederick gestured forward. "Please, be seated. I regret that our paths have not crossed since your aunt's death—I won't count that one time I saw you in

Gunter's, for we were hardly able to exchange pleasantries, much less speak. I am sorry I was unable to attend to you after the funeral. I know it was a great loss to you, especially. Tell me how you go on."

Phoebe sat with her usual quiet grace. Although she was identical to her sister, she had never attracted the same attention that Anna seemed to draw. Rather, she somehow managed to fade into her surroundings. It was astonishing, really, that one such as she could be forgotten, since she was obviously Anna's equal in beauty. And she had an air of calm competence that drew people's confidence.

"I go on well enough. However . . ." Phoebe knit her brows and fell silent.

Frederick waited, hoping she would open up. She could be difficult to read, and he wasn't sure how to prompt her. At last, Phoebe met his gaze. "I am just not sure what to do now. I find the thought of embarking on a fifth Season exhausting. It is all I have been trained for, of course, but the idea of making morning calls and going to more balls—and all to no purpose." She stopped and bit her lip.

"Why do you not marry?" Frederick intertwined his fingers on his lap. "You cannot hoodwink me into believing you haven't had several offers. Honestly, between you and Anna, I was certain you would marry first. If anyone was born to the role of wife and mother, it is you."

Phoebe gave a strange, painful twist to her lips and shrugged. "I will not say that I have had no offers, but I admit I have had few. And none which inspired in me any desire to accept." She pressed her lips together and surprised him with a candid look that was unlike her usual shy regard. "I must suppose I am not such a slave to the matrimonial state that I am willing to engage in it at all costs."

"Men are foolish," Frederick said, shaking his head. "Many girls on the marriage mart fly off the shelf with only a fraction of your beauty, calm, and good sense. I am sure this Season will prove more successful for you."

"I am sure you are right." Phoebe's voice lacked conviction.

Silence fell as Frederick pondered how different Georgiana Audley was to the gentle creature who sat before him. Even Georgiana had ended up married. With her dark hair and charcoal eyes, Georgiana was a striking beauty. She lit each room she was in until every man in it had gravitated toward her. She would never settle for an insipid London Season if she were not inclined to do so. Georgiana would not settle for anything in life, really.

Having taken temporary leave of his senses—he would later convince himself—Frederick exclaimed suddenly, "Phoebe, you are not a victim of your fate. You are the author of it. Why do you not do something unusual? Something daring?"

Phoebe lifted her eyebrows in surprise before the mask fell over her face again. "Daring! I cannot imagine what you might mean by that. What could *I* possibly do that is daring?"

Frederick looked at her meek expression, and the idea sagged before it had fully taken flight. He shrugged. "I don't know why I said it, but now that I have, I must stand by it. It is the very thing you need. Take an opportunity you would never dream of accepting, and seize it. I do not know what that will be. You must simply put your willingness out into the world, and let the world provide you the opening." Gaining steam, he added, "Show yourself game enough to step outside of your usual path, and the opportunity will present itself."

Phoebe did not look persuaded, but she nodded. "Something daring. Well, I suppose I could."

There were sounds of the front door opening, and after a murmured conversation in the corridor, Lydia and Fitz entered the room, ending Frederick's *tête-à-tête* with Phoebe. He stood. "Lydia, I have welcomed your guest for you, as you ought to have done."

"Freddy!" Lydia protested. Like Georgiana, she was a dark-haired beauty who had only grown more handsome as a married woman. Phoebe stood out next to her, as fair as an angel, with her blonde hair. "We never fixed a time. Although I *am* sorry, Phoebe. Fitz, will you have this sent to my room as well as the other packages?" Lydia handed the boxes to her husband, who accepted them in a docile manner that would have astonished the soldiers in his regiment.

Frederick took the opportunity to lean into Phoebe, catching her wide, blue-eyed gaze in his. "Tomorrow, I must leave for my estate for a fortnight, but I am sure to see you at the Stanich opening ball upon my return. Your family may not be here to support you, but our paths will cross many times this Season, my dear, and I am just as certain that you will receive an offer at the end of it. Remember what I've told you. Something daring." He grasped her fingers in his and pressed a quick kiss to them before turning to his sister.

"Lydia, I am sure you both have much to discuss, and I will leave you to it. We are to dine at eight. Cook is making syllabub."

"How thoughtful," Lydia replied, before turning to Phoebe. "Cook knows it's my favorite sweet. Let me show you what I've just purchased." Lydia pulled her toward the armchairs and placed Phoebe with her back to Frederick, putting an end to any further exchanges.

Chapter Three

The door shut behind her, and Phoebe exhaled noiselessly, attempting to regain her composure that had fled at the sight of Frederick Ingram.

"Oh, yes!" Lydia leapt to her feet again. "I must tell Sarah to put a second set of sheets in the trunk that will be traveling with us." She rushed out, leaving Phoebe alone in the drawing room.

Phoebe could not remain seated. She stood and walked over to the cool marble of the mantelpiece, staring above it at the large, gilded painting that was familiar from years of visiting the Ingram home. The painting was of a quaint country house that did not seem to belong in such an austere drawing room, and the bright flowers in the foreground had always charmed her. She ran her finger over the twists and scrolls on the bottom of the frame.

Well, that was not so hard, was it? Phoebe's heart twisted painfully, giving lie to her assurance, as the image of Frederick bowing his tousled, boyishly curled head to kiss her fingers flooded her mind. The moment had been over much too soon, but she had learned to suppress—with the greatest severity at her disposal—the desperate longing that came over her when she was in Frederick's presence. When months would go by without seeing him, she would think it too long. Within seconds under his careless, brotherly affection, she wanted to die rather than suffer the pain of unrequited love—or stamp her foot in irritation and send him away again.

Lydia blew into the drawing room, having accomplished her mission and sat on the couch, patting the seat next to her. "I'm sorry for the delay. I would have returned in time, except that the mantua-maker said she had almost finished my dress, and if I could just wait, I would not be required to send someone to retrieve it. Her assistant is sick, and she was quite on her own with so many orders, poor thing."

"It's no bother," Phoebe replied, sitting next to Lydia. "I have all the time in the world, unlike you. Have you completed your shopping for your trip then?"

Lydia frowned in thought, her eyes searching her memory. "I believe so, but I still have all of tomorrow in case something has slipped my mind. After Frederick leaves for his estate, I will make a list to be sure. I am going to ring for tea. Would you like some?"

At Phoebe's nod, Lydia went and gave orders to the footman and then returned to sit next to her. "It's a different sort of packing and not one I am entirely familiar with. When I was with Fitz in the Peninsula, we needed the sorts of things one cannot find in small villages and forests—a year's worth of tooth powder, for instance. Where we are going now is not likely to lack many things. The society will be refined, and I am told that anything might be organized, from picnics to balls. I will need to dress appropriately. This is what has me all on end."

"And who knows?" Phoebe added, "Perhaps there will be an entirely different fashion worn in Brussels—not that I am any judge of that sort of thing, having never traveled abroad nor wished to."

"I have thought of that but am not too worried." Lydia reached up and removed her chip hat, which she still wore. "I am told there are already so many English there, I believe we must set our own fashion. However, the one thing I've learned from travel is that one must never assume anything but rather be ready for all eventualities."

A servant came in, carrying the platter with tea and cakes. He placed it in front of Lydia, who put a generous pinch of tea in the hot water and let it steep. When the servant had gone, Phoebe accepted the cup Lydia handed her and sipped the delicately perfumed beverage.

"I cannot think how you can be so brave," Phoebe said, placing her cup on its saucer. "Your letters from Spain rattled on in your droll way as if there was no threat around you. You do not speak of it, but I am sure you endured such hardship. And here you are, about to travel again to another country. I could never be so bold."

Lydia lifted a shoulder. "I do not see it that way. As long as I am with Fitz, I am sure that everything will turn out well. There is something so solidly reassuring about him." She regarded Phoebe in silence, her gaze assessing. "There is this melancholy to you that I do not like to see. Do you fret that none of us will be here to share the Season with you?"

Phoebe set her plate on the table, her lemon cake scarcely touched. "The thought of another Season exhausts me, if I might own the truth. Last year, you, Stratford, and Eleanor were with me for much of it. I still had Aunt Shae to think of, and I was able to enjoy London's festivities with Mary Reading. She is married now and will stay in Worcester for the Season, and there is no one else I am close to." She met Lydia's gaze. "But I do not mean to worry you. It is only that Anna left today, and you are leaving the day after tomorrow. It is natural that I should fall into a fit of the dismals for a day or two."

Lydia clasped Phoebe's hand. "Anna told me that Mrs. Morris is not the gayest companion for you. Can you not go somewhere where you will not need her—to a country party or something?"

She tsked in impatience. "I suppose that is a stupid question. You must be here in London. But how I wish there was something for you to look forward to—some adventure. For no matter how staid one might profess to be, a bit of adventure is essential to one's happiness."

Phoebe laughed. "It is funny you should say so, because Ingram suggested something very similar. He told me to go do something daring."

Lydia's eyes flashed with mirth. "Daring? You, Phoebe?"

The words were not meant to be cutting. Lydia was a friend of long date, after all. However, Phoebe felt them like a blow, and it must have reflected on her face. *I must be dull, indeed, for everyone to have such a view of me.*

"I am sorry," Lydia groaned. "That did not come out how I wished it. Of course, you could do something daring. Why should you not? And what's more besides, why should you do what everyone expects of you and stay in London—"

She broke off and gasped as her hand flew to her mouth. "Phoebe," she said, her voice low and throbbing with excitement. "I have just had the very best idea—and I am astonished I did not think of it before. You must accompany me to Brussels."

"Brussels!" Phoebe's eyes grew wide, and a helpless laugh escaped her. "I couldn't . . . "

Lydia's eyes burned with the thrill of her idea, and from what Phoebe knew of her, it meant she had latched on to it and would not easily let it go. "Listen to me. This is *exactly* what you should do. I am told Brussels is like London but on a smaller scale. There are parties and routs . . . picnics—or there will be when it's warm enough. There is the opera. Everywhere you go, English is spoken, and some of the best families might be seen there. This will be a chance for you to do something out of the ordinary—to not accept fate as though you had no hand in it."

Lydia's words rushed out, one upon the other. "And you can keep me company. I cannot tell you how I long to have a friend on the journey and for all the parties there. Do say you'll come."

As Lydia laid out the possibilities, Phoebe felt the blood drain from her face. Her heartbeat sped, and she could not contemplate the proposition with the fear that had overtaken her. Anxiety grew like a buzzing in her ears that blocked out all other sound. There was simply no possibility she could leave England for a foreign country. Phoebe was not the adventurous kind. If anything, Anna was.

She put out her hand to stop the outpouring of Lydia's words. "I am sorry to disappoint you, but I cannot go. Mrs. Morris needs me."

Lydia drew back, and her brows snapped together. "I thought it was supposed to be the other way around. Don't tell me that you feel an obligation to Mrs. Morris. She is merely a hired companion until you get married."

"Yes, but I could not let her go so quickly after having engaged her services. What would she do?" Even as the words left Phoebe's lips, she knew it was just an excuse. Mrs. Morris did have family she could return to. Her presence was more to lend respectability to Phoebe as an unmarried woman than it was for Phoebe to support an impoverished companion. Still, a person did not simply fly off to Brussels on a moment's notice.

Lydia frowned and shook her head. "That need not signify. As I've said, you have no obligation to her. Just consider the idea, Phoebe. Don't give me a final answer now. We have all day tomorrow for you to make plans. And you will not need to procure anything difficult—I have enough of everything to spare whatever you might need. Besides, I am convinced that we will not find anything lacking in the shops there. Brussels is reputed to be quite a modern city. You will only need your clothes and personal belongings, and I will see that all else is taken care of."

Phoebe pinched her lips together, but Lydia forestalled her. "Do not give me an answer now. Call upon me tomorrow to bid me farewell. Or"—she gave Phoebe an engaging smile—"to deliver good news."

Phoebe knew that her visit would be to bid farewell, but she relented. "Very well. I will give it some thought." They turned their attention to the latest London gossip, with Lydia interspersing their conversation with all the delights Brussels could hold.

It was not very subtle.

Inside Stratford's home on Grosvenor Street, Phoebe untied the strings of her bonnet, and Mrs. Morris appeared at the upstairs railing.

"Miss Tunstall," she cried out, her voice tinged with disapproval as she descended the stairs. "I received your note, but you should not have gone off without me. I am your companion, and I've been engaged for a reason."

Phoebe did not answer right away and turned to hand her bonnet to the butler. She removed her cloak and handed that to him as well. When she felt composed, she faced Mrs. Morris. "Shall we sit in the drawing room?" Without waiting for an answer, Phoebe began to climb the stairs with Mrs. Morris trailing after her, her words flowing without pause.

"I cannot claim to have been doing anything of use all this time, fretting and worrying myself to pieces as I was. What else have I to occupy myself other than concern for your welfare? That is, after all, why Lord Worthing engaged my services. And when I am not with you, why, anything might happen to you."

But only after noon, Phoebe thought with bitter irony. Her breath came quickly as much from climbing the stairs as the sudden urge to snap at Mrs. Morris, but she forced herself to reply evenly. "I was perfectly safe as my note indicated. I merely wished to say goodbye to an old friend before she leaves for Brussels."

"For Brussels!" Mrs. Morris exclaimed. "Why would anyone wish to leave this great country and go live among heathens?"

"I have heard that Brussels is a lovely city, and that it attracts its share of English men and women of rank. I am sure it must be a genteel place to live. I wonder if the spring is as cold there as it is here," Phoebe mused, seized by the whimsical idea of viewing it for herself.

"I am sure it must be a dirty, nasty place," Mrs. Morris said, following Phoebe into the drawing room. "I will ring for tea. I did not want to take any while you were not here. I would not presume to encroach upon your goodness. However, now that you have arrived, I am sure it must do you some good."

"None for me," Phoebe replied, sitting and picking up a book that lay on the table in front of her. "I have just taken tea with Mrs. Fitzwilliam. But you may order some for yourself if you would like. There is no need to deprive yourself, as I find it perfectly natural that one should wish for tea over the course of a day."

Mrs. Morris hesitated before sending Phoebe a look of studied resignation. "No, if you are not to have any, I believe I may wait until dinner. It is true, I have had nothing since breakfast this morning, but let it not be said that I was eating you out of house and home." She gave a titter that had Phoebe clenching her teeth.

"Really, Mrs. Morris. Ring for tea if you would like some. As I said, I have no objection to your taking tea even if I am not here or should not care for it."

Mrs. Morris shook her head resolutely and sat on the chair next to Phoebe. "Oh, no. It would not be right to do so. But the moment you should care for some tea, you need only say the word, and I will order some."

Phoebe wrestled within herself. There was a perverseness in her that seemed to spring up out of nowhere. If Mrs. Morris chose to go hungry after she'd been urged to order tea, what could Phoebe do? And there was an accompanying obstinacy in her to do as she wished, no matter whether or not it inconvenienced Mrs. Morris. But Phoebe's habit of effacing herself for the comfort of others was strong, and that voice was hard to shrug off.

"We may ring for tea, for it will be several hours before dinner," she said at last.

"I knew you would change your mind," Mrs. Morris exclaimed brightly as she went over to ring the bell. She left to confer with the footman then returned. "Tea will be just the thing for you. Shall I go on with reading Fordyce's sermons?"

"No, I believe I had enough of that yesterday. I have a novel I would like to read. But you may read your sermons if you'd like. In this way, we are both of us pleased." Phoebe lifted her book in front of her face, providing herself with the only barrier at her disposal.

She was desperate for quiet so she could think. It would even be worth having tea she did not wish to drink if she could just read her novel in peace. Phoebe had found that if she spent too much time in her room, Mrs. Morris would hound her later, desperate for company, and keep her up much too late. Better to give Mrs. Morris the dose of attention she needed now so that Phoebe could go to bed early.

"I think I should read one or two sermons to you. It will be much more edifying than a novel. Besides, that is what a companion is meant to do." Mrs. Morris reached for the double volume of *Sermons to Young Women* sitting on the table in front of her. "I should not be so selfish as to read my own book and drink tea while I'm doing nothing to aid you."

"Silence would restore my mind," Phoebe said firmly. "By allowing me to read in quiet, you would be lending me the greatest assistance."

"You must trust my judgment for how a young lady should spend her time," Mrs. Morris replied, undaunted. "I am wiser and have lived many more years than you. What is the novel you are reading? If you should not care for Fordyce, I can read the novel to you instead."

It was a novel by Maria Edgeworth that Phoebe very much liked and was reading for the second time. She had no desire to hear the words read in Mrs. Morris's nasally tone.

"I feel a bit of a headache coming on," Phoebe said as she stood abruptly. She needed to leave now, or she would be unable to check the hasty words that were bubbling up inside of her. "I had better spend time in my room to be restored for dinner."

"But you have not had tea," Mrs. Morris replied, intercepting Phoebe as she aimed for the door. "I know you said you do not wish for refreshment, but you must have tea first." Mrs. Morris put her hand on Phoebe's elbow.

Something in Phoebe snapped. The thin cord that seemed always to hold the fragments of her resolution together had become so tight and brittle over the past months, it pulled apart with a sharp twang. Phoebe slipped her arm from Mrs. Morris's grip and leveled a gaze at her. She inhaled through her nostrils and turned to resume her place on the settee.

"Perhaps you are right about the tea. It will give us time to discuss something, for I have come to a decision."

The servant entered at that moment, and Mrs. Morris hurried forward to gesture him to the small round table in front of her chair. She doused the leaves in the teapot and, while it was steeping, cut two large slices of cake and set them on two plates, handing one to Phoebe. She poured the tea, then reached for her cake, picking up her silver spoon. "Go on, then. I am eager to hear what you have to discuss."

Phoebe ignored the cake and sat on the edge of the settee, pivoting to face Mrs. Morris. "I was invited by Mrs. Fitzgerald to travel to Brussels, and I have decided to join her."

Mrs. Morris could not immediately speak as her mouth was full, but her eyes told Phoebe of her sentiments on this announcement—surprise laced with outrage. When she swallowed, it was only to protest. "But I cannot travel to Brussels. I could never leave London. This is a fool's scheme, and you must abandon it at once."

Phoebe ignored the impertinence with her mind on the greater goal. At Mrs. Morris's decisive pronouncement, the idea of travel that had earlier seemed an impossibility to Phoebe now became a certainty. There was no wavering in her breast when she said, "And yet, the matter is quite decided. I will depart the day after tomorrow. I will see that you are paid through the trimester to give you time to seek another engagement should you wish it."

Mrs. Morris's hands trembled, and Phoebe almost felt sorry for her. It could not be easy for someone of Mrs. Morris's age and situation to face change with equanimity. And yet, Mrs. Morris seemed to possess an evil genius for uttering precisely the thing to kill Phoebe's compassion.

"Lord Worthing will never approve. I shall write to him at once."

"You may do so," Phoebe replied, one eyebrow raised. "I plan to do so myself. However, my brother has no hold over me, as I am of age and have an independence. I make my own decisions now."

Mrs. Morris's brow furrowed so deeply her eyes glittered. "It is a drastic idea and one that will bring you to no good end. I forbid it."

Phoebe stood. "*You* forbid it?" she repeated with icy calm. "You forget yourself, ma'am. I am not your charge to order about. I will be taking dinner in my room tonight. I expect you to leave by tomorrow."

"Well, I have never—" Mrs. Morris sputtered. "You will regret this absurd notion of yours. Mark my words. You will regret it!"

Phoebe did not glance at her as she swept out of the room. She kept her composure in place as she passed a servant on the way to her bedroom. But once she closed the door to her room, she walked to the bed and threw herself face down on the mattress, and screamed into it. When she lifted her face from her hands, her arms still tucked underneath her, she was laughing and trembling.

I cannot believe I did that. I cannot believe I did that. But I did! And I am free.

Chapter Four

The next day at Lord Ingram's residence, Phoebe followed the butler into the drawing room still wearing the hat and cloak she had been too impatient to remove. She found Lydia seated at the desk near the fireplace writing a letter.

Lydia set down the quill and looked at Phoebe, a hint of melancholy in her expression. "Have you come to bid me farewell?"

Phoebe's pulse beat in her throat, and she found herself unable to give voice to the monumental step she was about to take. She remained frozen as the butler quietly withdrew.

"Lydia, were you in earnest about my accompanying you to Brussels?"

Lydia's eyes widened, and she placed her hand on the back of the chair. "How can you doubt me?" She stood and hurried over to Phoebe. "Of *course*, I was in earnest. Have you decided to accept my invitation, then? How did this come about? Oh, I am thrilled beyond words. But here I am peppering you with questions, and I must give you a chance to answer. Come sit with me."

A nervous laugh escaped Phoebe as she allowed Lydia to draw her to the sofa where they had sat together only the day before. "I imagine my decision must come as quite a shock. It is only that I've decided to take you up on your offer. That is, if Fitz is able to secure a passage for me at such last-minute notice." She turned her questioning gaze on Lydia. "Can he?"

"There is no doubt that Fitz will succeed. My husband is capable of anything he sets his mind to." Lydia darted to her feet again and paced in front of Phoebe. "I never dreamed you would change your mind. You are not one for spontaneity. What happened?"

Phoebe raised her palms and shrugged. "I hardly know, myself. It was just . . . I could not stand the thought of another day in Mrs. Morris's company."

"I should say not!" Lydia gave an exaggerated shudder. "I cannot fathom how you were able to stand her for as much as a day. But . . . will you be ready? There must be a thousand things to do before tomorrow."

"The most pressing thing is finding a maid." Phoebe chuckled. "Gertie turned as white as a sheet when I proposed she join me."

Lydia waved that worry away. "You shall share mine for the journey, and we can engage another in Brussels if we need one."

Phoebe nodded. "That relieves my mind. Otherwise, Gertie has begun packing my trunks. I have only to apply to Stratford's banker for funds and send off a letter to Stratford and Anna. Mrs. Morris is having her trunks packed as well and will take herself off before the afternoon is through, and Stratford will surely send instructions to his butler regarding closing the house. As for anything else . . ." Phoebe stopped to think. "I believe I have everything I need, unless you wish to recommend some items for me to purchase?"

"No." Lydia's response was decisive. "There is nothing you need, apart from your clothes and personal effects. Oh, we shall have *such* fun together. I will see that Fitz purchases your passage as soon as he returns. We leave tomorrow at the unfashionable hour of eight o'clock. Can you bear it?"

"Easily! I shan't sleep a wink." Phoebe filled her lungs to combat the breathless feeling that threatened her. "But . . . might I come and stay with you tonight after I finish packing and accomplish my errands? I believe it will help calm my nerves to be here."

"The very thing. I will send a carriage for you at seven o'clock if you think you can manage to be ready. I am sure Fitz will be just as delighted as I am when he hears the news."

This proved to be true. Lieutenant-Colonel Fitzwilliam was an amiable man, although his troops would not have described him as such despite their esteem for him. Once assured that Stratford would not mind Phoebe's going abroad without her brother's prior approval—and rightfully blame him for aiding her—Fitz could only applaud the fact that she would provide his wife with such excellent company while he was going about his military duties. Of course, Phoebe wasn't sure how Stratford would feel about her sudden decision, but she was not going to waste the opportunity by delaying her journey so she might find out.

With that out of the way, Lydia informed Phoebe of the good news that her maid had a cousin, Mary, who was also eager for the adventure and could be ready "in two shakes of a lamb's tail." As she readied Phoebe for dinner, Mary showed herself to be cheerful and efficient, and Phoebe liked her immediately.

Over dinner, Phoebe asked the question that had been occupying her mind whenever her thoughts weren't absorbed by the business of leaving. "What is the purpose of having a military presence in the Low Countries?"

Fitz signaled for the footman to take Phoebe the dishes that lay out of her reach before answering. "As you might know, before Napoleon came to power, the Dutch owned Brussels and all the land surrounding it through to the coast. The French then conquered the region and extended their border to include the Dutch territory. Now that Napoleon is safely away on the Island of Elba, we must establish the borders that were set by the Congress in Vienna. We also have some small part in reestablishing the French royalty who were dethroned when Bonaparte crowned himself emperor. And of course, there are still local Belgic people who remain loyal to Napoleon whom we must keep an eye on." He smiled at Phoebe. "I assure you, there will be plenty to keep us occupied."

Phoebe returned his smile, relieved that the military presence there seemed to be more of a formality than anything else.

The next morning, they set off by carriage to Ramsgate, where they joined the packet boat heading to Ostend on the Continent. The packet was filled mostly with British gentlefolk and their servants, all thirsting for pleasure and adventure in the city of Brussels, where a British presence meant safety. A few soldiers could be identified by their regimentals, and Fitz said more would be coming later on transportation provided by His Majesty. At Ostend, they crossed the sandy bay on foot before switching to a narrow boat that traveled in a meandering fashion on the canals to Ghent. They could have traveled all the way to Brussels like that, but Fitz had been ordered to stop first in Ghent and pass on a message to the quartermaster-general stationed there.

Lydia knocked on the door to Phoebe's cabin in the canal boat. "I believe the weather will be fine enough today that if we dress warmly we may dine above-deck and watch the scenery. Be sure to cover your throat, for there will be a breeze."

Phoebe reached for her cloak and followed Lydia out of the cabin, where they climbed a steep set of stairs that was more akin to a ladder. "A luncheon outdoors sounds delightful. I can hardly believe it is no longer English soil that I see through my window."

A breath of adventure lifted Phoebe's spirits as she stepped on the protected deck above the cabin suite, where a table awaited them. The wind billowed her cloak about her as she followed Lydia and Fitz. For the first time in her life, her movements were not dictated by someone else. She was the complete master of her destiny. They took their seats at the table, and her stomach did a little flip. The newfound freedom frightened her as much as it thrilled her.

The boat's progress engulfed them with a chilly breeze, but the sun beat down hard enough to keep them warm through the time it took to eat their simple meal. A servant brought fish seared in butter that set up wafts of steam in the cold air, accompanied by a side dish of boiled potatoes and one of spring peas. A second servant carried up bread with a plate of hard cheese on the side. And there was Flemish ale, which Phoebe sipped at laughingly, murmuring that she did not think it at all the thing for a woman to be drinking ale—a notion which Lydia and Fitz shot down without hesitation since it was watered down. The melody of flavors from their simple fare mingled on her tongue, and Phoebe thought she had never tasted anything so delicious in her life.

The sights that met Phoebe's eyes as they drifted by on the canal were of lush meadows and vast pastures, separated by small rows of hedges or alleys of trees. Collections of houses with roofs of thatched reed or red clay tiles came into view, and often there was a thick wall of stone or brick that enclosed a more prosperous farm, with its telltale smoke rising somewhere from out of sight. There were tall spires signaling a church or, more occasionally, the parapet visible from the top of a château. In some respects it did not seem so very different from the English countryside.

They did not dine again outdoors before arriving at Ghent, as the fickle spring weather lowered the temperatures enough to threaten snow. They stayed overnight in Ghent at a house that was rented for officers who passed through, and the next morning when Fitz's business was concluded, it was quick work for the groom to ready their carriage that had traveled with them from England.

They reached Brussels in little more than four hours, arriving mid-afternoon, and just as Phoebe had begun to doze off, Lydia touched her arm. "We have arrived."

Phoebe blinked and tried to swallow but found her mouth had gone dry. Her neck had begun to ache on the side where she leaned against the squabs. However, the charm of all there was to discover outweighed the fatigue from days of travel, and she peered out of the window as they pulled up in front of a simple yet spacious brick house.

The carriage came to a halt. Fitz did not wait for the footman but opened the door and assisted both ladies to alight. "Welcome to your new home. It is on *rue des Feuilles*, in case you should lose your way. Might I congratulate you both on what excellent travelers you are. But on that head, I'd had no doubts."

Phoebe lifted her gaze to study the windows of the house that revealed nothing of its interior, then turned back to smile at Lydia. The servants had followed in a second carriage, which was pulling up behind theirs, and it contained the bulk of their trunks.

The agent was waiting for them inside the house and, having bowed to the newcomers, began showing off its charms and explaining where to obtain items they might find necessary. As they made their tour, the footman and groom brought the trunks up to the rooms, and the maids set about unpacking. After having completed their tour of the house, Fitz said he would accompany the agent to his office. He wished to learn his way around the city and announced his plan to make his superiors aware of his arrival. He would not put it off.

"And let us do the same," Lydia said, turning to Phoebe. "Explore the city, that is. There is time enough to go junketing about before it grows dark. Shall we have our own Brussels tour once we've changed out of our travel dresses?"

"Can we do so?" Phoebe asked, doubtfully. "We will not have Fitz to accompany us."

"Never mind that." Lydia swept aside Phoebe's doubts with a wave of her hand. "Fitz likes for me to be independent, and I am a married woman. I might do as I please."

Lydia's spirit of fun was contagious, and Phoebe hurried to change. She was accustomed to a more spacious bedroom than what she had been given, but the large window looked out over the quiet street, and its ledge was lined with geraniums. There was a smooth, comfortable-looking wooden chair with an embroidered footstool in front of it, placed before the rough stone chimney. The room was brightened by pink flowered wall hangings, and she thought she would spend many happy moments here.

"Mary," Phoebe said, turning from the window. "Take my jonquil dress from the top of the trunk and shake it out. I will wear that one, and the chip hat with the broad rim."

"Yes, miss." With efficient movements, Mary set down the darning basket she had been holding and walked over to the trunk, pulling out the yellow dress with care.

Phoebe studied her for a minute, then added with a smile, "And once you are finished unpacking the trunk, you may visit the city with Sarah, if Lydia can spare her. I shan't need you before dinner."

Mary's eyes lit at the prospect. "Yes, miss," she said with real enthusiasm.

With a blessed freedom and the world at their feet, Phoebe and Lydia set off with a guidebook in the direction of the *Palais de Justice* and then walked along the *rue de la Madelaine*. They marched over the worn cobblestones, chatting without cease until they had crossed several streets and entered what looked like the older part of town. Buildings were wedged next to one another, none of them very tall, until the tight medieval streets opened onto a plaza. Phoebe gripped Lydia's arm and stopped short.

There, in front of them, was an enormous open square whose edifice of connected buildings had arcades bordering it on all sides. The central building was distinguished by its tall spire, and the more prominent among the others were decorated with painted emblems and gilded statues—their façades adorned with rows of what looked like hundreds of panes of glass. Although the magnificence of the buildings stole one's breath and demanded Phoebe's full attention, the market taking place in the square's center did not permit it. Shouts in a foreign tongue accosted them as merchants haggled with buyers over the price of anything from vegetables to cotton to tools. Rays of sun lit a row of stands filled with flowers of all types and colors.

"This is not the Brussels of my imagination," Phoebe breathed. "Not after seeing the quaint farmhouses and long stretches of pastures. I was quite deceived."

Lydia laughed. "It is rather magnificent, isn't it? I, for one, would not dream of criticizing the great nation of England, but I am not sure we have anything like this."

They walked to the opposite end of the square and entered more of the smaller streets, one of which led to a bridge perched over a narrow canal. On the other side, they discovered a variety of shops and vendors, some selling what looked like a stew of unknown origins. Phoebe wrinkled her nose as Lydia whispered, "I believe that is blood sausage. *Not* my favorite."

They passed another stall with a more tantalizing scent, presided over by a wiry woman who set out rows of crisscrossed baked pastries, with a spiced apple interior visible through its lattice crust. She shooed away an urchin who had drawn too close, but without any real rancor. Lydia had been given some francs to spend, and she purchased some of the tarts in perfect French. Phoebe spoke fluent French too, of course, but she knew her accent was deplorable and did not relish speaking it. She was torn between longing to experience everything with Lydia's boldness and wanting to run and hide in their house among her possessions, which were now the only thing familiar to her.

More shops were open farther down the street, and there was an energy to the bustling crowds that gathered there. Customers waited patiently, but the shopkeepers hurried to meet the demands, giving each one their full attention before turning to the next person. Most of the shops had a foreign look to them with signs in both French and the Flemish language and roughly hewn façades that stretched up from the packed dirt streets. Some of the low windows drew Phoebe's eye to the odd trinkets on the shelves behind them that she immediately wished to purchase and send to Anna and Eleanor.

Occasionally, there was a shop that had such an English feel to it that Phoebe could believe herself to be back in London. They entered one such shop and found that the owner was indeed an English woman who had recently moved to Brussels to sell hats. Phoebe eyed the designs that, while pretty, were nothing out of the ordinary from what they would see in London.

"What brought you to sell your hats in Brussels?" Lydia asked before the urge to do so could occur to Phoebe. There was something about being abroad that broke social rules that might otherwise exist, such as asking a personal question of a stranger.

"I had nothing to keep me in London, and I thought the competition might be friendlier here." The milliner spoke in the recognizable accent of a London merchant. She turned a bright smile toward Phoebe and Lydia as she wrapped a package and set it aside. "And I turned out to be right. Ther've been so many customers, I can't regret my decision to leave England. The Belgic people're keen to try new fashions, and the English like to have someone who speaks their language. I've been here for six months."

"And you don't miss England?" Phoebe asked.

"No, I've found that people are more pleasant here than they are in London." She reached up and pinned a hat to display on a wire hanging from the ceiling. "Like I said, I don't regret my decision to come."

Lydia and Phoebe left, promising to return when they were ready to purchase something. They circled back toward the part of town where their house was located, and the streets grew wider as they neared home. On the way was a coffeehouse with the placard *Au Cygne Noir* swinging on metal chains. Inside were polished wooden tables, where some sat drinking coffee or tea. The patrons all looked to be dressed in the height of fashion, even by London standards, and Lydia turned to Phoebe. "Shall we go in?"

Phoebe squeezed Lydia's arm. "Why not? We have time at our disposal."

As soon as they entered, all eyes turned to look at them, and Phoebe gulped. Not a single face appeared familiar to her, and she hated the unknown. Until now, their journey had been almost constant amusement, but suddenly the endless possibilities of the unfamiliar wore a shroud of constraint. What was she doing here in this place where she heard not just English, but strains of French, what was possibly Flemish, and even other foreign tongues? How would she cope in a place where she knew almost no one?

"Mrs. Fitzwilliam!" a voice called from the darker corner of the coffee shop and had them swiveling toward it. Lydia smiled up at the handsome gentleman dressed in civilian clothing, who was approaching them. Phoebe's first thought was that he looked to be of marriageable age, which both made her want to laugh at herself and blush for the direction of her thoughts. It was a good direction, though. Perhaps here she could at last relinquish her impossible dream of having Frederick's love. Coming to Brussels was exactly what she needed to start fresh.

"Mr. Conroy," Lydia said. "I did not know you would be here. It's been an age since I've seen you. May I present to you my good friend, Miss Phoebe Tunstall?"

Mr. Conroy laid his hand over his breast and bowed before Phoebe. "I am delighted to make your acquaintance. Are you—no. Of course, you cannot be an officer's wife if you are Miss Tunstall. How came you to be in Brussels? If . . ." Mr. Conroy's broad smile faltered as he seemed to catch himself. "If that is not too impertinent a question to ask?"

Phoebe returned his smile, instantly liking his easy manners and address, which managed to chase away some of her trepidation from knowing no one. "I decided to come with Lydia and her husband for a visit. The thought of a London Season did not delight me, but this adventure did."

Mr. Conroy's sandy lashes, which matched his hair of a similar color, framed a set of warm brown eyes. "I hope you do enjoy it. Brussels society will be the richer for having you here." He turned to Lydia. "You may not have heard, but Mrs. Marshall is in town, and she is hosting one of her famous soirées tonight. There is to be dancing."

"Is she now? Famous!" Lydia clapped her hands together. "I hope she may be persuaded to send us an invitation, late though we are. I am sure she will be glad to do so, once she knows we are in town, for we are old friends."

"That is capital." Mr. Conroy beamed at them and glanced back at the small party sitting at his table. He bowed again to both women, but his gaze lingered on Phoebe, his eyes alert—and interested. "I'm afraid I must return to my friends. But perhaps I shall see you tonight."

"Why, yes . . . perhaps." Phoebe's lips drew up of their own accord. She was unaccustomed to being the center of such focused attention, especially from someone as handsome and agreeable as Mr. Conroy.

When Mr. Conroy returned to his friends, Lydia took her place at an empty table, and Phoebe followed suit. A servant stepped forward to take their orders. When they had requested tea and the spiced cake the shop was known for, Lydia set the ivory cloth napkin on her lap. "So you see, our adventure in Brussels begins *right away* with a soirée that is sure to be amusing. I am confident our stay here will be all you could wish for."

"I have not a doubt," Phoebe returned and leaned back as the servant placed a selection of jams and jellies on the table. She peeked at Mr. Conroy and found that he was looking at her as well, whether by accident or by design. She again fixed her gaze on the platter of jellies and decided she would risk no more looks in that direction.

Chapter Five

*F*itz came out of the library as soon as Phoebe and Lydia arrived home. He held a gilded card in his hand.

"I happened to meet Mrs. Marshall, who is in Brussels, my dear. I suppose the news will not surprise you, as you have undoubtedly obtained everything there is to know about life in our new city in the few hours you were out." Fitz's wry smile included Phoebe, and he added, "Her house is a stone's throw from the Hôtel Royale, and she insisted I accompany her inside so she could send me home with an invitation for tonight. Do you feel fatigued?" he asked, looking at Lydia and Phoebe in turn. "We can stay in if you prefer."

"Oh, Fitz, how could you tease so? Of course we are not going to miss a soirée of Mrs. Marshall's, especially when she is bound to have some of the old brigade with her, whom we have not seen since we traveled together in the Pyrénées."

"The happy days of campaigning, my sweet?" Fitz returned in an equal mix of drollery and affection.

"I was happy campaigning because it meant we were together. And then you went off to fight that horrid war in the Americas where I could not come." Lydia removed her cloak and bonnet and handed them to Sam, the footman, who had accompanied them from England. "I want to see some old faces, and I am excited to show Phoebe off. We saw Ensign Conroy today, and I believe he is already smitten."

Phoebe smiled at Sam as she handed him her cloak. "There is nothing to show off, Lydia. Do not put me to the blush, I beg of you."

She had said her words lightly to diffuse the attention, but Lydia rounded on her with perfect sincerity. "You have been sitting on the shelf long enough. And there is absolutely no reason for it. I am determined to see that you are valued at your proper worth. I promised you would be diverted in Brussels, and I intend to fulfill my promise."

Fitz pulled his pocket watch out and glanced at it. "If you wish to keep your promise, you had better dress. We will need to dine before we go."

Phoebe and Lydia exchanged a glance and hurried up to change. When Phoebe was dressed in her evening gown, she attached gold drop earrings on to her ears as Mary brushed her hair. Her new maid turned out to have a deft hand at coiffures and had been making small changes in the way Phoebe styled her hair. In the past, Phoebe had always had her maid style it with no fuss—brushed back from her face in what Anna called "her governess look" and pinned up in a chignon that might have the addition of a few curls if the occasion called for it. It felt more natural to keep to such a simple look.

But as soon as the earrings were in place, Mary lowered the brush and scrunched her eyes as she examined Phoebe from all angles. "Miss, I think we might cut more of the sides here if you'll permit. It'll hold the curls better."

Phoebe stared at her face in the glass, frozen at the thought of so drastic a change. She glanced doubtfully in the reflection at Mary, who demonstrated what she'd had in mind by holding sections of Phoebe's hair up to frame her face. Phoebe hesitated still. Could she do such a thing?

Frederick's words filtered through her mind. *Do something daring.* He surely did not have a modish hair style in mind when he said that, but . . . why should she not? *If I can't do something as simple as cut my hair, what sort of courage will I ever have?*

"You may do it."

Mary had been heating curling irons in the fireplace, and after she cut some strands as short as Phoebe's chin, she pulled one of them out and curled the short strands to frame her face. The curl sprang to life next to her cheek, which had the effect of softening her look. Phoebe couldn't explain why, but the blonde curls so close to her face caused her eyes to sparkle with life. *Goodness. Not even Anna has attempted such a hairstyle!*

She continued to study her reflection as Mary curled the last piece of hair, and she wondered . . . *oh*, she wondered what Frederick might think if he saw her hair. Would he discover an interest in her? Phoebe's stomach lurched in the old familiar way it did whenever she thought of him, but this time it was accompanied by a feeling akin to grief. Her coming to Brussels heralded the end of long-cherished hopes. He would look for her in vain in London—at least she hoped he might think of her at least once after he found out she had left—but she would be here in Brussels, where she was likely to find a husband who was not he.

There was a knock on the door, and Lydia poked her head in. "Cook has set out a dinner for us. Are you ready?" Phoebe faced her, lips turned up in a self-conscious smile, and Lydia gasped. "Oh, you *do* look lovely. And Mary has cut your hair. Well done. We should have thought of this ages ago. My goodness, but I believe you will have scores of gentlemen flocking to your side tonight."

Phoebe stood and brushed the folds out of her dress to distract herself from the attention. She bit her lip and tried to stop grinning like a fool. "We shall see about that. I am ready."

"Mary, Miss Tunstall will need her warmer cloak, as the air has grown chilly. Bring that downstairs, for we shall leave right after we finish eating."

"Yes, ma'am."

Phoebe followed Lydia to the dining room, where their conversation jumped from one thing to another as they recounted to Fitz all they had seen that day. Phoebe could hardly recognize herself as she laughed and fought Lydia for her share in the conversation. She couldn't believe that right upon arrival, they already had somewhere to go. If being in a foreign country had not filled her with promise that this Season would be different, a party with an entirely new set of people—and, if one were being perfectly honest with oneself, where the men would far outnumber the women—gave her all the hope she needed.

Fitz had given orders to the groom to bring the carriage around at nine o'clock. The weather had indeed grown chilly without the sun to warm them, and Phoebe wrapped her cloak around her white dress. Wishing to make a good first impression on Brussels society, she had chosen a gown with short puffed sleeves and gossamer-thin Indian muslin that extended to her wrists. Under her bust was tied a gold ribbon with pearls sewn in tiny rows. It was not a dress she often wore because it seemed such a shame to waste it on smaller affairs. But this was a new life. A new adventure. And sometimes one need not wait for a grand occasion to look and feel one's best.

To the more spiteful gossips, of which London abounded, Lydia had come down in station when she married Lieutenant-Colonel Fitzwilliam—or Major Fitzwilliam, as he had been at the time. Lydia was sister to a *viscount*, her mother had been quick to remind her when she attempted to forbid the match with Fitz. In the end, it was her brother, Frederick, who'd countenanced it, and Lydia was allowed to marry for love and follow Fitz off to the Peninsula. After all, Lord Ingram had inherited the viscountcy, and his decisions about family matters outweighed his mother's, even by Lady Ingram's own standards.

Tonight, for a woman married to a career soldier, officer though he was, Lydia did not look like one who had come down in station. Her dress in rich Damescene purple offset her dark curls and lent a regal air to her bearing. And as Lydia had surely known from experience, standing at the side of her red-haired husband, the color set him off to advantage, as well.

In the carriage, Phoebe clutched her hands on her lap, looking out the window in the dark as they rode to their destination. They were staying in Upper Brussels, along with most of the English, and the houses here were made of brick, not so dissimilar in style to the British with wooden doors and iron *garde-corps* on the windows. Nearer to the park, the houses and hotels were grander and built with cut beige stone.

If it were not for the unusual foreign smells that filtered into the carriage, the nasal sounds of French, and more guttural sounds of Flemish—which she could not understand—she might think herself still in London going to a ton party. All of a sudden, Phoebe was seized with a frisson of nerves, and some of the daring left her at the thought of attending a party with complete strangers.

However, here they were again in Fitz's own barouche, which had made the journey with them on the packet boat from England, the canal boat after that, then carried them from Ghent to Brussels that morning. Phoebe had ridden in it a couple of times last Season, and it seemed an odd juxtaposition to sit in such a familiar carriage in a foreign country. Fitz and Lydia talked of commonplace things as they rode, and Phoebe forced herself to focus on what they were saying, and thus calm her nerves.

The carriage stopped, and a footman from the Marshalls opened the door. Fitz hopped down and held out his hand for his wife and Phoebe. Sounds of conversation and the clinking of glasses poured through the open doors, and light flooded from the window onto the street, beckoning to them. Her legs trembling from nerves, Phoebe followed Fitz and Lydia up the stairs, where the servant took their names and announced them. There was a slight lull in conversation as their party walked in, for the gathering was too intimate to let newcomers arrive unnoticed. Faces, both curious and friendly, turned their way, and Phoebe's heartbeat sped up again. Would she ever be at ease with all eyes on her?

Mrs. Marshall walked forward. "Lydia, how delighted I am to see you again. I knew you were coming, but I was sure we could not expect you until next week."

She and Lydia kissed each other on the cheek like old friends, and Lydia answered, "No, your information must have been wrong, for we were always meant to arrive today. May I present my friend, Miss Phoebe Tunstall?"

"You are most welcome." Mrs. Marshall turned her warm smile on Phoebe, even as her eyebrows lifted. "But did you say you arrived today? Fitz neglected to tell me this when I insisted you come tonight. You must be dead with fatigue."

"I assure you, we are not, ma'am," Phoebe said, surprising herself for having been the first to answer and—if she were not mistaken—surprising Lydia as well. "At the very least, *I* could not wait to begin exploring Brussels and discovering everything there is to do here."

"Well, there are a great many officers, who I am sure will be vying for your attention," Mrs. Marshall leaned in to whisper.

As if in answer to the summons, Mr. Conroy, whom Phoebe had spotted from the side of her vision, came forward. He was dressed in civilian clothing, but Lydia had informed her over dinner that he was an ensign with the 69th regiment and knew Fitz.

"Mrs. Fitzwilliam, Miss Tunstall," he said with a crooked smile as he bowed before them. "You did come after all. There is supposed to be dancing tonight, and as you may see for yourself, ladies are in short supply."

"For once." Lydia turned to Fitz. "This is your chance to hide in the card room, my love. You can escape the dancing if you wish it, and no one will trouble you over it."

Fitz took his wife's hand in his and bowed over it with a kiss. "I shall not add to the competition of gentlemen begging for your hand then. In any case, I am the one who gets to bring you home." He winked, which made Phoebe smile. If only she could have a love match as perfect as theirs. What it must be like to have a man look upon her with such open affection.

When Fitz left for the card room, Mrs. Marshall turned once again to Phoebe. "Let me bring you over to meet more of the gentlemen. They will be wishing for an introduction, I am sure. Yes, Mr. Conroy, you may come as well. I would not dream of whisking such a charming young lady out of your reach without inviting you to join us."

Phoebe turned a startled gaze to Lydia, who smiled and raised an eyebrow, as if to say, "Go." Within minutes, she found herself surrounded by gentlemen who were as attentive as Mr. Conroy, except that he seemed to consider himself to have a prior claim on Phoebe and paid her a most flattering attention. Laughter and conversation came readily to Phoebe's lips, situated as she was in the center of a group of men who clamored for her attention.

For the first time in her life, Phoebe had the novel experience of being interesting. She'd certainly had little chance to experience *that* sensation with a twin sister whose charms added sparkling wit to her self-possession. Phoebe set her gloved hand in a soldier's, not feeling any of the fatigue she ought. From there she went from one partner to the next without sitting out one dance.

There was a pause between a set of dances as the musicians rested, and Lydia came over to Phoebe. "Are you having as much fun as I hope you are?"

Lydia's bright eyes twinkled, and Phoebe could not help but respond with a broad smile and a nod. *This* was exactly what she needed to forget Frederick Ingram. She needed to be courted and admired and to be seen as somebody who possessed womanly grace, rather than a little sister who was timid and cowardly and not interesting at all. The memory of how Frederick viewed her threatened to sink Phoebe's spirits, and she forced herself back to the gaiety of their surroundings by sheer will.

Phoebe opened her mouth to comment on how amiable the officers were, when she was interrupted by the arrival of a broad-chested, hook-nosed older woman. She approached them and neatly blocked their view of the shorter man trailing her. He moved to the woman's side, revealing an attire sadly out of fashion, which included a wig, ornate waistcoat, and—Phoebe thought—hidden stays.

"Mrs. Fitzwilliam," she exclaimed. "You have arrived in Brussels. I heard rumors you would be here."

Lydia's smile grew forced, and Phoebe had an inkling the woman was not a favorite of hers. "Mrs. Parker, Mr. Parker, how delightful. What brings you to Brussels?"

"We go where the regiment goes, even though our son has sold out. And Brussels is simply *full* of opportunities. I shall see if I can secure you an invitation to one of the Duke of Brunswick's parties."

"How kind," Lydia replied. "But I do not find it necessary to attend exalted gatherings. I much prefer spending time with friends."

"And who is *this* friend?" Mrs. Parker asked, gesturing to Phoebe in a manner that bordered on crude. With such a direct question, the introductions had to be made. Lydia was neither so cruel as to give a cut direct—nor did it appear to be a practical thing to do in the small circle of Brussels society.

"This is Miss Phoebe Tunstall." Lydia gave Phoebe a close-lipped smile that seemed apologetic.

Mrs. Parker turned her calculating gaze on Phoebe. "You simply must come for tea. I insist. We are staying on *rue de Flandre*. I shall be sure to introduce you to anyone you might wish to meet. And of course, you will be wanting to find a husband. This sort of thing you must leave up to those of us who are married."

Phoebe had the sensation of being trapped by such forced friendliness. Mr. Conroy came to ask for a second dance at that opportune moment, and she was able to escape. "If you will excuse me . . ."

The encounter left Phoebe tired, although she regained some of her energy from Mr. Conroy's attention. As she performed the steps of the quadrille, she reflected that she could not escape difficult people just because she was in a different country. They would be found wherever she went. Phoebe would just have to steel herself against their attempts to encroach, and surely anyone with the least amount of gumption could do *that*.

The fatigue of the journey began to press upon her. And although Mr. Conroy was smiling at her in such an attentive way that was nothing like the brotherly treatment Frederick Ingram usually dealt her, Phoebe thought she might suggest going home on the earlier side. Lydia had urged her to say the word when she was ready to leave. Perhaps tomorrow, when she was rested, she would remember Mr. Conroy's look and her heart would flutter.

Regardless, she was determined. This was going to be her Season.

Chapter Six

$\mathcal{F}$rederick spotted the tall buildings, spires, and fog rising up from the city of London as his carriage drove through Lambeth and rambled down the road toward the Thames. He pushed aside the book he had brought for his journey—a fruitless attempt at distracting his mind from the restlessness that did not seem to leave him night or day.

He rubbed the bristles on his chin and squeezed his eyes shut as an unbidden image of Georgiana in the arms of some unnamed gentleman rose to haunt him. It was done. She was no longer his—never had been. And if he were a man of sense, he would begin thinking of his own future.

The carriage sped on. Frederick had stopped overnight at Croydon and would be in London by midday. Plenty of time to look over his correspondence and dress for the Stanich ball, which was to open the Season that night. Now that he was free from the hope of securing a love match—for without Georgiana it could not be so—it was time to look over the matrimonial prospects with a more practical eye. Lydia had been gone a fortnight, but Phoebe would be there tonight. She was a warm reminder of happier days visiting Stratford, when Frederick would bring Anna and Phoebe candy, just to coax one of their bright smiles. That first visit they were still small enough to be tossed over his shoulder—and their family informal enough to let him do it.

Now that Lydia was settled and Frederick had no other family to see to, he would keep his eye out for Phoebe and see that she was suitably wed this Season. It would be about time, as she was too desirable to be left on the shelf. He could look after her needs alongside his own.

When Frederick reached his house on Grosvenor Street, Hartsmith came forward in a hurry and went to take his cloak, which he immediately handed over to the footman. In the butler's hand was a letter that he extended to Frederick.

"Mrs. Fitzwilliam requested that I give this to you as soon as you arrive. She said to tell you that it is most surprising and agreeable news."

It was so like Lydia to have some last-minute gossip to share with him. It was unlikely to be urgent, however. No sooner had Frederick taken the thick paper in his hand than there was a knock on the door, and Hartsmith opened it to reveal a soldier, standing stiffly and wearing the colors of the 1st regiment.

Frederick waved for the butler to let him in, and upon catching sight of him, the soldier bowed and handed Frederick a missive. "I am sent from the Secretary at War. You are requested to report there as soon as you may."

Frederick skimmed the missive, which did not add any other details than what he had just been told. The matter appeared, then, to be both secret and urgent. "You may tell Lord Bathhurst that I will need two hours to ready myself since I have only just arrived, but will come as soon as I am able."

"Yes, my lord." The soldier bowed again and turned to leave.

"Hartsmith, put Lydia's letter in the study on top of the rest of my correspondence. I will read it upon my return." His valet had followed him in and was directing the footman with Frederick's trunks. "Caldwell, have hot water brought up. I will want a shave before presenting myself at the War Offices, and be quick. I cannot delay."

"Very well, my lord." Unruffled by the sudden orders, Caldwell left the footmen and made his way toward the kitchen.

When Frederick had changed into a crisp olive-drab coat and a starched white cravat, he called for Joseph and directed the groom to ready his phaeton to take him to Whitehall. Joseph was another servant who had accompanied Frederick on campaigns where the use of several horses had been required. Joseph and Caldwell were on easy terms with each other and both performed their tasks well, whether in London or when following the drum. Neither one were men Frederick could easily part with.

At Headquarters, his former assistant, who had been transferred to the Southern Department, exited the building as Frederick hurried in. He had handled the military correspondance while Frederick convalesced after being attacked by a man spying for the French. As a result, they shared a rich history, but Frederick had no time to exchange news just now. He greeted him with a wave before climbing the steps and entering the office attached to that of the Secretary at War.

Giles Craint dipped his quill into the inkwell and continued writing at a furious pace. He did not look up when Frederick dropped his hat and gloves on the desk. "Well, Giles, what's afoot?"

The aide-de-camp looked up from his letter. "What's afoot, you ask? Why, only that the Corsican upstart has escaped from Elba."

Frederick furrowed his brows as he took a seat across from Giles. "What, Napoleon? How in the deuce did he manage that?"

Giles didn't bother to return an answer, and Frederick could hardly blame him. At times, it seemed as though there was nothing Napoleon couldn't do.

"Where is he now?"

"News has it he is in the south of France and is being welcomed rather than rebuffed."

Frederick exhaled. They were back at it again. "Did they not set a guard upon him? How is this possible? No, never mind. Don't answer that. He has the devil's own luck. Well, I must say I'm not surprised the people welcome him back as their savior. The Bourbon king has done nothing to win the people over. No wonder I was summoned."

Giles glanced at the door to Lord Bathurst's office, which was still closed, but there were sounds of conversation as the men inside drew near the door. "Yes. I have no idea what it's about, but I would be surprised if you were to remain in London, all things considered."

Frederick nodded. He had been thinking the same thing. His responsibilities since the war had ended had been increasingly to respond to requests by Sir Hudson Lowe, stationed in the Kingdom of the Netherlands as quartermaster-general. Although Frederick had no desire to act in the capacity of assistant, his knowledge of the troops' locations and requirements made him a valuable man to have on the ground.

Lord Bathurst exited with Sir William Howe De Lancey, who had served in the Peninsular War as deputy quartermaster-general. His interview today caused Frederick to narrow his eyes in consideration. De Lancey was a capable man and well liked, whereas it was commonly known that Wellington disliked Sir Hudson. Frederick wondered if the meeting had anything to do with Napoleon's march and whether De Lancey would be replacing Sir Hudson. Of course, it was all speculation at this point.

Lord Bathurst glanced at Frederick sitting across from Giles. "You're here, Ingram. Good. Come in." He shook hands with De Lancey and bid him farewell as Frederick walked forward. Lord Bathurst entered the room and gestured to the chair in front of his desk before taking his seat. "How is everything at the estate?"

"It was time I went, but all is well. Affairs are in order." Frederick wasted no time in bringing up the issue at hand. "I just learned that Napoleon is in France again."

"Yes, and given the news, you will not be surprised as to why I have called you here. However, even without this recent news, which is likely to reach Lord Wellington at the same time it reached us, the last letter I had from him included a request that you join him. He has need of you on staff to coordinate communications between the quartermaster-general and himself. I imagine with this news the need will be even greater."

"Lord Wellington is still in Vienna. Am I to go there?"

"The timing is most inconvenient, as he expressed an urgency, but this was before he had learned of Napoleon. If it were merely up to me, I would send you directly to Brussels. However, I think we must wait to hear from his lordship. My guess is that he will not delay in traveling to Brussels and will wish to have you secure suitable headquarters for him and see that he has everything he needs. Sir Hudson is in Ghent and cannot perform the role. But we must wait to hear from Wellington now that this news has come."

Frederick was not sure how suited Sir Hudson was to his position, now that he would be forced on to the duke's path. He had a pedantic, questioning tendency that would only exasperate Lord Wellington. "So, you are of a mind that Napoleon will march upwards to Brussels?" Frederick asked, adding after only a moment's pause, "I suppose it would make sense. He won't attempt Russia again, and all his threat is based in the north."

"Even if he does not go north, that is where we intend to head him off. It's where the royal family is at the moment. If he is to reclaim *la France*, he must establish himself over the Bourbons. Therefore, we must ready ourselves either to go into France to meet him or wait and rebuff him at the border. However, I think it likely that he will come to Brussels and then attempt to go to Vienna himself."

"Winning supporters along the way," Frederick added with irony.

"He will at least attempt it. So, my recommendation is to get your affairs in order and be ready to set off on the first packet to Ostend as soon as I hear from his lordship."

"You may be sure I will," Frederick said.

Frederick left the War Offices, his head so full of the startling news he had just received that he had been home for several hours before he remembered the letter from Lydia that was supposed to contain important news. She could not have had news of Napoleon, however—not that this news could be counted in any way as surprising or agreeable.

As soon as he remembered the letter, Frederick dropped the latest list of supplies and expenditures he had been studying and reached for the stack of correspondence. Hartsmith knocked softly and carried in a glass of brandy, but Frederick waved it away and asked for tea. Sitting at his desk, he slid a knife through the seal of Lydia's letter.

Fred,

We are at last ready for our departure to Brussels tomorrow, where I have no doubt the gayest time will be had. From everything I've heard, it is just like Europe of old when the Grand

Tours were taking place. I expect it will be a far cry from a wet billet in a tent in the Peninsula.

Frederick looked up from the letter, an odd grin lifting his lips. He had spared little thought for his sister who would be traveling abroad. After all, what was Brussels after Portugal? She had shown herself to be highly intrepid there. If Lydia had surprised him at first with this hidden strength, she did so no longer. However, it was a sobering thought that she was in for more than she'd bargained for when contemplating the move. Life would change in Brussels as England readied for Napoleon's attack, and she might find herself in as much of a battle there as she'd encountered in the Peninsula. He read on.

But the most delightful thing imaginable has occurred. I have invited Phoebe Tunstall to join us on our trip to Brussels, and she has accepted. In fact, we are likely all of us to be there by the time you read this letter.

Frederick grasped the letter, his jaw going slack and his heart racing a staccato beat. Although the Stanich party had slipped his mind, he would have remembered in time to go and see Phoebe. There, he would have announced the news of Napoleon's escape to her as an old friend, as it was sure to cause her some distress. He would have slipped his arm around Phoebe to comfort her, reminding her that she had nothing to worry about as long as she was on English soil.

He froze at the thought. Now, she was *not* on English soil but instead was directly on the probable path of the enemy. She would learn the news before Frederick could tell her of it, and she would have no one to reassure her that all would be well. Lydia could not possibly be up to the task. It was one thing for his sister to be there with Fitz at her side, capable and accustomed to difficult conditions in the war. It was another thing for Phoebe to accompany her—she, who had no such experience. He focused his eyes back on the words.

Phoebe said no at first, which I am sure you must have guessed had you known of my offer. She has never possessed the spirit that Anna has. (Not to say she is any the less loved for all that.) However, to my surprise and delight, she saw the wisdom of such an adventure and overnight has changed her mind and said she would come. Would you care to know what prompted her? She said it was to escape that disagreeable Mrs. Morris, but I am convinced she decided to do something daring because it was what you suggested she do. Phoebe—daring! So of course, I told her Brussels was the very thing for her.

Is that not just the most delightful news? I knew you would wish to know because we've always been close to the Tunstalls, and now you will not see her for the London Season. I am sure she will be missed. I must say how proud I am to see Phoebe doing something so out of character. I am confident she is going to amuse herself to no end, and I only wish you could be here with us. Well, I said we were ready, but there is always a hundred last-minute things to do, so I will leave you with this.

And with all my love,
Lydia

Frederick leaned back in his chair, prey to a state of numbness that was something like shock. Something daring. Those were his words! *Devil take it.* Phoebe in Brussels just at the moment when Boney had escaped from Elba. That was the last place Frederick could wish for his tender-hearted friend to be, even if she was with Lydia. Frederick cursed the carelessness that caused him to suggest such a thing to her. As soon as he arrived in Brussels, he would find a way to get her back home again. Stratford would never forgive him otherwise.

Chapter Seven

Phoebe and Lydia sat in the drawing room with a comfortable listlessness as they recovered from the days of travel and a first evening spent dancing. Phoebe had ordered Mary to loosen her stays, and she allowed herself the luxury of leaning back on the sofa as she drank her tea and took tiny bites of scone that melted on her tongue. The sofa and green upholstered chairs with the broad seats and narrower backs were placed in a circle with an opening at one end to the fireplace. And even if the dark stained-wood floors gave the room a dim aspect, the low furniture and tasteful frames hung on beige walls made it cozy.

Lydia held her cup of tea with two hands and stared out of the window with a vague expression before fixing her regard on Phoebe. "Fred must have got the letter I left, telling him that you came to Brussels with me." She smiled suddenly. "How I would have loved to see his face when he read *that*."

Phoebe's stomach leapt at the mention of Frederick's name, and she scolded herself for the involuntary reaction. Her decision to come to Brussels was tied to her having relinquished all hopes of winning his regard. She lowered her plate to her lap lest her trembling hands give her away. No one knew of her long-held feelings for Frederick Ingram—not even her own twin. It was time to put this childish fantasy behind her. If only her body wouldn't betray her.

When she was reasonably sure of her poise, Phoebe answered. "I am sure he shall not give it a second thought."

"Of course, he will," Lydia countered. "Why, when we dined together the night before he left, he said he was going to take you under his wing this Season."

"Indeed!" Phoebe did not wish to read anything into the revelation, but her heart ticked a steady rhythm in her chest.

"Indeed," Lydia mirrored. "He said it was high time for the last Miss Tunstall to be married off and that he would see to it himself. It is the kind of thing he hoped Stratford would do were the roles reversed."

Once again, Phoebe was plunged back into the role of little sister. She should not have been surprised. When had Frederick ever viewed her as anything but that? Sharp fangs of disappointment poked at her, despite her resolve to put him completely out of her mind.

At the sound of the knocker, both ladies sat upright. Phoebe set her plate on the table in front of her and brushed a crumb from her dress. Their footman opened the door and stepped into the drawing room, closing the door behind him. It was needed for privacy as the drawing room was on the ground floor, only steps from the front entrance. "Mr. Conroy is here to see you, Mrs. Fitzwilliam."

Lydia sent a mischievous look to Phoebe. "To see me, is he? Send him right in." When Sam left the room, she murmured, "In town for so short a time, and already you've made a conquest. Fred's kind offices will not be needed, I believe."

Phoebe had no time for a rejoinder before Mr. Conroy was shown in and was bowing over their hands. "I had hoped I might find you both at home today. Would you care to accompany me to the Royal Park? This is where the fashionable set gathers in Brussels, and you are sure to find pleasant Society there."

Phoebe glanced at Lydia before turning back to Mr. Conroy. "I believe we are unengaged for this afternoon, are we not, Lydia?"

"Perfectly at liberty. We have nothing pressing at the moment. We need only the time to finish our tea and change. Shall I pour you a cup?"

"With pleasure." Mr. Conroy sat on the chair closest to Phoebe. He turned his smiling face toward her, the slightest flush on his pale cheeks. "Are you worn through from dancing? I admire your fortitude in attending parties each night—and so soon after arriving in Brussels."

"We are tired, but nothing a walk in the fresh air won't cure." Phoebe passed the tea from Lydia to Mr. Conroy. "Lydia, will Fitz be joining us today?"

"No, I imagine we won't see much of my husband during the day, as he's been put in charge of the 2nd battalion of the 33rd Regiment of Foot." She smiled at Mr. Conroy. "You likely already know that."

"I do. Your husband is well liked among the infantry, ma'am." Mr. Conroy stirred his tea and added with a laugh, "He may inspire respect bordering on fear, but I don't believe there's a soldier who knows him that doesn't sing his praises."

"It is good of you to say so." Nothing gratified Lydia more than compliment paid to her husband.

Mr. Conroy stayed and finished his tea, promising to wait while the two women changed into their walking dresses and donned a warm pelisse. It was still early enough in March for spring to be a mere promise. Phoebe and Lydia exited their rooms at the same time and linked arms as they walked to the stairs to meet Mr. Conroy.

No thrill of anticipation in walking with Mr. Conroy filled Phoebe, but she hoped that this might change. She could not help but be flattered by his obvious interest. And upon that, she told herself, was enough to base a potential match. Mr. Conroy stood as soon as they reentered the drawing room, and he picked up his hat and the cane that was leaning against his chair.

"We've only been to see Lower Brussels where all the canals are," Phoebe told Mr. Conroy. "My maid told me they are not to be found in the upper portion. Where is the Royal Park located?"

Lydia answered as she buttoned her coat. "We rode alongside it on our way to Mrs. Marshall's party, so we did have a glimpse of it from the carriage. Fitz pointed it out, but you must not have been paying heed. Of course, the gardens require a visit during the day, though, where we can see more of them."

"And this is where I come in." Mr. Conroy gestured for the women to precede him out of the house.

"I am sure we will know Brussels as well as London by the time summer has arrived." Phoebe stepped behind Lydia into the cold air, the sun's rays not quite reaching them in the narrow street. In the intersection ahead, the sun shone gaily and Phoebe's heart matched its light. Here she had gained the attention of a man, who seemed as honorable as he was handsome. The likelihood that her days as a spinster would soon be behind her began to dawn on Phoebe, and she did not need the sun for her to be flooded with hope.

They set out, walking down *rue des Feuilles* and discussing the three parties they had thus far attended and the theater performance that would be held later that week. Mr. Conroy assured them that the opera must not be missed, as they were to have a special performance by Miss Nash, who had come expressly to Brussels for the purpose.

"So, you see, you did not err in your choice to come if even Miss Nash has done so," he said gaily. "Brussels will be all the rage this Season."

They entered the Royal Park, which was laid out in broad avenues. On either side of the paths were sculpted bushes and marble statues, and regular plots of earth showed splashes of color where early spring flowers poked through. Phoebe was struck by the number of people dressed in elegance, strolling or riding along the avenues, despite the chill. She could almost think she was in Hyde Park if she based her fancy on the sight of the people alone. There were even one or two faces that seemed familiar to her, whom she must have seen in London, although she could not say who they were.

They had not walked very far in the park when Phoebe noticed a figure advancing toward her, whose short stature and untamable blonde curls were all too familiar. *Martha Cummings.* It would appear she was not to benefit, simply by having left London, from the removal of one who taxed her good graces. The poor girl had done nothing to deserve Phoebe's dislike. It was only that Phoebe could scarce utter a word in edgewise whenever they met.

"Phoebe Tunstall! I had no idea you would be in Brussels, too. You are the very last person I expected to run into here." She turned to walk in Phoebe's direction. "I was sure you would wonder where I had gone when you noticed I was not to be found in London this Season. I was planning to write to tell you of my surprise. My brother, Albert—that is he, just greeting an acquaintance there—

announced that he had need of me to run his household here, and although I have no taste for adventure, I assure you, I could not tell him no. He positively *begged* me. And now, I find that you and I shall *both* be here. The prospect of enduring a Season in Brussels shan't be so hard after all."

Albert Cummings walked toward them, looking very much the male version of his sister. He was of a compact, portly build that spoke to his love of fine dining, and whose freckles were only slightly less evident than Martha's. His curls were tamer for being all the shorter, and he could not be considered a handsome man. Phoebe knew she was not being kind, and she could not identify why. Determined to repent, she offered a smile to Mr. Cummings when he came upon them.

Martha, clutching one hand to Phoebe's arm, reached her other hand out to her brother. "Albert, this is Miss Phoebe Tunstall. Isn't it the greatest joke that *she* should be *here* like I am? Phoebe, this is my brother, Mr. Albert Cummings."

"Good afternoon." Phoebe curtsied, then turned to search for Lydia, but saw that her friend had fallen behind in conversation with Mr. Conroy.

Mr. Cummings and Martha moved forward again, and Phoebe stepped beside them, remembering Anna's joke. Since Martha had greeted her without any evidence of surprise, she must have learned about the existence of her twin. "My sister, Anna, informed me that she had made your acquaintance."

Martha let out a healthy laugh that caused some of the other people strolling down the lane to turn and stare. "Your sister was such a tease and had me all turned about. She had me believing that you . . . that she was you, and that you had not only married but were with child! I was utterly at a loss to account for it as it would be so unlike you to keep such a secret."

Mr. Conroy and Lydia had been detained by people they knew, and Phoebe slowed her pace to wait for them. Martha had glanced more than once at Lydia and Mr. Conroy. Although Phoebe had no desire to introduce them and further the connection she had tried so hard to discourage in London, such a thing would be impossible to avoid. Brussels was small. They would always be meeting, and Phoebe was not a hard-hearted person.

When Lydia and Mr. Conroy came abreast, Phoebe performed the introduction. "Martha, please allow me to introduce you to my childhood friend, Mrs. Fitzwilliam. And this is Mr. Conroy. This is Miss Cummings and Mr. Cummings."

Martha curtsied. "Were you walking this direction? Shall we go on together?" Without waiting for an answer, she took Phoebe's arm again and began moving forward. "How did you decide to come *here*? I can't imagine what brought you to Brussels, as I was sure you would be eager for a London Season where all the eligible gentlemen are. I, myself, had resigned all hopes of a match when I came here, but now I'm beginning to wonder if I was wrong to do so. Why, there are so many soldiers, even if the only eligible among them are officers, which must be scarce—although it does not *seem* as though they are. I can hardly believe we are both here. What an adventure! One day our children will beg us to know all about it."

In this way she prattled on without seeming to expect an answer. Phoebe did not dare to look at Lydia for fear she might be tempted to go off into gales of laughter. She was reminded why she did not seek out Martha's acquaintance. Phoebe was already cast into the shade with a sister like Anna, and even with a friend like Lydia. But at least she loved them. She did not need someone in her life who talked to her as though she were a wall. Mr. Cummings appeared to be more reasonable than his sister, for he made conversation when called upon but did not burden his companions with profuse talk as he walked alongside them.

The conversation required little from Phoebe, and her thoughts began to drift when Martha pulled her out of the reverie by asking what their plans were for that week.

"I . . . I do not know our plans yet. We have only just arrived earlier this week—" So much had happened since then, the concept was hard for Phoebe to grasp.

"This week! You must be utterly exhausted after the travel. I know I was when I arrived, and Albert almost feared I would not be up to the task of running the household just when he needed me. Everything is so dreadfully foreign. But we have been here *two weeks*, and knowing a bit about Brussels Society as I now do, I believe you should not miss the dinner being given tonight by Mrs.

Darnell. That is, if you have received an invitation. I find I like Brussels Society ever so much more than London's. There is never a shortage of things to do, and as we are not numerous, we're nearly certain of being received everywhere."

"How nice," Phoebe replied, fighting to remain gracious. She had not come to a foreign country just to frequent the same set of people who had not delighted her in London. She paused to examine a bed of flowers, where early blooms poked out courageously, giving time for Lydia and Mr. Conroy to reach their side. Martha had gone on to describe the parties she had already attended as Phoebe's gaze drifted to the gates of the park.

There, an officer in regimentals entered the park at a clipped pace and, ignoring some of the people strolling by him, stopped at a small crowd of people he appeared to know. He relayed urgent news from the looks of it, as some of his spectators put their hands over their mouths and began to speak with animation among themselves. He moved on from them, and the same scene played out in two other groups nearby. Phoebe could not remove her gaze from the bearer of news and the effect he left behind. Something was amiss, she was sure of it. Even Martha had stopped talking.

One such group contained two soldiers, and afterwards one of them raised his hand to flag Mr. Conroy. He led the others up to Phoebe's group. "Conroy, you will never believe the news we have just received. Boney has *escaped*. He landed in the south of France and is making his way up toward Paris."

Napoleon escaped? It didn't seem possible. The only reason the English were safe on the Continent was that Napoleon had been captured and sent away. Phoebe felt the cold seep through her pelisse and moved ever so slightly closer to Lydia, who had not shown any reaction. She appeared to be digesting the news as she examined the soldier's face, surely understanding the implications better than Phoebe. After all, she had followed her husband to war against Napoleon.

Phoebe knew she was safe in Brussels. After all, the emperor would have no interest in coming here, would he? He would go to Paris and reclaim his seat of power. And . . . if he wished for anything more, the brave British soldiers would come to Brussels to defend them. But to be on the same continent as such a monster did not sit well. The Season's promises palled before the news.

Martha was peppering the unfortunate soldier with questions he could not answer, and Lydia took the time to pull Phoebe closer. "Do not fret. We are in perfect safety here, and if I fear otherwise, I will make sure to hasten you back to London, even if I have to accompany you there myself. Fitz will have heard the news by now, and perhaps he will have more to tell us at dinner."

Mr. Conroy separated from the group of soldiers and glanced at Phoebe. "Miss Tunstall, I am sure you must be as shocked by the news as we all are. I had thought Napoleon's threat to be a thing of the past." His look grew pensive and then he met Phoebe's gaze. "He almost seems to be a myth, does he not? A legendary sort of fellow who cannot be held by a simple gaol. But we'll see to it that he doesn't get very far."

"Perhaps a true gaol is what he needs," Phoebe said. "I am not sure he had such a thing on the Island of Elba. He could not have or he would not have been able to escape."

"You must be right," Mr. Conroy replied. "I believe Campbell will have a lot to answer for."

The officer left to tell others of his news, and Lydia laid her hand on Phoebe's arm. "Give me a moment, my dear. I've just seen Mrs. Marshall, and she may have more news."

Phoebe stood in place waiting for her to return, and Mr. Conroy plastered on a smile. "Well, it is not news I could wish to hear. And we are so newly relieved of our trouble in the Americas. But . . . I am sure all will be well. Let us focus instead on what a delightful afternoon you have offered me by allowing me to walk in your company. I have heard Mrs. Darnell is throwing a dinner party tonight. Might I dare to hope you and Mrs. Fitzwilliam will attend?"

Phoebe glanced after Lydia, who, if her drawn brows were any indication, appeared to be discussing the latest news and not receiving much reassurance in return. "I cannot say until I find out what Lieutenant-Colonel Fitzwilliam has planned for us, but"—she turned to him, attempting to recapture the hope and excitement from their first night in Brussels—"I do hope we might be able to attend."

Mr. Conroy offered his arm to bring her to Lydia. "Good. I will look out for you, then."

In the end, they did not attend the dinner that night because, although Fitz was unable to enlighten them with further information on Napoleon's escape, he had much to occupy him. He had been tasked with apprising certain officers in Ghent and Bruges of the situation, and when finished with his correspondence, he sent the letters off with aides on horseback.

They dined late that evening with just the three of them. The only additional communication Fitz brought concerned the Duke of Richmond, who had sent off an urgent letter to Vienna to find out what Lord Wellington would have them do. There was plenty to discuss about what the news might imply, but some of Phoebe's fears had begun to die down as a more practical turn of mind took over. She thought that they could very well continue with their life in Brussels since nothing was likely to happen at present. And that meant more parties, operas, and dinners.

This led Phoebe to spare a thought for Mr. Conroy, and she wondered if he had suffered a stab of disappointment at not finding her that evening.

Chapter Eight

At last, Frederick received word from the duke that he was to go directly to Brussels. It was what he had expected and desired, and he leapt into action to prepare for a departure the next day. A fortnight had already passed where he'd had to sit on the news and wait for orders, and there was little he liked less than that.

The journey to Brussels was scheduled to take a week. Frederick booked passage on a packet boat at Ramsgate heading for Ostend. The winds were favorable, and he arrived later that day. From Ostend he boarded the narrow boat that would carry him along the picturesque canals to Brussels. He would make the entire voyage that way, disembarking at last in the Grand Bassin just inside the ramparts. He sailed with his trunks and carriage, jealously guarded by Caldwell, along with four horses that Joseph would care for. Frederick feared he would need them should it come to war, and he had no confidence in his ability to find good cattle when he was there.

The canal boat was filled with more soldiers than civilians, which came as no surprise. The Secretary at War had spoken of their immediate plans to build up their forces in Brussels, even though they were not certain what Napoleon's final move would be. Frederick had made some acquaintances among the officers on the boat, but as he kept largely to himself, was given plenty of time to think.

Persistent thoughts of Georgiana with her faceless new husband intruded Frederick's well-ordered mind, and he quickly banished them with a sense of irritation. Nothing was more pointless than pining over what could not be. But Frederick was also thinking ahead to what awaited him. He knew he could trust his sister to handle nearly any challenge. Lydia had shown herself to be of much more fortitude than he ever could have imagined growing up with her. She would manage the news of Napoleon's arrival on the Continent with courage. But Phoebe?

The only image he could summon of his childhood friend in face of such a threat was one of a tongue-tied maiden. He could easily imagine her cowering in her room, fearing to leave it while tales of that monster Napoleon Bonaparte circulated. He knew no one else in his intimate acquaintance who was so retiring as Phoebe Tunstall. What spirit of mischief had prompted him to propose that Phoebe do something so contrary to her nature when—had he said nothing at all—she might still be safe in London? Only he was to blame for her present predicament, and no one would convince him otherwise. He needed to set it right.

From the moment they had set foot in Brussels, their life had been a flurry of activities. During the day, Phoebe and Lydia invariably went to the Royal Park, missing only one day when there had been a downpour. They began to cross paths with the same people, and in such intimate Society, introductions were a simple thing to obtain. They made morning calls and received them, and every night went to a different event. One night it was to hear Miss Nash sing, another it was to attend a soirée; there was a dinner the evening after—and their evenings continued in the same vein. There was simply no time to worry about the looming threat of a French invasion, besides such a threat seeming so very distant.

It was not long before Phoebe was made to feel quite the belle of each gathering. Officers and gentlemen remembered her name, sought her out, and remained at her side when there was no dancing. Admirers sent flowers each day, and the variety of them brightened the drawing room with their colors and scents.

It was a novel experience. In London, Phoebe had always given up the center of attention to her more dazzling twin. She had been content to hang back with Aunt Shae. Or, perhaps . . . content was not the right word. She'd felt it to be her responsibility—and a heavy one at that—as someone needed to stay with her elderly aunt. The lot naturally fell to her.

But here, Phoebe had the heady sensation of having all of Brussels at her feet. She prepared for the largest ball yet to be held in Brussels for the Season; and as she stood in her shift, examining the contents of her wardrobe and waiting for Mary to arrive with the curling irons, she chuckled to herself. *I am beginning to believe myself a desirable catch—advanced age, notwithstanding.*

Baroness Turton was holding the ball in her rented lodgings on *rue de la Madeleine*, and Phoebe chose her gown with care. In general, she gave little thought to what she wore. After all, Anna cared enough for the two of them. But this time, Phoebe imagined what kind of splash she would make if she were to put on something surprising. The gown she was thinking of was one of the newer ones in a bold color that Anna had convinced her to have made up when they were in London.

The carmine-red gown in silk taffeta had a lower neckline than she was accustomed to, but it was in no way indecent. Its bodice was cut in the form of a square, and the thin sleeves on either side came up just over the shoulder with tiny seed pearls sewn into the seam. A thin gossamer-like fabric overlay in the same color as the gown added a shimmering effect in candlelight. The result was magnificent, and Phoebe thought that no woman could be cast into the shade while wearing such a gown.

It was not just the gown that was so new and out of character. Mary arrived with the irons and styled Phoebe's hair in the new, shorter curls. Apart from that first night when her maid had cut the sides of her hair, Phoebe generally wore them pinned back. It seemed easier to slip on and off bonnets that way.

Tonight, Mary curled the strands in front, then crimped the remaining hair on the sides to form waves, which she pulled into a softer chignon behind. She attached paste diamond pins strategically throughout her blonde curls to make it seem as though Phoebe's entire ensemble was bejeweled from head to toe. The toilette was complete with a ruby necklace set in gold around her neck, and gold and ruby drops in her ears. She dabbed her favorite lavender scent on her collarbones.

Phoebe pulled on her long white gloves, her nerves jumping in anticipation. She glanced one last time in the looking glass as Mary tugged at the overlay from behind the dress to smooth it. Tonight was going to be different—Phoebe just knew it. *I am going to this party to be admired, and I am going to have fun before finding a husband and settling down.* If evidence of the past week had proven anything, Mr. Conroy was looking to be the leading candidate. But Phoebe was not going to choose too soon. She was going to enjoy her Season.

She entered the drawing room, and both Fitz and Lydia looked up from where they were sitting. Lydia stood with a satisfied smile. "Phoebe, I swear, I have never seen you look so well." She came over to examine Phoebe's gown, fingering the red overlay of her dress.

"You look very fine," Fitz said. "As I am, to a degree, responsible for you, I shall have to make sure all your suitors behave with the utmost propriety. I must have my work cut out for me, though. I am sure there will be many vying for your attention."

Phoebe felt her cheeks grow warm under such attention, but she was determined not to shrink from the praise. "I daresay Anna was right about this color. She did not imagine where I would be wearing it when she recommended it, though."

"Assuredly not," Lydia replied with a laugh.

Fitz glanced at the clock on the mantel. "Shall we set out?"

Phoebe stared through the window of the carriage as they rode, comparing the streets she knew with the ones she had yet to discover. Before long, they turned on *rue de la Madeleine,* where the noise of the guests reached them as they pulled up. A footman stood in attendance, and he assisted the ladies to alight. Fitz gave instructions to the groom, who then drove off, and the three of them joined the milling throngs up the stairs.

"Lady Turton, Sir William," Fitz said, bowing. "You know my wife. May I present her friend, Miss Phoebe Tunstall?" He stepped aside and exchanged a few words with Sir William.

Lady Turton was young, though married to the baron, who was much more advanced in years. Despite her youth, she assumed her role of hostess with poise. "Miss Tunstall, it is a pleasure to make your acquaintance. As Brussels is so small, I am sure we will have a chance to further it before long." Having bestowed a warm welcome, she turned to the next guests crowding in.

The ballroom was not yet fully crowded, and Phoebe stopped to see who was there. She saw more than one person glance her way, and she turned to Lydia as a sprig of fear seized her. Might there be something wrong with her appearance, or was the dress too bold? She thought she had conquered all insecurities over such a trifling thing as her appearance.

Lydia knew her well, for without even meeting Phoebe's gaze, she leaned in to murmur, "You are turning all heads tonight, my dear. I am glad."

Phoebe remembered to lift her chin and throw back her shoulders. *I will not be able to find a husband if I hide in the shadows as I usually do*, she reminded herself.

Mr. Conroy wasted no time in coming up to Phoebe as soon as he spotted her. There was a light to his eyes and a smile to his lips—a singular focus that set her nerves on edge again.

"Why, Miss Tunstall, I find myself at a loss for words when I behold you like this." He held out his hand, and she placed hers in his as he bowed over it.

Phoebe wasn't sure she was ready for Mr. Conroy's focused attention, but she forced herself to look him straight in the eyes in keeping with her determination not to shrink back. "How kind of you to say so, even though I am sure you must be very skilled at flattery."

Their gaze held a beat too long, and Mr. Conroy's eyes widened a fraction. He took a step closer, as if drawn by an invisible thread. It took Phoebe an instant to understand what it all meant and almost laughed when she realized with a start that she was *flirting*.

Mr. Conroy remained fixed at her side, but Phoebe did not have time to examine how she felt about his attention because other men began to take notice, too. They flocked over, forming a small group.

"Miss Tunstall, I hope you mean to save a dance for me this evening."

"Miss Tunstall, you are a vision. I believe I had your word at the last assembly that you would dance with me at this one."

"Why of course," she said, responding to the first officer who had addressed her, adding to the other gentleman, "Why, yes, Mr. Mann. I remember, and I would be delighted."

"Miss Tunstall," a lieutenant called out, starting forward.

Mr. Conroy held up his hand, and Phoebe thought she detected thinly veiled annoyance. "You will get your chance, I am sure. But first Miss Tunstall is promised to me." He held out his arm, and Phoebe rested her hand on it, offering an apologetic smile to the other gentlemen as Mr. Conroy led her to the dance floor.

There was a set still in progress, and as they waited Mr. Conroy leaned down to speak. "I believe I am partnered with the most beautiful woman at tonight's ball."

Phoebe returned a smile, unsure of how to respond. It was flattering, but she could hardly agree with him by thanking him. She hoped he had other topics of conversation to entertain her with than how she looked.

"Are you finding Brussels to your liking?" he asked when the silence stretched.

"I am. I find it vastly amusing." She darted another glance at him, unwilling to meet his gaze head-on a second time. She could not afford to be direct in her attention until she could be sure of her own heart. If only their conversation could leave the realm of commonplaces, she might be less nervous.

"I am glad to hear it. I was afraid you would wish to rush to London once you heard that Bonaparte is back on the Continent. Brussels would seem a dim place if you were to leave."

Ignoring the direct compliment, which came too fast for her liking, Phoebe knit her brow. "Do you think Napoleon will come to Brussels? It seems unlikely that he should do so when he is so uncertain of his welcome in France. Surely there is no reason to leave that you know of?" Her throat went dry as vague fears mounted. Could they be in danger here? Of course, Fitz would look out for her along with his wife, but what could be done against a tyrant, hungry to conquer more lands?

"There is not the least need for you to feel worried," Mr. Conroy assured her. "I will let you know if there is any cause for concern. In any case, I will be here should you need anything."

The set ended, and the couples moved off the floor as Mr. Conroy ushered Phoebe into the center. He had spoken directly to Phoebe's fear in saying he would be here if she needed anything. Mr. Conroy was becoming determined in his pursuit. That was what she wanted, wasn't it? Yet, it did little to bring her comfort. She couldn't imagine running to him if she needed help.

She hoped her feelings would change with time. Or maybe it simply meant he was the wrong one for her. Phoebe had little experience with such matters, despite having made her debut four Seasons ago. The music began and Mr. Conroy smiled at her and held out his gloved hand for Phoebe to place hers in it.

She would not show any strong preference until she could be sure, but that did not mean she could not throw off all of her cares and enjoy this dance.

Frederick arrived in the late afternoon to Brussels. He had his horse saddled and went directly to the Hôtel Ducale, where Lord Bathhurst had recommended he take lodgings. He left Caldwell and Joseph to follow with his personal effects. The Duke of Richmond rented an office in the hotel, and Frederick was determined to make his acquaintance without delay. He would be best-equipped to guide Frederick in preparing for Wellington's arrival. As much as he was looking forward to surprising Lydia and Phoebe, his sense of duty prompted him to report to Lord Richmond first.

"My lord, I believe you expected to see me here," Frederick said as he was ushered into the Duke of Richmond's chamber.

"Indeed. Lord Bathhurst sent a letter that you were coming. I was gratified that his lordship sought fit to send someone immediately. I am told we are to expect De Lancey as well. Did he come with you?"

Frederick shook his head. "He is to be married first but will not tarry after the happy event, I believe." Talk of De Lancey had brought to mind Frederick's speculation that the current quartermaster-general would soon be replaced. That led him to ask about the man currently holding the position. "And . . . Sir Hudson?"

If Lord Richmond knew of changes in personnel, he did not communicate them to Frederick. "He has begun making arrangements. Troops will be arriving by the boatload."

Frederick nodded. "I traveled over with a boat full of soldiers, myself."

"Sir Hudson has had his hands full setting up lodgings for the men." The duke looked up when a servant appeared, and he ordered him to bring refreshments.

"I am to assist Sir Hudson to some degree," Frederick said. "While his focus is the troops, mine will be scouting out appropriate headquarters for the officers."

Lord Richmond gestured to the spacious room. "You will find plenty suitable. There is a house on *rue du Parc* that should suit Lord Wellington. It's spacious, but there are several rooms where he might hold meetings. I would try there first. But do that tomorrow. Tonight, unless you are dead with fatigue, I suggest you present yourself at Lady Turton's ball. Everyone is going to be there, and it would be good to let Brussels Society know you have arrived. I will have my servant procure you an invitation to it. Of course, there will be a flurry of invitations to follow, but we can't have you tucked away, sight unseen, in the gayest city on the Continent."

Frederick looked at him curiously. "Is it as bad as London? Something every night?"

Lord Richmond laughed. "Worse," he exclaimed. "It is such a blasted intimate Society that everyone notices whether or not you are in attendance, and it becomes fodder for gossip. One feels almost *compelled* to make an appearance. I don't know how we all bear it, but we do manage to amuse ourselves here."

The servant brought in drinks, and Frederick took a sip of his, leaning back in his chair. "Has there been a change of mood since you had word of Boney's escape?"

"There is some undercurrent of nervousness—or perhaps *excitement* is a better word," Lord Richmond admitted. "But there is no talk of leaving. People do not see Napoleon capable of dislodging the king as easily as that. Or they wonder in the case that he can regain power, whether the upstart will be ready to begin marching into other territories after such a resounding defeat in Russia. Why, he can hardly have men left for the task."

"I am somewhat of this mind." Frederick rubbed his chin as he gathered his thoughts. "Yet a man of his stamp, who once thought to rule the entire Continent, and England besides, will not so quickly change his spots. And he does have an unfortunate knack for successful warfare."

"Well, we shall see. In any case, it is good to have you here. Lord Wellington will have enough tasks to hand off to you, but you are a capable man for the job." Lord Richmond cocked his head and said with a glimmer of a smile, "You are so like your father, you know."

Having finished his drink, Frederick met Lord Richmond's gaze and put his hands on his knees before standing. "That is always a fine compliment, although what I wouldn't give to have him here in my stead."

"Well." Lord Richmond offered his hand. "I believe we will be seeing much of each other in the coming months."

"I presume so," Frederick replied, giving the duke a firm handshake and turning to go. He had hoped to call on Lydia and Phoebe before he did anything else, but with Lord Richmond's advice in mind, he decided he would have more success looking for them at the ball.

Caldwell had directed the hotel servants to bring Frederick's trunks to his room, while Joseph brought the phaeton to the stables. His trunks open and half-unpacked, Frederick stood in front of the glass where he whipped the end of his starched cravat through the loop he had created and gave a series of tugs until he had achieved the effect he was striving for.

He wore a burgundy waistcoat and black breeches, and Caldwell helped him on with his black coat. The shoes appropriate for the ball had been buried in the bottom of his trunk, as Frederick had not anticipated needing them so soon upon his arrival, but they were found and Frederick set off at last.

It was late when he climbed the steps to the Turtons and went to greet the host and hostess, who were no longer at their places by the door. He thanked them for the last-minute invitation that had arrived as he was getting ready. Lord Richmond could be spotted in conversation on the other side of the room.

The duke had been right. All of Brussels appeared to be at this party. Frederick greeted a few people he knew as he searched the crowds for Lydia. There was not a chance that his sister would be absent from such a gathering as this.

He finally caught a glimpse of Lydia and made his way over to her. She hadn't yet turned Frederick's way when the crowd opened before him, catching his attention and revealing the most ravishing beauty in the center of it. The woman wore a red dress, exquisitely molded to her form, that shimmered in the candlelight, along with the jeweled clips pinned throughout her curls. Her profile was partially hidden, but Frederick could see her laughing and extending her gloved hand for a gentleman to bow over it.

He froze in his steps. The fact that he could notice another woman boded well for being able to put the sad story of Georgiana Audley behind him. And this one arrested his attention completely, as he was unable to take his eyes off the enchanting creature before him. Although she had still not turned, there was a decidedly familiar air about her, and Frederick waited. He found himself holding his breath as she ducked her head shyly—a movement so familiar it plunged him back into his early youth. Was it . . . could it be?

The woman turned fully in Frederick's direction at the same time that Lydia spotted him, crying out, "Fred! *You*, here in Brussels. I can hardly believe my eyes. You gave no warning that you were coming. What brought you here? Although—I think I must guess." Frederick glanced at his sister but dragged his eyes back to the bewitching creature in his path, his voice seeming to have fled in his complete and utter surprise. That ravishing creature in front of him was none other than Phoebe Tunstall.

Chapter Nine

*P*hoebe had finished her dance with Mr. Conroy. He had not yet had a chance to relinquish her to another when she was surrounded once again by a circle of eager suitors. It was such a novel experience for her. She had been told countless times that she and Anna were very pretty girls, but it had always been Anna who received the notice. Attention made Phoebe uncomfortable.

Now, for the first time, attracting the regard of others was gratifying rather than a curse because she felt they were truly interested in her. They were not using her to get to Anna or standing up for a set with her for lack of a better partner. They seemed to genuinely seek her out.

Mr. Conroy was persistent in his attentions, but the other gentlemen were no less so. It was only that Mr. Conroy held a slight advantage over the others. Phoebe had not yet walked with them or gone riding together in the park. There had been no conversations with them beyond the merest pleasantries. With Mr. Conroy, there had not been many conversations, but there had been some.

Phoebe turned from Mr. Conroy to the gentlemen who had gathered around her when a tingle on her spine made her want to turn. She had the uncanny sensation she was being watched. It was so strong that she did turn—slowly—and there, directly in her path, stood Frederick Ingram, his eyes on her.

Phoebe willed her expression not to change, although the blood drained from her face so quickly she was afraid for the briefest moment that she would faint. She would not give Frederick the satisfaction of knowing what a shock it was to see him there.

After a brief, numb moment where she could only blink stupidly, she turned back to Mr. Conroy, who was still at her side. "Thank you for partnering me for a dance."

He looked at her for an instant, but his gaze was drawn to Frederick, who had not moved. Phoebe ignored the questioning gaze Mr. Conroy sent Frederick, then her, and she instead turned to the other gentlemen, suddenly at a loss. It would not be right to accept one of the dances now that Frederick had come. He would wish to speak to her, and having seen him, Phoebe could not snub him by going off to dance on someone's arm. And if she was being honest with herself, she wished for nothing more than to talk to him.

However, none of that could be voiced, so she merely smiled at the other gentlemen and shook her head. "I beg you will excuse me. I have something I wish to say to Lydia."

"By all means." She heard this and other responses like it but would not have been able to say who spoke them.

Despite having conjured the excuse, Phoebe did not know how she was going to make her way over to Lydia, who stood at Frederick's side. Her feet did not seem to want to obey her, and she turned away in confusion. She had always kept a rigid hold over her emotions, training herself to be perfectly natural in front of Frederick. Never had his appearance thrown her in such a way that she was frozen in place. But her beleaguered brain asked why he was here, and it demanded: *He must come to me.* Why should she fall into the same pattern she had from childhood of running to him? There were plenty of other gentlemen who found her interesting, even if Frederick Ingram still looked at her like a child. Maybe it was time to show him that she no longer was one.

Enough. She must walk to where Lydia and her brother were standing, and Phoebe took a deep breath and turned to go. It was unnecessary. Frederick Ingram was standing right in front of her.

"Phoebe, I don't believe I've ever seen you look quite so ravishing." His voice was clipped, and she wondered if she had done something to bother him. He glanced at the other gentlemen who had not moved from their close circle after being dismissed, and she little knew how much time had passed since she had spoken to them. It had seemed enough time for them to go elsewhere.

Frederick took matters into his own hands. "Gentlemen, indulge me a few moments of time with Miss Tunstall, will you? We are old friends and have some catching up to do."

He did not give them a chance to respond but took Phoebe's hand and slipped it under his elbow, leading her—not toward Lydia as she expected—but to a corner, which held fewer people.

When he stopped and faced her, his expression was grave. "Phoebe, I beg you will forgive me for my suggestion when we were in London. I should never have counseled you to do something risky. I have been reproaching myself these past weeks for my thoughtless words. After all, it is what *I* said that led you here, I believe. And this is the very last place I could wish to see you."

Phoebe went cold at his words. She knew Frederick did not look at her with any sort of interest, but now he would not wish for her presence in Brussels? He must think her a sad bore. "I am sorry you are not happy to find me here," she said in a stilted voice.

A look of confusion crossed Frederick's features. "No, you misunderstand me. In ordinary circumstances I would be delighted to see you here. In fact, I am astonished to see you at a ball, and quite sought after if I am not mistaken. But I had assumed the news of Napoleon's escape would make social engagements unpalatable for you. What I mean to say is, I'm sorry for encouraging you to do something risky and daring—and so out of character, because it led you here. If . . ." He paused, faltering. "If that makes things clearer."

Phoebe did not have to remind herself to throw her shoulders back when she answered him. "Fred, I may not be as outgoing as Anna, but I am not so fearful as that. I am disappointed that you think so little of me." She realized belatedly that she had slipped into using the nickname his sister used—the one Phoebe sometimes called him in her head. She had always questioned whether using his Christian name was correct after she had reached her majority, but he had insisted upon it. Using a nickname that no one else used but family was the outside of enough, but it had slipped from her tongue.

Frederick did not seem to have noticed. "No, it is not that I think you cowardly. But I don't know how I will face Stratford the next time

I see him. I have not communicated with him since we've had word of Napoleon's escape, but I don't need a letter from him to know that he will have my neck when he finds out I sent his little sister to the country that harbors the world's most notorious escaped prisoner. I think you should go back to England, while we quell the threat."

"Stratford can hardly wring your neck," Phoebe countered. "He will be too busy, as Eleanor is to be confined any day now. And allow me to assure you, I do not plan to go anywhere. I'm enjoying myself." Phoebe gestured to the packed ballroom. "For the first time in years I'm finding amusement. I do not regret for an instant having accepted Lydia's invitation, so you may put the idea of my going home to rest."

Frederick did not answer right away but exhaled and stared over Phoebe's shoulder as if to garner his patience. She knew he would likely attempt to get her to see reason—but not before he considered what *she* had expressed. It was a quality that endeared him to her. Even when she was young, Frederick did not talk over her but considered her feelings and opinions, despite being ten years her senior.

"I have no authority over you," he said at last, bringing his gaze to meet hers. "You are not my sister, and you are no longer a girl."

Well at least you realize that.

"But I hope you will trust me enough as your friend to hear me out. And if, at any point, I think you should leave that you will listen to me. Stratford would never forgive me if anything happened to you, and I would never forgive myself."

Phoebe was touched by his concern, but she set her lips in opposition. "Are you telling Lydia to leave as well?"

Frederick glanced at his sister, and Phoebe followed his gaze. At that moment, Fitz came to Lydia's side. He saw Frederick across the room and lifted his hand in greeting, not showing any surprise at seeing his brother-in-law. Frederick returned it and then brought his attention back to Phoebe. "I suppose I would tell her if I thought she would listen. But the truth of the matter is, she is Fitz's responsibility now, not mine. And Fitz is not a man to take kindly to another man telling him how he should handle his wife—even a well-meaning brother. You, however, are another story."

Phoebe's defiance took on the form of a bright smile that she pasted on her face. Frederick was not her husband to order her about, nor did he seem to have any interest in taking on the role. "I beg you will not trouble yourself. Even if Stratford were not to agree with my decision to remain, I am old enough to know my own mind and make my own decisions. I don't intend to revert back to girlhood and start handing over my independence now."

Frederick opened his mouth to reply but had no chance. Lydia had grown tired of waiting and came over, bringing Fitz in tow. "Fred, you arrive and barely spare me two words before rushing off to talk to Phoebe. You didn't write to tell us you were coming either. What a start you gave me. Have you come on military business or for pleasure?"

Frederick broke Phoebe's gaze to face his sister, then nodded to her husband. "Fitz. Good to see you. I wasn't even sure until the last minute that I *was* coming, so I didn't bother to write. What purpose would there be other than to say I might be? And you would eventually learn that for yourself. Wellington has asked for my services on staff. How are affairs in Ghent?"

"I have not been since we've had word of Boney's escape," Fitz replied. "Half the population there is loyal to him, so I imagine his escape will be met with some cheering. It's going to be an interesting game to see whether he comes this far north. It will make our stay here that much more memorable."

Frederick glanced at Phoebe, then asked Fitz, "Do you think Phoebe should go back to London? Do you plan to send Lydia?"

It is as though I am not even here, Phoebe thought with indignation.

Lydia let out a gasp of protest and rounded on her husband. "You are not thinking of sending me home, I should hope. I was with you in the Peninsula, and that was vastly more uncomfortable than here. This is no different than London."

"Well, it is likely to be *a little* different than London if Napoleon heads north. But no, my dear. Truth be told, it is so much more pleasant with you here. I would find it hard to go on without you." Fitz slipped Lydia's arm through his and pulled his wife closer. Phoebe was not often prey to jealousy, but there was something intimate and reassuring in that gesture, and it made her own lack of intimacy—her own loneliness—that much more acute.

She fought against the hollowness inside. "So, you see, Frederick, Fitz does not think there is any need to run back to England. I hope we shall be able to put this topic to rest."

Lydia raised her eyebrows at her brother and added her mite. "I am surprised at you. Why should you recommend we go home? Brussels is full of amusing things to do. We are surrounded by soldiers who would warn us away if there was a threat—with you two at the head of the list."

Frederick glanced at Fitz and furrowed his brows. It seemed to Phoebe that an unspoken message passed between them. When Lydia put her hands on her hips and waited for him to speak, Frederick said, as though offering his last protest, "I just don't think Stratford would like Phoebe to be here. I merely suggested—"

He was unable to finish his words because Lydia shook her head. "No, Fred. Phoebe will have a much nicer time in Brussels than she would in London. There is something every night and so many people to meet." She glanced at Phoebe with an air of mischief. "So many *gentlemen*. Besides, who would take her back? You?"

Frederick raised both of his hands. "I know when a battle is lost. Forgive me for even suggesting such a thing." Phoebe stared at him, stung. Of course, he wouldn't want to take her back to London himself.

Lydia slipped her hand out of Fitz's arm and into Phoebe's. "We are going to get something to drink so you two can talk about military things, which I know you wish to do."

They walked forward a few paces, where Lady Turton gestured to Lydia. "I wanted to introduce you to the Hansens," she said, before presenting Lydia and Phoebe to the couple.

Lydia was drawn into conversation, but Phoebe's attention was still on the men behind her. She heard Frederick say, "There is no talk of anyone leaving, I assume. But surely you are not blind to the concern. It will only continue to grow more tense here as Boney makes his way to Paris. Truly are you not worried?"

"I don't like the idea that we are close to action," she heard Fitz answer. "But I don't think it right to deprive my wife of being at my side if that is where she wishes to be. If I believe there is imminent danger, however, I will send her off."

Phoebe didn't hear any more because Lydia finished talking with the Hansens, who had wished for an introduction so they could invite her and Phoebe to their musicale—even if it was generally known that the evening was to showcase their own daughters' musical talents. Lydia accepted for them both, and then they pushed their way through the crowds again. This time they were waylaid by Martha Cummings, whose plump, eager countenance always lit up when she saw Phoebe and left her feeling guilty. It could not be denied, however, that once Martha began talking, there was no escaping her.

"Who is that charming addition to your party?" Martha gushed, her eyes fixed on Frederick.

Phoebe knew to whom Martha was referring, and it only reminded her that Frederick was a man dashing enough to catch anyone's eye. She rather wished he were not so handsome. The chances of her catching his eye had always been slim.

"Lord Ingram is my brother," Lydia replied. "I am not sure how much you will see of him, however. He is here to prepare for Wellington's arrival."

"Pity."

For once, Martha had nothing to add. It was perhaps for the best, as Phoebe would have been hard pressed to respond. She had no idea what to think about the sudden appearance of the one person she had both longed to see and for whom she had completely given up hope of sharing a future. She risked a glance back at Frederick, who was still talking to Fitz, and the hopeless weight of love threatened to crush her. Just when she had been about to break free from it and turn her attention to someone else, here he was again. She did not know quite what she should think about that.

Chapter Ten

*P*erhaps it was the fact that he had just arrived in Brussels and was not in the proper frame of mind for a ball, but Frederick had found this particular ball to be of the most insipid variety. There was something about Phoebe Tunstall in a bold red dress that drew the eye to her slender form and the creamy skin above her bodice. And there she was, surrounded by a circle of eager suitors . . .

Then when he got her alone, it was only for her to defy his advice. *He*, an old friend! It unsettled him to have her question him like that. He was only looking out for her interests, and she refused him.

He was used to the version of Phoebe who weighed his words and treated him with deference. Anna had always been the defiant one. He and Anna had always got on well together but despite that, he didn't consider his friendship with her to be on quite the same level. Even as a girl, Phoebe was more mature than her years, and the few times they'd shared a deeper conversation, it had stayed with him. Once, after his father's funeral, they met by chance in Stratford's library and she asked him how he fared, her glowing eyes settling on his face as she listened. With her full attention on him, Frederick had ended up telling her more than he told most people—like how he had been afraid to step into his father's shoes.

It was a rare thing to get Phoebe's unsolicited point of view, and it was something of a treasure when it came. Although a subtle shift had occurred when she left the schoolroom, for all that, she

76

had always remained a girl in Frederick's eyes. The last thing he had expected was to find her at a ball, surrounded by men whose gazes were fixed on Phoebe as their object, and she looking very much like a woman.

By Jove! Stratford was going to kill him. And he would deserve it. Phoebe Tunstall was definitely off-limits for any other thought than the purest, most sisterly way—not that he thought of her in any other capacity.

The next day, Frederick spoke to the landlord of the house on the park and engaged its rooms for Wellington and the staff. He assumed it would not be long before Sir Hudson Lowe paid a visit to Brussels to see to the housing and supplies for the troops which would soon be coming in droves. He then paid a visit to Lord Richmond's house in Lower Brussels, but the visit was unprofitable as the general was out. Having nothing further to occupy him, Frederick set out for the Royal Park, where he was sure to see people he knew.

There had been a frost on the grass in the early part of the morning, but it had melted away and only a chill in the air reminded one that it was late March. Frederick entered the park on foot and followed the pale gravel path, bordered by green hedges on one side. The grounds were crowded, but he didn't see anyone he knew.

He took the time to appreciate the gardens that were more in the French style than the English. The hedges were cut with precision, and there were benches placed for discourse or trysts at regular intervals—innocent trysts as the park was only frequented by polite society in daylight and the seats were open enough. Frederick wandered down the main avenue, wondering if he would see a glimpse of Phoebe and wondering further whether she would look more like herself today. When he turned down a narrower avenue, he was gratified by the sight of her, dressed in a brilliant white gown, paired with a royal blue Spencer.

She was looking up at the gentleman at her side, and although Frederick could discern the usual reserve she kept for strangers, there was a smile on her lips that Frederick did not like in the least. It would not do for Phoebe to fall in love with somebody here. She should be back in London, where a courtship might take place in the regular fashion. In a city like Brussels, any gentleman might think himself worthy of her, no matter who his family was. As he studied her profile, Frederick thought of her innocence. *She should not be here where there might be a war*. He wasted no time in going to her and bowed before the gentleman and Phoebe.

"Frederick," Phoebe called out, whether from surprise or pleasure he could not tell. "Mr. Conroy, may I present Lord Ingram to you? We are old friends, so you will not be surprised that we greet each other by our Christian names."

"Pleasure," Frederick replied curtly when Mr. Conroy bowed. "What regiment are you?"

"I am an ensign with the Sixty-Ninth," Mr. Conroy answered.

"South Lincolnshire? When did you arrive?"

"We've been in place since January. We came to hold the borders, but it seems as though events beyond our control are turning our mission into quite another." Ensign Conroy gave Frederick a polite smile.

"It would seem so," Frederick answered vaguely.

There was a pause as the three of them cast their gazes around the park. Frederick knew he was likely intruding on the *tête à tête* that Mr. Conroy had envisioned, but he didn't want to leave Phoebe to the exclusive care of this gentleman. Stratford would not like it, as there was no chaperone to be seen. Not that this was in a secluded corner of the park, but still.

"Where's Lydia?" Frederick asked.

Phoebe looked around and gave a tiny shrug. "I am not sure. She should be here any minute. Mr. Conroy invited me to go walking, and Lydia planned to meet us here but said she wished to pick up some spiced cakes and has not yet arrived."

"The pace does not lift at all in Brussels, does it?" Frederick asked Phoebe wryly, but it was Ensign Conroy who answered.

"Not one bit. But when you find such charming company as Miss Tunstall, one looks for every opportunity to be amused." Mr. Conroy's smile toward Phoebe was possessive, and it irritated Frederick to no end. Phoebe should be under the protection of one of her own family members. Or in default of that, a close friend. Lydia had offered to bring her to Brussels, but she was certainly not doing her job. He would have to talk to her.

At that moment, Lydia entered the park from the entrance on the far side. Her brisk pace and purple redingote identified her yards away. She was swinging a parcel in one hand, and she raised her other hand in greeting. Frederick crossed his arms and waited until she arrived. "You are retrieving your own packages now? Have you no footman or servant to do this—or a maid to accompany you places?"

Lydia laughed. "It's the most charming thing. Not only does Wouters have the *best* cakes in Brussels, there is even a little area where one might sit and take tea and sample them. Mrs. Foster invited me to sit a bit, and I thought it would do no harm since Phoebe was in good hands. And you see, I was not long in coming."

Frederick gestured forward, hiding his irritation. "Shall we go on?"

Phoebe turned and walked alongside Mr. Conroy, who thankfully did not offer his arm. Had he done so, Frederick might have happily throttled him. He was probably a nice enough fellow, but Frederick wasn't sure the man was good enough for his friend's sister.

He and Lydia fell back a ways behind Phoebe and Mr. Conroy, and he waited until there was enough distance to murmur, "Lydia, are you sure you should be allowing Phoebe to entertain gentlemen on her own without a proper chaperone?"

Lydia sent him a look of impatience. "Do not talk fustian. Phoebe is two and twenty. She's been out for four Seasons, and she is walking with a gentleman caller in broad daylight in a public park that is packed with all of Brussels society. There is absolutely no danger to her person or her reputation."

There was truth in what his sister said, and Frederick knew it would not be wise to insist, so he merely said, "I would just like to remind you that Stratford will not be happy if we allow her to give her heart to somebody who is not worthy of her. What do you know of this Mr. Conroy?"

Lydia pursed her lips. "Fitz has nothing to say against him. In truth, I think Phoebe old enough to make up her own mind about a gentleman. I do not consider the matter too closely at all, other than to wish her happiness in her choice."

Frederick looked ahead and was deprived, due to the brim of Phoebe's hat, of the sight of her profile when she turned to speak to

Mr. Conroy. But he knew Mr. Conroy could see Phoebe's face. He couldn't say why, but he didn't like the man studying her so closely. The ensign was being entirely too familiar.

A sudden breeze pulled blonde curls free from underneath the back of Phoebe's straw poke bonnet, and it reminded Frederick of when she was much younger. But then the breeze picked up and hugged her gown to her body underneath the spencer. An inexplicable urge to grab a cloak and drape it over Phoebe—*and perhaps pull her into an embrace*—came over Frederick but he dismissed it quickly. Such errant thoughts had no place in his mind.

This was Stratford's *sister*.

"I still cannot get over Fred appearing in Brussels without giving a clue to his impending arrival. Were you never more surprised than when he made an appearance at the ball?" Lydia spooned jam onto her bread and took a bite. They had not seen Frederick again in the days since they had crossed paths with him at the park, nor had she and Lydia had much of a chance to discuss anything at length, as they were so often in the company of others. "He has never been the best at letter writing, but to not tell me he was planning to travel to the Continent is beyond anything."

"He seems to have grown extremely protective of you," Lydia added when Phoebe had remained silent. "He pulled you aside the night he arrived, after barely offering me a greeting, and then growled at me for leaving you alone with Mr. Conroy at the park."

What could Phoebe reply? She was unwilling to look too deeply into her thoughts on Frederick's arrival. She felt as though her heart had stopped beating when she saw him. The shock had been so great, all her good resolution to find a husband among Brussels society fled in an instant, and she had trouble reclaiming it again. Once more, she became the schoolgirl in his presence—tongue-tied with secret love. It had taken all her efforts to focus on what Mr. Conroy was saying after Frederick had shown up at the park. Phoebe was all out of patience with herself.

"He did not say anything of importance at the ball or the park."

Phoebe curled her fingers around the teacup and looked across the table at Lydia. Fitz walked in and greeted both ladies as he filled his plate on the sideboard.

"Good morning, dear." Lydia moved the coffee pot from where it sat beside her so her husband could set his plate down before turning her attention back to Phoebe. "By the way, what did Stratford say to your impulsive decision to come? I saw you had a letter from him two days ago and have forgotten to ask. It was so careless of me, but when I thought of it we were in mixed company, and our social engagements have not let up." She stifled a yawn. "Was he pleased to have you here? I expect we will also receive an answer from Eleanor to the letter we sent her."

"I have not had word from him since Napoleon's escape, although he must have heard about it by now. Truly, I don't know if that will change his opinion. He expressed some surprise at my impetuosity but said he knew I would be in good hands with Fitz."

Lydia gave a derisive snort. "But not with Fitz's wife. He believes he knows me too well to think me capable of taking good care of his sister."

"All that matters is the truth," Fitz said, spearing a bite of ham and putting it in his mouth.

Phoebe laughed. "I will not pretend that my brother has a glib tongue. But I am sure that if he had thought more carefully before writing, he would've praised your ability as a chaperone as readily as Fitz's." She took a sip of tea and reflected. "I do not know what he will think when he does find out that Napoleon is on the Continent, but I expect Eleanor will give us more details on that head when she writes. I have no desire to leave." She glanced at Fitz, frowning suddenly. "Unless you think I should do so? My desire to remain is unchanged, but Lydia and I have been hearing of more officers' wives removing to Antwerp."

Lydia also kept her eyes trained on Fitz, and he took some time to answer. "The only thing we can do at this point is to see how things progress. In any case, there is no imminent need to flee, and I believe if the Duchess of Richmond decides to stay in place you ladies might do so as well. We can always reconsider the matter as the situation evolves."

The marital state had been good to Fitz. He was not more than ordinary in the way of looks, but Lydia saw to his attire, and a complacency from being happily married added to his natural self-assurance and made him more handsome. He sipped his coffee, turning to his wife. "I must make a short trip to Ghent, and I will be staying overnight. I trust you will do well enough without me as escort for your social engagements?"

"You need have no fear for us, as you well know," his wife replied, giving him an indulgent look. "Did you time your visit to Ghent with the musical revue you had so little desire to attend?"

That coaxed a laugh out of Fitz. "I would like to tell you that the musicale had no bearing on the timing of my visit, but I might have been able to put the visit off a day or two had it been anything else."

"We shall do very well this evening without Fitz, won't we Phoebe?" Lydia gave her a conspiratorial smile and glanced at her husband under her eyelashes.

Phoebe drank more of her tea but was unable to touch her breakfast. It had been the same yesterday. She wondered if Frederick would be at many of the society events or if he would be occupied with military affairs as much as Fitz was. She was tempted to ask Lydia whether he would attend tonight's musicale, but she had worn the willow for Frederick Ingram for half a decade, and she was not about to give up her secret now. If Frederick was going to be there, she would learn about it eventually.

Chapter Eleven

*T*hat evening, Phoebe stood in front of the selection of new dresses in her wardrobe, wondering which one might best attract notice should some . . . particular gentleman make an appearance. The choice of gowns was not a concern she often entertained. She did not care overly much what she wore since Anna usually wore it better. She just wanted to be noticed for who she was, despite being the shyer, quieter twin. It did not mean she was content to fade into the woodwork.

At last, she chose a Saxon-green dress, edged with cream lace around the neckline and trimmed with green braid everywhere else. There were tiny rosebuds sewn in at regular intervals on the cloth, and as soon as she'd seen it, it had reminded her of a spring garden. She could only thank the heavens her paid companion had bored her so greatly in London, for she'd spent much more time at the dressmaker's shop than usual. It had paid off, for the contents of her wardrobe had never been finer. Mary styled her hair and wove a green ribbon around the cluster of curls, and Phoebe suppressed the errant thought that *surely* Frederick must notice her in such a dress.

The carriage brought them to the revue at Mrs. Hansen's house, where a collection of matrons gathered with their daughters in hopes of displaying their talents. Anna had once made a joke that such an event was no different than purchasing a horse at Tattersall's.

Phoebe had never sung before anyone unrelated to her, although she enjoyed singing very much. Anna had no such talent and would always answer for both of them, saying that neither of them could carry a tune. It was not done in a spirit of malice. Anna knew Phoebe was painfully shy and would not wish to bring notice upon herself by standing up in front of everyone.

Phoebe followed a woman in who was quietly advising her daughter on which piece to perform, and she wondered what it would be like to sing in front of a group of people. Her heart beat faster at the thought. There was no one here she knew—no one she needed to impress—unless Frederick came, and nothing was more unlikely. The hostess ushered them into the anteroom and instructed them to write their names down on the paper if they wished to sing.

Lydia laughed. "No, not for me. I am here to support and applaud the efforts of others. I will not inflict my voice upon anyone." She began to walk away, and Phoebe hesitated in front of the paper. In London, she would shrink from attention, but here, in Brussels . . . *I can be anything I choose.*

In a sudden movement, she picked up the quill from the ink pot and wrote her name at the bottom of the list, which already contained about a dozen other names. She set the pen down and turned to Lydia, who was staring at her with wide eyes.

"My word, Phoebe. I believe Brussels is going to be the making of you." Lydia's smile grew broad. "Never once have I heard you speak in front of a gathered audience, much less sing. I am looking forward to such a treat."

Phoebe bit her lip. "I suppose I can always back out if I lose my nerve." She was already losing her nerve.

Mr. Mann stepped forward upon seeing her and bowed. "Miss Tunstall! Mrs. Fitzwilliam. Did you see how many names were on the list? I have a feeling we're in for a long evening," he teased. "But I am sure to be delighted by all the talented ladies here tonight. I don't suppose I shall have the pleasure of hearing either of you sing."

Lydia glanced at Phoebe before replying. "You will have that pleasure. Phoebe has agreed to sing for us."

"Will she? Why, that is delightful." Mr. Mann's expression of pleasure was genuine, and Phoebe smiled weakly in return.

There was no backing out now. With Mr. Mann, she supposed she could be perfectly at ease since he was an unassuming gentleman. Even if Mr. Conroy should appear . . . She had not had time to complete the thought when Mr. Conroy entered the room. Phoebe took a deep, silent breath. Even with Mr. Conroy here, she *could* do this. It was not as though she were going to be singing in front of the London ton. With such intimate Society as was found in Brussels, Phoebe was becoming known. It was time she gave up her timid past.

"Shall we sit?" Lydia moved forward to the rows of chairs without waiting for an answer.

Phoebe followed, and they slid along the first row of unoccupied seats and took their places in the center. Mr. Mann took a seat at her side, and Mr. Conroy took the one next to Mr. Mann. He leaned around him and smiled at Phoebe and Lydia. "Good evening, ladies. Mann, here, has the best seat in the house. But eventually, he will need to offer to bring you refreshments. I need only be patient." Phoebe smiled at his light sally and then turned her face forward, squeezing her hands tight on her lap as the hostess came to the front of the room.

Mrs. Hansen welcomed her guests and introduced the man who would be providing the accompaniment on piano for those who chose to sing. She checked her list and invited the first young lady to make her way forward. It was Miss Foster who, although not quite on the shelf, was no longer in her first bloom of youth. She appeared to be singing because it was the proper thing to do rather than because she wished to cast out lures. She began Handel's "Silent Worship," and her pitch was correct, even if there was no passion in her voice.

As the second, then the third young lady took her place to sing, Phoebe began to grow overly warm. Her turn would soon draw near. She was not sure she would be able to go through with it—to stand up in front of a crowd of near strangers and sing. *What in the world came over me to contemplate it?* She leaned over to whisper to Lydia. "You must excuse me. I am going to get some punch."

Lydia gave her a look of compassion, likely knowing how nervous Phoebe was. Mr. Mann glanced up as Phoebe stood, and Mr. Conroy lifted his head. She made her way down the aisle, hoping he would not follow her. She needed time to think.

Phoebe went to the table in the side room and asked for a glass of punch, which she took and sipped. Thankfully, it had been iced and was cool, which helped steady her nerves. She brought her silver cup over to the double doors opening into the room where everyone was seated, and she stood in the back watching the crowd. A familiar voice came from behind, entirely too close to her ear.

"Do you plan to sing, Phoebe?"

Phoebe jumped and almost spilled the punch on her dress. Thankfully, she had drunk most of it and was able to save her dress from ruin. Frederick now stood beside her, grinning, and the sight of him made her knees weak. She froze, keeping her gaze ahead as she tried to collect herself.

He lifted his arm and leaned against the doorjamb behind her, so that were she to tilt her head back it would be resting on his arm. She was at once conscious of his presence, delighting in it. At the same time, she wished to show him she was no longer a girl who would come trotting after him just because he threw her a smile.

"I am astonished you came," she replied—coolly, she thought with inner pride—after briefly meeting his glance. "I did not take you for a man who would consider a musicale entertainment."

She felt rather than heard him laugh at her side, and he leaned in to speak in a low tone to avoid being heard over the song that Miss Yates was currently singing just a half-tone above the piano. His words vibrated in her ear. "I admit that desperate times call for desperate measures. As of yet, I have few friends here to send me invitations, so I am forced to accept whatever entertainment I can find."

Phoebe remained silent. She was never someone who had a ready answer on her lips, but she decided not to worry about that. It would serve him right to work a little harder to gain her attention. It did seem to produce a result because after Mrs. Hansen had introduced the next young lady, who began to sing, Frederick leaned in again. "This one is not so bad."

Phoebe raised her eyes to the young lady singing. She was pretty and clearly not older than twenty. But there was a self-assurance to her that must please any gentleman who was interested. Phoebe was tempted to look at Frederick to see whether she would see such interest in *his* eyes. When she tilted her face, she found his eyes on her. Their gaze held for a moment.

Very carefully, Phoebe turned her head forward again and took the remaining sip of her punch. "She does have a most delightful voice. Have you given up on the idea of my returning to London?"

She felt him shrug and forced herself not to lean against the arm that was still perched behind her. Frederick's warmth radiated next to her, but it was a comfortable warmth rather than a stifling one. He leaned in again, and she waited in exquisite torture. Did he do so to speak quietly? Or did he wish to be near her?

"I am not keen on the idea of you staying here, but I recognize that I have no authority to bid you do otherwise. I merely accept when it's time to retreat."

"Good," she said. "I'm glad to know you are a man of sense and not one given to lost causes."

There was a round of applause. "Shall we sit?" he asked, and Phoebe glanced at him before looking at the chair he indicated. Mrs. Hansen held up her list and put up her spectacles before calling out, "Miss Phoebe Tunstall."

Frederick pulled back in astonishment, and Phoebe felt her courage desert her completely. However, several members of the assembly had turned back to look at her, and she had no choice but to move forward. She handed her cup to Frederick, who took it, his brown eyes not leaving hers.

Every eye in the room was on Phoebe as she took her place in front, and her breath was coming quickly. She had planned on singing "Captivity" by Stephan Storace, about Marie-Antoinette's days in prison before her death. She wondered if she would remember the words and the tune—if she could sing it without her voice croaking. Would she be obliged to run out of the room in complete failure?

"Tell Mr. Primrose what you wish to sing," Mrs. Hansen encouraged, gesturing to the accompanist.

Phoebe tried to speak, but her lips would not obey. She turned her gaze to Lydia, who smiled and nodded in encouragement. Her eyes then sought out Frederick at the back of the room. He had not taken the seat he had suggested but stood, unmoving, in the place she had left him. His intent gaze stiffened Phoebe's spine. He was really seeing her now. Perhaps for the first time.

She would not sing "Captivity." No, she had something else in mind.

Frederick stood unnoticed behind the crowd who had their eyes trained on Phoebe. He detected a stillness in the air—an attention that had not been there for the other ladies, and he couldn't decide if it was because others were as shocked as he was that Phoebe Tunstall consented to sing in front of an audience, or if it was because she was as lovely to look at as a rose in bloom.

Frederick stood upright. *A rose in bloom?* Where had that poetical turn of phrase come from? He hadn't thought to enter his dotage at such a young age. He must be going mad.

Phoebe had paused and, for just a moment, was the timid thing he had known from childhood. Then she looked straight at him and turned and murmured something to the pianist. When she stood straight again, the candles behind her created a halo of glory that lit her blonde curls and made the spring-green threads on the fabric of her dress shimmer.

The first notes sounded, and it took a minute for Frederick to realize what he was hearing. "Greensleeves"! He was surprised at Phoebe's choice. While the music wasn't uncommon, it seemed odd coming from a lady. And from what he remembered about the lyrics, it was something about falling in love, or being lost in love, or something like that. Something rather vulnerable for Phoebe to sing in front of a room full of strangers.

She took a breath and opened her mouth, her voice both strong and sweet as the melody joined the chords on the piano. The sound of it pierced and pulled at his inner being. The mournful tune, combined with the surprise of the words—once he paid attention to their meaning—left him immobile.

Alas, my love, ye do me wrong
To cast me off discourteously
For I have loved you oh so long

Delighting in your company.

Greensleeves was all my joy
Greensleeves was my delight
Greensleeves was my heart of gold
And who but my lady Greensleeves

Your vows you've broken, like my heart
Oh, why did you so enrapture me?
Now I remain in a world apart
But my heart remains in captivity

I have been ready at your hand
To grant whatever you would crave
I have both wagered life and land
Your love and goodwill for to have

Phoebe did not look at anyone in the audience as she sang. She certainly didn't look at him. But there was such a melancholy sound to her singing that the verses seemed to take on a personal significance. Did she love someone? Was he here? Frederick glanced at Mr. Conroy, who sat stock still, his jaw slack. Frederick folded his arms and brought his gaze back to Phoebe.

If you intend thus to disdain
It does the more enrapture me
And even so, I still remain
A love in captivity

Well, I will pray to God on high
That thou my constancy mayst see
And yet that once before I die
Thou wilt vouchsafe to love me

The doleful tune died down, and there was a brief silence before a roar of applause. Phoebe blushed and smiled, dropping a curtsy before walking over to where his sister sat and taking her seat between Lydia and some soldier. The man leaned over and whispered something in her ear, and Frederick saw her cheeks lift in a smile and the nod she returned in reply. Mr. Conroy also leaned forward to say something to her. Phoebe's back was rigid, as though she was tense and exhausted from having given her all. She must have been spent. He had not known she had such a thing in her.

Phoebe had not come back to stand by him after she finished her song. *And I have loved you oh so long, delighting in your company.* The words teased at Frederick. Perhaps it was just the verses of a song chosen because it amply set off the lower tones of her voice; but somehow, he didn't think so. She'd closed her eyes when she sang those words.

There was only one more performance after Phoebe, but the spell of enchantment ended when Phoebe took her seat. When the last young lady finished, there was a polite applause before the audience got to its feet and made its way to the tables that had been set out with a light supper.

Lydia spotted Frederick at the entrance to the drawing room and came over to him. "You must be desperate for company if you are here."

Frederick pushed away from the door where he had been leaning as he ruminated on the surprise that was Phoebe. "I am not sure I will have much to do until Wellington arrives. In the meantime, I have few acquaintances here, and I find myself at a loss for things to do. This was a diversion."

His eyes found Phoebe again, and she was flocked by the two gentlemen who had been sitting beside her, as well as four others who had come up to her. *Why are there only gentlemen at her side? Where are the ladies?*

Lydia followed his gaze. "Phoebe was quite an astonishment. Did you know she could sing so well?"

Frederick kept his regard trained on Phoebe and shook his head. "How could I? Stratford never mentioned it, and Phoebe was not likely to sing in front of *me* if not even you were aware of her talent. I don't believe she has ever sung in front of a crowd before. What do you think changed this time?"

Lydia lifted her shoulder. "I cannot be sure, but something in

Brussels seems to have altered her. Phoebe is coming into her own, I daresay. For too long she has been under the shadow of Anna, and then she hid herself in the background by accompanying her aunt everywhere and remaining fixed at her side. Here, no one distracts her by needing anything, and she has no one to amuse but herself. I suppose everyone is seeing Phoebe for her real worth here, and that encourages her."

Lydia leveled a gaze at Frederick. "Perhaps *you* should notice her, too. Did she not have the most enchanting voice? I declare, she was *a sirène.*"

Frederick was not about to admit to the sensations that had pierced his heart as he listened to her song. He would not confess that he had felt bewitched as though she *had* been a *sirène.* "Phoebe is like a little sister, nothing more," he said.

He knew it was not quite true, but he was not about to let his sister think he had any interest whatsoever. For all he knew, she would rush over and tell Phoebe on the spot, and then Frederick would be stuck. He would not hurt Phoebe for the world, and he would end up asking for her hand in marriage just to spare her feelings.

Better to nip this little fancy of his in the bud right away. Besides, more likely than not, their paths would separate again and this evening's enchantment would fade into memory. Phoebe would go back to London, and he would do whatever he needed to deter Napoleon. Their paths would cross a few times over the years as he settled down with some chit he did not very much care for and Phoebe went on to marry, have children, and grow stout.

As soon as he conjured the image, Frederick found fault with it. Phoebe was delicate-boned and had a gentle, graceful air about her. Rather than imagining her stout with a parcel of offspring, he could better imagine her sitting in a chair with a couple of angelic children at her feet, holding the latest one in her arms . . .

What the deuce! He was definitely going mad. He was starting to have thoughts that were entirely inappropriate about Stratford's little sister. Frederick glanced over at Phoebe again, who was engaged in an animated discussion, and he could see for himself that every man encircling her had been snared. She no longer quite fit into the mold of little sister.

Lydia nudged him. "Where have you wandered off to in your thoughts? I asked you a question, and you did not even hear me."

Frederick mentally shook himself and looked at Lydia. "What was the question?"

"Fitz has gone to Ghent and will not be back until tomorrow night. Would you like to go walking with us in the park tomorrow afternoon?"

That would have been an agreeable prospect, but he had spoken with the general, who wished to do a review of the existing troops in Brussels and had enlisted Frederick's help. "I cannot. I have things I must see to tomorrow. Perhaps we might go for a ride next week."

"An excellent idea," Lydia replied. "I am not sure I will be able to encourage Fitz to come. You know he is not overly fond of pleasure riding. But if not, I will see if one of those gentlemen wishes to join us so we can make a foursome." She sent a glance at the crowd around Phoebe.

Frederick thought he saw mischief in his sister's glance. She was probably trying to provoke a jealous reaction in him by inviting someone like Conroy. It would be just like her to attempt to arrange a match with Phoebe, but he would thwart her noble intentions. Phoebe belonged with a different man—not Conroy, but someone else. And he . . . well, it was not the time to be thinking of marriage. Besides, Frederick wasn't sure at this point that he belonged with anyone.

Lydia gestured to Phoebe to come, and she left her crowd of admirers and walked over to where they stood. When she came near, Lydia slipped her arm around Phoebe's and drew her close. "You have the voice of an angel, Phoebe, and you have been hiding it from us all these years. Never once have I heard you volunteer to sing. Besides, Anna always said neither of you could sing."

Phoebe laughed, and the sound enchanted Frederick as much as her singing had, but for a different reason. He had heard the carefree sound from her little enough over the years. Phoebe's laugh settled into a soft smile. "In truth, singing is not one of Anna's accomplishments. I simply allowed her to imply that neither of us possesses the talent because I could not imagine myself singing in front of everyone."

Exactly! "I'm curious," Frederick said, drawing her gaze to him. "What prompted you to do so tonight?"

Phoebe bit her lip. "I do not know."

There was a small pause. Lydia looked ready to say something, but Frederick impulsively put a hand on her arm to stop her. There was more to Phoebe's response, he was sure, and he wanted to know what it was.

At last Phoebe lifted her eyes. "I have been hiding long enough. A friend told me to do something daring." She studiously avoided Frederick's gaze and added with the barest hint of a smile on her face, "And now that I have begun doing so, I am afraid I cannot go back to what I once was."

"We should not want you to," exclaimed Lydia.

Frederick remained silent. Although he did like seeing Phoebe come out of her shell, he wasn't sure if he approved of this new version of her. The version he had urged her to be! He wished he could send her back to London where she would be safe. Safe from any potential danger that might come to the city and safe from the attentions of soldiers who would attempt to win her hand in a rushed courtship. Contrary to what Frederick had professed when he'd promised to find her a husband, he was realizing he did not want her won by anyone. At least not for the moment. He wanted her to stay quietly in the background where she had always been.

But he supposed that was not fair.

Chapter Twelve

In the end, the promised ride was delayed by two weeks. The Duke of Wellington arrived in Brussels at last on April 4, and Frederick was taken up with the flurry of orders that followed. He was glad to greet his friends among Wellington's aides-de-camp—Wrotham, along with John Stewart, Anthony Pinkton, and George Sutherland, who had traveled with him from Vienna.

They introduced Frederick to Herbert Dalrymple, who was the youngest of the duke's ADCs but whose father was an intimate of the Prince Regent. Dalrymple looked young enough to still be in school, but he showed himself to be full of pluck and asked questions without fear of showing ignorance. They called him Dolly—or *cawker*, depending on the level of teasing. The other ADCs in Wellington's staff numbered up to thirty.

"It took you longer to arrive than I expected," Frederick said when he entered Headquarters and found them there. "What kept you?"

Wrotham lounged back on one of the chairs, sipping coffee. "Long, you say? We rode like the devil. Barely stopped to rest. Wellington needed to reach an agreement with the Allies on the best manner to repress that 'enemy and disturber of the world' before we could set off, however."

He moved his legs to allow Frederick to sit down. "He and Blücher also spent some time sorting out strategy. Or rather, the duke told him what he expected, and the Prussian blustered well enough before finally agreeing. The Prince of Orange had his say, and Wellington will have to assign him to a regiment of honor, along with a general he can look up to. All of that took some time and finesse."

"But we are here now," Pinkton added, standing near the windows that overlooked the park. "And your holidays are over. I am sure you will be running around in no time just as we have been."

"Is Slender Billy here, then?" Frederick asked, referring to the Dutch prince and heir to the throne. The Prince of Orange had been Oxford-educated and was known to prefer the English as company. He was amiable enough, and not at all high in the instep, but he was impetuous and had to be reminded of his responsibility to the Dutch people.

"He's here and eager for action, as you might guess," Sutherland said.

Wellington entered the room then, trailed by Sir William De Lancey, who had come from London in time to meet the duke. Rumor among staff was that he would indeed take on the role of quartermaster-general, though nothing was official. He and the duke were discussing the most logical place to store provisions in Ostend, which would need to be sent as soon as it could be arranged. Wellington glanced at Frederick and walked forward, extending his hand. "Mighty glad to see you, Ingram. These quarters are perfect. You know Sir William, I trust. I will have some instructions for you to take to Ghent on Monday. However, you should be back in time for the theater performance on Thursday night."

Frederick nodded, not bothering to give a response, for he knew Wellington would not wait for one. The duke stepped forward and continued his discussion with De Lancey, and they disappeared into the office that had been reserved for him.

Frederick turned to Sutherland with a grin. "He is not easily fatigued, is he? I had almost forgotten. It has been some time since I've served under him."

Sutherland gave something between a snort of laughter and a grunt. "No. And let it not be said that we, who are his juniors, are any more fatigued than he is for *that* he should not accept, I assure you."

Before Frederick traveled to Ghent, he visited the troops stationed near Brussels and took note of what provisions had been allotted to them. He was to coordinate efforts with the acting quartermaster-general, but not in the role of assistant. He would remain ADC to Lord Wellington and pen the communications with London that did not require the duke's personal hand.

When Frederick returned from Ghent, he was sent on another errand that was closer to Brussels, but which took the whole day. Wellington and his staff then went to review the newest troops that had arrived and sort out which regiments could fight on their own, and which ones had too many foreigners or raw recruits to be relied upon. They would need to be bolstered by combining the regiment with more experienced troops. Throughout all this, thoughts of Phoebe edged in on Frederick's consciousness whenever there was a lull in the activity, usually when he was riding or on the edge of sleep.

It was too long before Frederick saw her again for more than a brief exchange at their house or at some social event. It was not until Frederick grew short with Sutherland after receiving another assignment that would take him out of Brussels that he realized how much he had been hoping to see Phoebe again for more than a few minutes. He actually *missed* her, and that was something that was new.

Frederick had not entirely neglected his sister and Phoebe with Lord Wellington's arrival, but when they did see him, he was always on his way to do something else. The lack of time in which to share a deeper conversation was frustrating, but Phoebe had to be glad that he at least came when he could. It seemed to her that something had shifted between her and Frederick in those brief encounters, subtle though it was. She felt his regard when she wasn't looking at him, but when she turned to face him, his gaze flitted away.

For as long as Phoebe had known Frederick, he had given her his undivided attention whenever circumstances brought them together, but he had never sought her out. Not—she reminded herself—that he was doing that now. He and Lydia were close, so it was likely that he came to the house for that reason. Or perhaps the lack of his usual peers elevated Lydia and Phoebe to a higher status. In any case, whenever he came, she had the sensation that he held back from expressing everything that was on his mind.

One day, Frederick stopped at the house over breakfast to share with Lydia the news of their cousin's marriage and was just on the point of leaving when he said, "Do not think I have forgotten about our ride. The weather has grown warmer while I have been so busy, and if the sun holds I promise I will find time to escort you soon. It will be more agreeable than it would have been when I first proposed it." He tipped his hat with a smile and walked out the door.

"Good heavens," Lydia said, rising from the breakfast table, having left much of it untouched. "I have never so frequently had the pleasure of Frederick's company, even when we lived together." She walked over to straighten the curtain, whose hem had gotten caught on one of the potted plants. "How entertaining Brussels has proven to be! Even if half the Society has come here on an economizing plan, there is just the right type of company to be had. Not so few that you feel to be forever meeting the same people, but not so many that you are unable to form any intimate connections. I did not err when I invited you, don't you agree?"

"Hm?" Phoebe looked up. She had been reflecting on how dashing Frederick had looked that day in his well-fitting coat, and Lydia's words had barely registered. Frederick was growing seasoned—no evidence of gray hair or lines to be seen, of course, but there was a maturity to him that became him well. When Frederick had been younger, he was on the thin side. With age, he had filled out, and she frequently thought how nice it would be to wrap her arms around him and squeeze him tight.

She gathered her thoughts from that distracting image and managed to focus on Lydia's question. "Why, yes. I do not know where I would be if you had not proposed the idea. Truly, I have never before been so vastly entertained."

There was a glint of humorous speculation in Lydia's eyes when she replied. "Might it have anything to do with the number of officers who are interested in courting your attention? Or . . . one officer in particular?"

Phoebe smiled but did not return an answer. It was true that

Mr. Conroy paid her a very flattering attention whenever they met. She enjoyed the time they had together, but there was still no stirring in her breast when she saw him. Once Frederick had come on the scene, her heart had refused to open to anyone else. Mr. Conroy must have sensed a reticence that had accompanied Frederick's arrival, because he had also pulled back in his courtship. At the beginning, he had been quite open about his intentions. Now, although he was willing to seek her out at public assemblies, he no longer came for morning calls or hinted about a future together. Either he had seen the competition and cut his losses, or he was simply not interested enough to pursue her at all costs.

"Shall we go shopping?" Lydia asked, her hand on the doorknob to the corridor.

Phoebe rose from the table. "Again?" she returned with a teasing smile. "Lydia, the packet will not hold enough trunks for all the things we are managing to accumulate. We cannot transport Brussels back to London."

"But the prices! Can you not believe your eyes? Silk and satin dancing slippers for less than four shillings, and gloves and fans for the merest pittance. We should take advantage while we are here to seize these treasures. We shall be the envy of the ton when we return."

"Slippers and gloves, which you will declare sadly out of fashion by the time we arrive in London." Phoebe laughed and shook her head. "No, I don't think we need any more treasures. However, I will accompany you, for it is beautiful out, and the day begs to be enjoyed."

They arrived at their favorite millinery shop that had sweet calamine-blue wall hangings between the dark wooden posts. Lydia began examining the hats lining the shelf, fingering the ribbons that dangled from them as she compared the embellishments. She lifted one and examined the green silk, sewn with tiny stitches into the straw rims. The sound of a tinkling bell signaled someone's arrival, and Phoebe turned to look. It was Martha Cummings, wearing a yellow dress that, unfortunately, had not been chosen with an eye for her complexion or figure.

"Phoebe Tunstall!" Martha exclaimed. "I have not seen you this age. Weren't you to come to the *al fresco* lunch held by the May-fields?"

Phoebe resigned herself to the addition of her chatty acquaintance and tried to be more gracious. "We were to go, but Lydia's husband invited us to the review of the Gordon Highlanders, so we went to see that instead."

"Oh, that must have been so exciting, although I suppose one must be obliged to stand around forever and wait for something exciting to actually occur. I have attended a military review once before and swore I would never go again. Although, I suppose if one were to ask and it was a *particular* friend I would go just to oblige her. Isn't that the most darling hat, Mrs. Fitzwilliam? Is that the one you've chosen?"

Lydia was less tolerant than Phoebe of people who stretched her forbearance, but she was not unkind. She exchanged a knowing glance with Phoebe as she replied. "Yes, I've decided to take this and the Shako for riding."

"The tall blue one there? Oh yes, you *must* have two. I am just the same. I cannot stop myself from making a purchase, especially when everything is so dear in London, and here it is sold for a song." Martha laughed and continued along in this vein as Lydia purchased her hats and had them wrapped up.

Seeking to give some direction to Martha's chatter, Phoebe asked, "How is Mr. Cummings?"

"Albert? He is going on very well. He is still looking for a good partnership in Brussels. The soaps and shaving kits he's finding here will be snapped up in no time by the gentlemen in London, if only he can find a partner that will be faithful in sending the supplies once he returns. He did say he won't invest too heavily or commit to staying here long-term. Once we'd learned that Napoleon has escaped and is headed this way, we know no peace. What a monster he is, I am sure. We are prepared to fly at a moment's notice."

"Now that Lord Wellington has come, I feel perfectly at ease." Lydia picked up her purchases and began to walk toward the door, her voice holding a quelling timbre that Phoebe was certain only she could discern. "I don't think there is any cause for panic."

Martha stuck to Phoebe as she trailed Lydia. "Oh, yes, I am vastly relieved that the duke is here. However, who can trust Napoleon? I, for one, would not want to be here when he sweeps into Brussels with his cavalry. I am sure those French barbarians would think nothing of spoiling any virtuous young women in their path." They exited into the bright sunlight, and Lydia paused to wait for Phoebe, sending her an amused look when Phoebe came abreast.

She could imagine what Lydia was thinking: *Keep talking, and you will have nothing to fear. That chatter would drive any man away.*

Phoebe scolded herself for finding humor in something that was, after all, a serious threat. And Martha was harmless. She walked at their side, gabbing without cease and not seeming to expect an answer, leaving Phoebe to reflect more on the threat that faced them. In truth, she scarcely allowed herself to think of it, although there was an increasing number of soldiers that flooded the area. What had begun as a simple garrison in Brussels had grown to an outpouring of troops, and houses holding different regiments in uniforms of various colors.

But in everyday life, it was difficult to imagine that any threat really existed. The cream of British, Dutch, and Belgian society mingled at every event, bringing to them refined conversation and a bravado that could bolster even the most hen-hearted against any threat. So far, Phoebe had attended picnics and card games, dinners nearly every day, walks in the park whenever weather permitted, and short rides in the country. And she had only been here just over a month. It was hard to imagine that anything could cast a shade over such a gay city.

"Well." Lydia stopped as they reached *rue de la Fourche.* "I believe this is where we must leave you, Miss Cummings. Phoebe and I have another engagement."

"Oh." Martha seemed taken aback, and her shoulders slumped. Phoebe took pity on her and added with a smile, "But we shall meet at the Rawlings' tonight, will we not? They have promised us games, and you can join my team." Martha perked up at the idea and bid them farewell more cheerfully.

"That woman!" Lydia exclaimed when they had parted ways. "If only she left half a minute for others to *respond* to her prattle I would like her much the better."

Phoebe found herself much in sympathy with Lydia's point of

view, but she had taken hold of her thoughts and refrained from heaping on her own criticisms. "I believe she is merely lonely."

The day finally arrived for their picnic, and Frederick announced his presence at an early hour when he strode into the breakfast room. "Let us ride out past the Forest of Soigny. I am told there is an incline easily accessible for our horses and that at the top is a perfect location for us to eat and appreciate the countryside." He looked around. "Is Fitz coming after all? You said he might."

"I am," Fitz said, entering the room from the corridor.

Phoebe was glad it would be just the four of them, as old friends made up such a comfortable party, and they enjoyed that rarely enough. She tossed the long end of her riding skirt over her arm and peeked at Frederick, who was particularly handsome in a dark riding coat, pantaloons that molded to his thighs, and white-banded Hessians with black tassels. He held out his arm for her to slip her hand underneath as Sam went to have the horses brought from the mews to their front door. When they were mounted and had set out, Lydia and Fitz rode ahead, arguing with cheerful passion about something inconsequential, while Phoebe rode more sedately at Frederick's side.

They went on in companionable silence for some time when Frederick interrupted her reverie. "And how are you faring, my dear Phoebe?"

Shock pulled her gaze to his, but she immediately turned her face forward again. He had called her *my dear Phoebe.* That was new. Her mind did not allow herself to think that she had come to mean anything to him, but her heart did not obey her mind's logic. "Well, I'm very pleased to be riding out of Brussels if that is what you are asking."

She could hear the smile in Frederick's voice. "As am I. But that was not entirely what I was asking. Are you content here? Not afraid of the future?"

She turned to him. "Should I be? Are you?"

Frederick took some time before answering. "I am not afraid, no. But I own that there is an added element I don't like. When I was off fighting in the Peninsula years ago—before your brother had registered—we were on someone else's territory, and there were no loved ones to defend or worry about. Our victories or losses had to do with us alone. Of course, there was always a possibility that if we did not succeed in stopping Bonaparte, we would only have to come back to England and fight the same battle on our own soil. But that threat remained a distant one because it was all happening overseas." He paused and stared ahead at the path that bordered the forest on the left and had a row of trees on the right, creating a green canopy.

"But with Lydia here—and you," he continued, "the threat is more real to me. I am still of the mind that it would be better for you to return to London."

The words came at Phoebe heavily. He cared about her enough not to want harm to come to her, but he did not care for her in *that* way—where he could not bear to see her go. He lumped her with the same affection he felt for his sister. She bit her lip and stayed silent, though she knew he was waiting for an answer. No promise existed between them, but she could not extinguish the hope that sprang up every time his words seemed to hint that there was something more.

It was time she took the matter in hand and steel her heart once and for all. She would answer him in the most even, sisterly tone in her possession. "I understand your worry, but to own the truth, I do not see myself leaving without Lydia. I don't have anything to return home to, and that makes me more willing to stay and take risks."

She glanced at him and decided to continue in this vein of honesty. "I have Stratford and Eleanor, and I have my sister. But I would be putting off my hopes for a match and for a family of my own. That is something I want, Frederick. For the first time, I have not gone somewhere at the request or convenience of someone else. I am here of my own volition. And I'm not keen to change that just yet."

Frederick sighed, then looked ahead. "Fitz!" he called out, making Phoebe wonder if he had heard her at all. *Wonderful. I'm pouring my heart out to Frederick, and he's not even listening.*

Fitz pulled on the reins and looked behind him, and Frederick raised his voice to be heard. "At the end of the Soigny Forest, we must turn left and not continue along the *Chaussée de Bruxelles*."

Fitz lifted his hand in answer and rode forward, steering his horse to the left when the canopy of trees came to an end. Frederick and Phoebe rode in silence, and out of pique Phoebe refused to be the one to break it.

"You will have your husband," Frederick said at last. His voice sounded hard, as if she had angered him, but he had been listening at least. "It is impossible for you to pass by unnoticed. Whether it is in Brussels, a small town near Worthing, or in London."

Frederick steered left after Fitz, and Phoebe followed his horse's path. "Do you think so? I believe I was overlooked for years." She gave a feeble smile, not bothering to meet his gaze. "I am not so sure what you say is true."

The path went up an incline to the ledge, where Frederick thought they might have their picnic. He was looking at her, and Phoebe felt his gaze. When he did not relent and look away, she at last turned her eyes to his and encountered a measuring look.

"Sometimes men are blind to what is right under their very noses. Although blind at first, it does not mean they will stay so."

He broke the gaze, and Phoebe felt her stomach plunge and rise again in the most giddy way. It was almost as though he was giving her a message about his own heart, but . . . that could not be true. His tone had not changed, and he had not looked at her like a man who was in pursuit of her heart. But he looked at her and spoke to her with *intent*, and that could only mean she had captured his interest to some small degree. And they had this picnic together, where she might get a glimpse into his heart. That was enough to fill the day with promise.

Chapter Thirteen

Frederick tossed the reins over his horse's back at the top of the hill and assisted Phoebe to unmount. When her foot hit the ground, she fell forward into him and he caught her around the waist.

"Oh, forgive me. My legs are not steady after the ride." She did not meet his gaze but disengaged herself from his grasp and walked over to the edge of the land that dropped off into a steep slope, providing a clear view of the valley. Frederick remained with one hand on her mount, watching Phoebe and trying unsuccessfully to rid himself of the sensation of having her in his arms.

She removed her gloves and stared into the expanse as a breeze tugged at her bonnet. Frederick had meant what he said as they were riding. Sometimes a man might be blind to what is under his nose. It was not that he intended to pursue Phoebe. Their friendship was of too long a date for him to contemplate such an idea. He had watched her grow up and, until very recently, he had thought of her only in the guise of a sister.

The way she felt in his arms—and the way her dresses fit her—was entirely too pleasing for his own comfort, however. And if he were being honest, the memory of her in that red dress the evening of his first ball in Brussels had plagued his thoughts more than once. Even now, the sight of her standing at the edge of the outcrop—the world at her feet, it seemed—arrested his imagination. She seemed at once unattainable and vulnerable. He wanted both to win her and rescue her, pulling her into his arms.

Frederick wrenched his gaze away and caught Lydia peering at him with an expression of surprise—and of comprehension, he feared. His sister missed very little, and it would serve him no good turn if she began to tease. He would have to throw her off the scent. Besides that, the thoughts he was entertaining about Phoebe had accosted him out of nowhere, and they struck him as wrong. The heat of embarrassment crept up his neck as he imagined what Phoebe would think of him if she knew. She had always been so poised, it was difficult to read her thoughts. But he feared the attraction he was coming to feel for her would shock her.

"Fitz," he called out to distract himself and to turn Lydia's thoughts to a new direction. "I have brought the blanket, but we had better set it closer to the line of trees. There is more wind up here than I expected." He patted the mare's flank, and she joined his gelding in grazing along the grass that lined the ridge on top of the hill.

"You are right," Fitz replied, walking over to him. "Here, hand me this corner. Lydia, will you open the saddlebags and pull out the items Cook has prepared for us?"

Phoebe turned from the edge and walked toward them, the fresh air giving a rosy glow to her face and a sparkle to her eyes. Frederick glanced up at her, his lips turning up, but for some reason he looked away again, unable to fully meet her gaze. He busied himself with setting up the blanket and taking the dishes from Lydia, which he set in the center. He was about to offer his hand to Phoebe to sit, but she knelt and claimed a spot on the blanket near him, turning to face the view.

"It is a shame that it really is too windy to picnic right on the edge. The view is marvelous." Phoebe turned to Lydia, who was bringing out the last of their picnic lunch. "Forgive me. I should have helped you. You must see the view, though."

"I will after we eat," Lydia said. "I am simply famished and must have food straight away. Fitz, cut me off some of that ham, will you, dear?" She took a bite of her bread without waiting for Fitz to oblige. Frederick had never known his sister to begin eating before everyone else was settled and thought it odd.

"No wonder, when you didn't touch your breakfast," Phoebe said.

Frederick saw Phoebe's eyes drift to Lydia's middle and back up to her face in a speculative manner. He turned to examine his sister as well. *Could Lydia be with child?* The way Phoebe trailed her gaze to Lydia's middle made him think that she, at least, thought so. Or she knew something he didn't. Strange that Frederick had never wondered why Lydia had not borne an heir to Fitz. True, they had been separated for nearly a year while he was in the Americas, but they had also campaigned together before that. He guessed one did not generally think about one's sister in such a capacity. Still, the idea of being an uncle pleased Frederick. He would have to see if he could get Lydia to open up on the subject in a way that did not make her—or him—uncomfortable.

"Any news on Blücher's arrival?" Fitz asked as he bit into the rustic sandwich he had fabricated. A piece of ham fell out of the other side, and he caught it in his hands.

"He should be here any day now. Wellington is counting on his input when they begin talking strategy." Frederick hadn't realized how hungry he was until he began eating. He wasn't sure if a slice of bread with meat had ever been so full of flavor. Maybe it was the pleasure of the day that did that.

The sun warmed them but could not compete with the stiff breeze that came over the ledge and blew past them. It brought with it the scent of wildflowers and earth. Phoebe curled her legs away from him, and she leaned near him on one hand. It brought her close enough that their arms were nearly touching. It was a comfortable sensation, incorporating all the ease of their long-standing friendship with the womanly allure he was slowly becoming conscious of. She wasn't completely silent as they ate, but she contributed little to the conversation. He wondered if she could tell that her presence affected him. She leaned even closer and her arm brushed his.

Enough of this. Frederick was annoyed with himself for the temptations that crossed his mind that had absolutely no place with this woman. He stretched his legs in front of him and leaned back on his other hand, shifting slightly so he was not quite so near to Phoebe. He was going out of his mind.

"I have some news that should interest you," he told Fitz. His sister glanced at him but that was as much interest as she showed.

"Sir Hudson Lowe is being replaced as our quartermaster-general."

Fitz tugged at a cluster of grapes until it came free from the bunch and then looked up with interest. "By whom? He knows the Low Countries by now and should be well-suited to continue in his role. Unless it's because Wellington can barely tolerate the man?"

Frederick laughed and shook his head at Lydia, who was offering a plate of cakes. Phoebe had lifted the basket of dates, and she offered them to Fitz, a question in her eyes. He couldn't help but smile and take one, feeling a giddiness that baffled him completely. "I believe you have the right of it. The duke is bringing on Sir William Howe De Lancey, whom he *can* tolerate. That's why he's in Brussels."

"De Lancey!" Fitz's look of surprise turned to reflection. "Yes, I suppose that makes sense. He's young, but he can get things done and won't waste his time with useless arguments."

"Or waste Wellington's time either." Frederick chewed on the date, which was plump and as sweet as a *bonbon*.

The conversation turned to Brussels Society and the ball that Wellington would be hosting. Then it drifted toward Fitz's training schedule for his regiment, with Lydia complaining vocally about how rarely he was at home. As this complaint was uttered after they had made plans to attend two balls and a card party that week, Fitz teased her out of the sullens she was pretending to have.

"I am afraid I'm growing chilly," Lydia said, getting to her feet after their leisurely lunch. "Will you be too disappointed if we head back already?"

"No. I am of the same mind," Phoebe replied, and Frederick hoped the hesitation he'd heard in her reply was because she also desired to remain in his company a little longer. "However, cold though it may be, you simply cannot miss the view. Come." She took Lydia by the arm, and they walked to the edge of the outcrop.

Frederick followed, while Fitz packed up a few of their belongings. He heard Lydia say, "Magnificent. It looks much like the views we had when we were coming over on the canal boat, except here you can see farther."

Fitz joined them. "Much of the countryside in this part of the Lower Countries is the same, I've noticed. The areas surrounding Brussels are not as developed as some of the English countryside, for there are many more hamlets and small farms than there are villages."

He had brought a map, and he unrolled it, looking ahead of him and studying the terrain. He pointed straight ahead. "That hill in front of us—where the valley rises again and where you can see a small spire—is Mont-Saint-Jean. And over there to the right we can just perceive the hamlet of Le Mesnil." He glanced again at the map and pointed to the left. "And those woods there are an extension of the Forest of Soigny. It's always useful to know what we are seeing."

Lydia linked her arm through her husband's. "A military trait, I am sure. Now that we are moving again, I feel sure that I will not fall off my horse from cold. Nevertheless, I think it is time we went back. This wind reminds me that summer is not yet upon us."

She and Fitz returned to the blanket. Frederick held out his arm for Phoebe and was gratified when she tucked her arm under his. He was beginning to open his eyes to the depth of his longing to share a greater intimacy with her. Whenever he was away from her, he thought about when he could next be with her. This outing, with the four of them, was a good start, but he wanted more.

Phoebe looked up at him with a soft smile. "I enjoyed our afternoon. I am often reminded that I am living in a foreign country, but this outing today almost felt like I was right back at home."

With me, you are. Frederick held her glance for a moment too long, then laid his hand over hers on his arm. "I am of the same mind. I hope my duties will allow for more of these outings."

Chapter Fourteen

*I*t had been nearly a week since their picnic on the hilltop overlooking the valley and hamlets, and it already seemed a distant memory. None of their outings had brought them in Frederick's path. Phoebe supposed it was only natural, as his military duties must take precedence. But even Fitz had time to come home and sleep. Frederick seemed to have disappeared from Brussels altogether. It was probably for the best, since Phoebe's heart was even more in danger than it had been in her earlier years, for she'd had a taste of what it was like to have companionship with him on an equal level—to be appreciated.

She and Lydia sat at the breakfast table, and Phoebe watched Lydia fiddle with her fork before pushing the eggs away from her. She took a bite of dry toast and swallowed it before drinking some tea. Sarah bustled into the dining room, saw the plate of eggs, and removed it without another word. Then the breakfast room was quiet.

Phoebe cleared her throat. "This is a delicate matter, I understand, and I suppose I am not in the best position to ask it. However, I am the only female company you have here who is on intimate enough terms to bring up such a subject. And I know something of the changes"—she broke off suddenly, a self-conscious smile on her face—"the changes that come over one in a delicate condition. After all, I have also watched Eleanor and Anna fiddle with their breakfast and push away dishes with the more pungent odors."

Lydia took another bite of toast. "You have guessed, then? It is early enough that I had not thought to mention it. But I am finding it more difficult to hide my strange dining habits. Whereas at the beginning I felt only joy and an insatiable hunger, I am now starting to feel a disgust for anything but the blandest of foods." She met Phoebe's gaze. "To tell the truth, it is a relief to speak with you about it."

Phoebe reached across the table and lay her hand over Lydia's. "Do you have any idea when you will be confined?"

"It is still some time from now. I imagine in the winter or around Christmas." Lydia shrugged. "If we are still here, I shall have to find a midwife."

"What does Fitz think of the news?" Phoebe asked, leaning back and sipping her coffee.

Lydia looked down and pulled the toast apart with her fingers. "I have not decided when I should tell him. I do not wish for him to worry—or send me back to London. I know he said he would not do so, but I am afraid if he knows I am in a delicate way, he may insist upon it."

"He does not know then!"

Lydia shook her head. "And until I tell him, I know I can trust you not to spread the word."

"Of course." Phoebe thought that Fitz must not be very observant, or perhaps they had not shared enough breakfasts. She supposed he had weightier things to think about. "What do you wish to do today?"

Lydia sighed and, instead of returning an answer, said, "Have you noticed that we have not seen Fred in an age? I wonder where he is and when we shall see him next."

Phoebe received a jolt at the sound of Frederick's name, but she kept her face expressionless. He was never far from her thoughts. "I do not know. Now that Lord Wellington is here, I imagine he must have little time to spend on social engagements."

"True. Let's go to Wouters today," Lydia exclaimed. "I have a sudden desire for that *kruidenkoek* they have, and I imagine we will meet up with cheerful company there. It is just what we need."

"An excellent idea." Phoebe was about to stand when the footman entered with the morning post. He handed her two letters, and she looked at the handwriting—one was from Anna and the other from Eleanor. "Shall we go after we read our letters?"

Lydia nodded. She had also received two letters, and she lifted one of them. "I have one from Eleanor."

Phoebe smiled and lifted hers. "As do I." It was just like her sister-in-law to write two separate letters, which would require separate postage—an extravagance that Stratford could afford—just to make Phoebe and Lydia each feel special. Eleanor and Lydia had gone to school together, and Eleanor had been staying with Lydia for the London Season when she and Stratford fell in love.

Phoebe chose a clean knife and slit the seal on Anna's letter first, skimming its contents.

My dearest Phoebe—

> *I was enchanted at the idea of your leaving London to embark on such an adventure—one I would not be loth to have had myself. But I must confess my growing fear, now that Napoleon has fled Elba and has begun marching up the Continent, that I don't quite like the idea of you being so easily within his reach. Would you consider coming home? If you do, I promise to leave my poor Harry alone all Season just to spend it with you in London. True, I cannot bear to leave Peter, so perhaps it will not be quite the whirlwind of gaiety we might otherwise have together, but it will be better than you being in London all alone. Surely my proposal must be a temptation to you? Unless there has been a handsome soldier to sweep you off your feet. But even a handsome soldier must surely see the wisdom of sending you back to London forthwith. He will wish to protect you . . .*

Phoebe read the letter with a small degree of surprise. Anna rarely showed any but the lightest concern, although Phoebe knew her sister felt things much more deeply than what was apparent. If Anna hadn't, she would not have been able to marry a rector. But for her to spend the entire letter urging Phoebe to return to England (apart from a scant line or two at the bottom praising Peter's ability to toss a ball and speculating on whether the kick of this child in her belly could likely—most certainly must—be a girl) showed the degree of worry she felt.

Despite the concern that leapt off the pages, Phoebe allowed the familiar cadence of Anna's writing to reach across the channel and soothe her. Anna had been right about one handsome soldier wishing to send her back to England, but she had not been inclined to accept his proposition.

She picked up Eleanor's letter and read the more thoughtfully chosen words from her gentle sister-in-law, although she was fully capable of infusing humor into her letters, as well. Eleanor also worried for Phoebe's safety but wrote that she trusted Phoebe to know her own mind and what the best course of action would be.

> *I am growing so round, you would not recognize me. This child is to have one more month by the doctor's calculations, but truly I do not know how I can grow any larger. Do you think I am giving birth to a descendant of the Nephilim?*

Phoebe laughed. "Has Eleanor mentioned her size in her letter?"

"Yes, something about Stratford watching her belly with growing alarm," Lydia said, holding her letter up.

Phoebe chuckled as she looked back down again, reading until she got to the space where she recognized Stratford's hand.

> *Phoebe, I do hope you have enough sense to return to England, given the latest news. You cannot be unaware that Napoleon has reached Paris, and if I know anything of him, he will not be content until he has started pushing his borders again. I would rather not have my younger sister there when he tries.*

She sighed and folded the letter. "Stratford wishes for me to come home, as does Anna."

Lydia looked up, concern pulling at the space between her eyes. "Do you wish to leave?"

Phoebe brushed the crumbs off the white tablecloth and shook her head. "I am going to change into my walking dress. It will be just the thing to go out, for it is a beautiful day. I think it might be the finest day we've had yet." As she walked by Lydia, she set a hand on her shoulder, then went to her room where Mary was examining a spot of mud on the hem of one of the cambric gowns.

"Mary, we are to go out. Oh, I had hoped to wear that dress, but I see it is stained. Help me into the brown one instead, would you?"

As Mary pulled out the requested gown and assisted her into it, Phoebe thought about her family back in London. She could feel their anxiety—their love for her and their desire to have her back where it was safe. But Phoebe felt at home where she was for now. It was odd how one could feel at home and at the same time achingly empty. Despite how little time she had spent with Frederick, in those times they were together there had seemed to be a pull between them. It was becoming increasingly more difficult to remove him from her heart. But she had to try. If she meant anything to him at all, he would have found a way to see her.

When they arrived at Wouters, the tables were nearly all full. "Look," Lydia murmured. "There is the Duchess of Richmond. She is not reputed to be very warm, so let us take this table over here.

However, Lady Richmond looked up and spotted them and sent one of the servants over to Lydia. "Mrs. Fitzwilliam, Lady Richmond would like to invite both of you to her table."

Lydia turned her profile out of Lady Richmond's line of sight and raised her eyebrows to Phoebe. "What condescension she shows us," she murmured. "I wonder what she can wish to speak to us about." They crossed the room to Lady Richmond's table and greeted her with a curtsy.

"Mrs. Fitzwilliam, I know who you are. And this is . . ." Lady Richmond let the question dangle, and Lydia turned to Phoebe.

"My lady, may I present Miss Phoebe Tunstall, sister to Lord Worthing."

Lady Richmond nodded and gestured to the two empty seats at her table. "My instinct has been correct in calling you over. Please sit. I could tell from your air of breeding that you must have connexions to the peerage. How came you to be in Brussels?"

Phoebe leaned forward to answer. "Mrs. Fitzwilliam is here with her husband, Lieutenant-Colonel Fitzwilliam. She invited me to join her rather than attend another London Season."

"And how many Seasons have you had?" Lady Richmond inquired.

"I have had four." Phoebe's confidence fled. It sounded so pathetic.

"And no match after four Seasons?" Lady Richmond remarked. "I *am* surprised. You have the connections, and you are a very well-looking girl. How do you account for it?"

Phoebe hid all trace of annoyance and answered as simply as she could. "I can account for it because no one has made me an offer that I wished to receive. My brother and sister were married first, and I was concerned for the welfare of my aunt, who was our only close relation. I did not wish to abandon her by forming a match. I suppose it was not my priority at the time."

Lady Richmond indicated for a servant to serve the women cake, while another servant standing behind the duchess watched to see which cup Phoebe and Lydia would choose. Phoebe chose a teacup and Lydia a coffee cup, and the servant poured the corresponding hot beverages. Lady Richmond's empty plate and cup in front of her gave indication that she had already eaten, and she did not stay long after asking a few more questions that bordered on impertinence, such as how Lydia came to be married to Fitz and whether or not theirs had been a love match.

When she left, Lydia and Phoebe were alone at the table, and Lydia leaned over so that she would not be in anyone else's hearing. "Impudent woman," she whispered. But her eyes held a glimmer of amusement. "In any case, it would not do to make an enemy of her."

Phoebe smiled over her teacup and lifted her eyes to the entrance of the café, where she saw Mr. Conroy enter dressed in colors and greet someone who sat at the closest table to the door. She was glad to see him, for they had shared an interesting beginning to their acquaintance. Although her heart still belonged to Frederick, she had to admit it would not be wise to so quickly abandon other prospects. She did want to be married, and one could not be overly selective at her age.

Besides, Frederick still seemed to view her in the light of a sister. When she had purposefully leaned next to him at the picnic, their arms almost touching, he had pulled away and sat back. What other sign did she need to know the state of his heart? He probably saw right through her feelings and desires and pitied her. Whenever she thought about her forward behavior that day, she had been ready to sink with shame. It was the boldest move she had ever made. Not having seen him since the day of their ride did little to settle her conscience on the matter. No, it was time to focus her encouragement elsewhere.

Mr. Conroy stood upright and looked around the room, pausing when his eyes settled on Phoebe. When she put her cup down and smiled at him, he seemed to take that as permission, for he walked over and bowed before the women. "Mrs. Fitzwilliam, Miss Tunstall, are you expecting anyone at this table?"

Lydia smiled at him. "No, we are not. Won't you please join us?"

"With pleasure." Mr. Conroy removed his hat and put it on the chair beside him, looking around at the crowd. "It is good to come here again. Our training has kept us busy. Our regiment was one of the ones Lord Wellington reviewed this week. Every soldier is glad to see a glimpse of his face. However, woe to the soldier who presents a slovenly appearance."

"The sight of Lord Wellington brings relief to more than just his troops," Lydia exclaimed. "I imagine every English man or woman in all of Brussels must be reassured to know that the duke has things well in hand. I hope we may see him at one of our assemblies soon." She looked up as the door opened. "I see that Mrs. Marshall has just arrived, and I have needed to have a word with her. Would you mind very much if I left you for a few minutes to talk to her?"

Phoebe was not entirely sure the conversation with Mrs. Marshall was all that pressing, since she and Lydia had called on her the day before. She guessed the excuse was more to give her and Mr. Conroy a chance to be alone.

"Not at all," Mr. Conroy replied. A servant approached, and he held out his cup for the tea that was offered. He stirred in sugar, took a sip, and settled his eyes on Phoebe. "I have not come to invite you to go walking, as of late."

"I've noticed." Phoebe smiled and hid the tremor of nerves that came upon her.

"I will be frank with you, if you'll permit it," he went on, and Phoebe's nerves increased. His directness threatened to force her into an intimacy she was not sure she was ready for, but she nodded.

"I have been interested in furthering our acquaintance. However, I must confess that when Lord Ingram arrived, it seemed to me that you shared a prior attachment with him. As a result, I abandoned my suit. But now, meeting you here again, I am reminded of how much your company brings me pleasure, and I thought I would ask in a much more open manner than is generally considered acceptable whether I was wrong in my assumption." He glanced at Phoebe, and she saw a heightened touch of red in his fair features. "If you will forgive my presumption."

Phoebe inhaled quietly as she sought the wisest way to answer him. "Perhaps it leans on the side of presumption, but I appreciate honest communication and the courage such a thing requires, so I will not hold it against you. To answer your question, Frederick and I grew up together, and we have a close relationship as such." She fiddled with the delicate gold painted handle of her cup. "But we have no understanding beyond that."

Lord Conroy's shoulders visibly relaxed, and a smile lit his face. "I cannot tell you how glad I am to hear that. I hope I might convince you to attend the theater with me Thursday night. With Mrs. Fitzwilliam, of course."

Phoebe's first sensation was the flush of victory over having someone as handsome and honorable as Mr. Conroy show such decided interest in her. At the same time, her victory was alloyed. Part of her grieved for something that would never be. And she was not sure if that part of her would ebb enough for her to seriously consider Mr. Conroy as a suitor. But it was too early to tell, and she had sworn to herself that she would keep her mind open.

"I would be delighted, Mr. Conroy."

Chapter Fifteen

Frederick dressed for the theater, stretching out his arm so Caldwell could assist him into the sleeve of his coat. He tugged on the lapels, shrugging his shoulders to adjust the fit. He was overcome with weariness as he took a seat and slid his feet into his shoes, but he would not miss tonight for the world. Phoebe would be there.

That week, he had ridden to Ghent to assist in moving the quartermaster-general's office to Brussels, where De Lancey was to be based. He'd taken stock of the provisions there and created a detailed list for Wellington to review before the duke sent a letter to London with all he required. Frederick had brought numerous dispatches before Wellington for his review and had carried out his orders to rearrange battalions, mixing the hired soldiers with the seasoned veterans. Earlier that day, Frederick accompanied the duke on his diplomatic meeting with the Prince of Orange and the Belgian and Dutch nobility, before meeting with Blücher, who was setting up half of the Prussian forces east of Brussels.

Caldwell filed Frederick's nails in silence. Frederick submitted to the operation, knowing it was needed as he had been too preoccupied to take care of his appearance of late. His valet knew him well enough to leave Frederick to his thoughts, although he likely discerned all that distracted him since Caldwell was by no means a dull fellow. As soon as he was ready, he called for his carriage.

The Austrian and Swiss armies were situated close to the French border—although not as close as the troops in Brussels—and the

Spanish armies were set to move over the Pyrenees into the south of France. However, the Russian armies were located farther out and would not be ready to march on Paris until the beginning of July. None would act without the coordination of the Allies.

It was far from a sure thing that Napoleon would give the Allies the time they needed to move on Paris. It was more likely the emperor would decide to go on the offensive; and with Russia still so far away, the likeliest place for Boney to attack would be Brussels. Wellington said they would be ready, and Frederick thought that with the number of troops they were accumulating, *surely* they would be able to defeat the enemy. But the British troops were only second-line, with the more experienced troops still returning from the Americas. Their numbers were far inferior to the 150,000 troops promised by each member of the coalition, and they had to settle for paying to hire soldiers from some of their allies. The British Army would not be sending His Majesty's best.

But tonight, Frederick allowed himself to think about something other than the war they were preparing for, and he hurried to the carriage that would take him to the theater. The truth was, he missed Phoebe—or at least missed the opportunity of seeing her and exchanging a few words. He allowed himself the honesty of admitting *that* to himself. Before Wellington had arrived, Frederick had spent every day with Phoebe and his sister, and there were just enough moments—such as their picnic—to open Frederick's eyes to the fact that Phoebe possessed an allure that had hitherto escaped him. Now she rarely left his thoughts. In fact, he found himself increasingly considering her for the role of his wife. The thought made him swallow with sudden nerves. He ran his fingers through his hair and then turned to exit the carriage, taking the steps to the theater at a jog.

Frederick joined the hordes of people streaming in. The jovial atmosphere was a far cry from the military details that had consumed him for the last week. Everyone carried on as if there were no imminent threat of war. Once he was past the marble hall and up the stairs, Frederick easily found Lord Wellington, who broke off his conversation to say, "Good. You are here. I've been running you too hard, Ingram, and you need this diversion. We are sitting in that box there where you see Sutherland and Wrotham."

Frederick bowed his greeting. "I shall go to them directly."

The theater hall was too packed with people for him to seek out Lydia and Phoebe, especially when he did not know where they would be sitting. He entered the box reserved for Wellington's aides and greeted the men, taking a seat beside Dalrymple, who was being teased about an actress who had caught his eye.

"I shall obtain an introduction and you will all be jealous," Dolly retorted good-naturedly.

Frederick smiled and turned to Wrotham, engaging him in small talk while his eyes roamed the crowds. It was growing warm, and he was glad that the duke had a spacious box set a ways apart.

He could not spot Phoebe or his sister and was beginning to fear they had not come, until he turned to the boxes on his immediate right and found them occupying a small box. Phoebe was wearing her hair again in that modern, becoming style with curls close to her face just above the indentation of her cheekbone. The line of her slender collarbones dipped under the fabric of her neckline, which ended in small puffed sleeves on her pale blue dress. From where he sat, he could discern pendant earrings that swung as she moved and caught the light of the candles. She wore no necklace, but the expanse of skin across her shoulders and along her slender neck was a work of art that needed no adornment. He saw her smile, her eyes squinting in a way that brought an involuntary smile to his own face. He glanced at the person next to her who had inspired such a smile and noticed it was Mr. Conroy. His mood instantly soured.

"What—or shall I say whom—has captured your attention?" Wrotham teased. Frederick sat upright and shot his friend a look. He was being far too transparent.

"I am only looking at the box where my sister is sitting with her husband, and our friend Miss Tunstall, sister to the Earl of Worthing. I've known her since she was a child."

"And who is the fellow next to her?"

"That is Conroy, an ensign in the 69th. Heard of him?"

"We've met," Sutherland said, joining their conversation. "He's considered a genial fellow."

"I am very sure he must be," Frederick replied, hiding his ire. He was not required to say anything further because the curtain opened and the comedy sketch that preceded the main act began. Before long, laughter rippled through the audience. Frederick darted another glance at Phoebe in her box, willing her to look at him, and flicked his eyes to the stage when Conroy glanced his way. Frederick did not want to be obvious in his regard, but surely she must have noticed his presence. And it was not as though they had just seen each other yesterday. From Phoebe's expression, it seemed she did not find more than mild amusement from the play, and she did not glance his way.

When intermission came, Frederick told Wrotham and Sutherland he was going to take a stroll. He had decided he would go to Phoebe's box to see her. Lydia would wonder what had become of him, and it was only natural that he would spend the intermission with such an old friend. If Phoebe had known he was at the theater that night but had never come to see her, she would find it odd

As he was about to enter their box, Mr. Conroy exited into the hall, where crowds of people milled in both directions. Phoebe trailed him up the two steps that led to the corridor. Frederick nodded a greeting to Conroy, who returned it with a stiff nod. He caught Phoebe's gaze, pleased to see the smile that lit her face.

"Phoebe," he said with a private vengeance, taking full advantage of the liberty he had in saying her Christian name. "It has been an age since I've seen you. Duties have kept me busy, but I will be able to come see you tomorrow if you are free."

Phoebe looked away, as if attempting to muffle her pleasure, but the smile was back in full bloom when she answered. "That would be delightful. I am not engaged at present. Are you going to greet Lydia and Fitz?" she asked.

Frederick's first priority was not necessarily to see Lydia. What he would have liked was to plant himself between Phoebe and Mr. Conroy, who had her on his arm, and take Phoebe's hand for himself. However, he obviously could not do that. At least not without making a cake of himself and embarrassing Phoebe besides.

"Yes, I came to see them, too. I will let you go on and have your refreshments."

Mr. Conroy gave a small bow and turned with Phoebe to join the crowds gathered around the refreshment table, and Frederick walked into the box. "Evening, Fitz, Lydia. Are you well? You looked peaked."

"Fred, where have you been hiding? We have missed you at the house. Although"—she glanced at her husband—"I must say that Fitz has been nearly as busy as you. When do you plan to come and see us?"

"I just told Phoebe I would come tomorrow—" Frederick broke off suddenly and clapped his hand to his forehead. "Good heavens. I forgot we are to have a cricket match tomorrow at the park. If I don't see Phoebe before the intermission is over, make my excuses for me, will you?"

"Who is playing? We never have cricket matches anymore," Lydia cried out. "That would be fun to see."

"That is likely because we have a shortage of men," Fitz answered mildly. "They are at present playing at much more deadly games."

Lydia's brow furrowed before she faced Frederick again. "Why, all the more reason to embrace such a simple pastime. Where are you playing tomorrow, and with whom?"

"The duke wants his aides and other staff members to play against the officers from various regiments. And we had better not lose," Frederick said, meeting Fitz's gaze, who laughed quietly. "We are playing in the park next to the king's palace. You and Phoebe will come and see it?"

"We certainly shall," Lydia exclaimed.

Frederick began to think that this change in plans might work in his favor, for he knew he was a fast bowler, besides being pretty skilled at fielding. He certainly hoped Phoebe would be impressed by him.

Frederick hammered in the stumps with the broad side of the bat, looking up from time to time to see if Phoebe had arrived. He spotted her well before the general crowds began to assemble, and his lips lifted as he stood upright. He tucked one of the bats under his arm and went over to see her. Lydia raised her hand in greeting and pulled Fitz away to talk to a nearby officer and his wife.

Frederick held out his hands to Phoebe, and she put hers in

them. He lifted her hands to his lips and caught a look of surprise in her eyes at the unusual gesture. It would not do to scare her away. He had no idea what she might feel for him; he knew only what he was beginning to feel for her.

"I did not get a chance to speak with you as much as I would have liked yesterday, but I see that Lydia has explained why I could not come and visit you today. I'm glad you came to see the match."

Phoebe tilted her head up at him, allowing her gentle gaze to meet his. "I am eager to see it. Can you believe I have never once seen a cricket match? I do not even know how it is played."

"Do you not? There are eleven players on each team," he said. "And the goal is simply to get all eleven batsmen out on the other side, then score more runs than them. And there you have it. As you can see, it requires great cunning." Frederick laughed.

"And shall you win, do you think?" Phoebe grinned up at him, her eyes twinkling with humor in something very like flirting. He loved it.

Frederick smiled back, the flirtation coming easily to him. "If you give me a token of your favor, I engage to win."

A determination came over him. He had spotted Mr. Conroy on the edge of his vision and hoped the man had not come at Phoebe's invitation. He edged sideways so that Phoebe was forced to turn as well in order to face him. From there she could not see Mr. Conroy.

At his request, Phoebe had turned a charming pink, and she raised her brows over doubtful eyes. "What token shall I give you?" She tilted her head to the side with an assessing gaze. "What would be enough of an inducement to cause you to win?"

"Whatever you decide," Frederick replied. *A lock of your hair*, he thought, but he would not voice such a thing, besides it being highly inappropriate to ask—and impossible to claim in so public a place.

Phoebe's face grew pinker and her smile broader. "Hmm." She appeared to give it some thought. "I believe the only thing I can offer you is my embroidered handkerchief."

Frederick pretended to consider the offer. "Did you embroider it yourself?"

"I did, as a matter of fact. It is silk, so more decorative than functional, I suppose." Her lips trembled as though she wished to hide her smile, and she looked adorably confused.

"Then that will do very nicely. I shall place it next to my breast, and I am sure to win that way."

Phoebe startled at his words and avoided his gaze as she searched through her reticule for the handkerchief. Her face had grown more scarlet, and she had no glib words for Frederick in return.

He had done it now. His words could not be taken in the same brotherly manner in which he had always treated her. But somehow his feelings for Phoebe had fled the realm of brotherly and had marched on unbidden into something else all together. Phoebe pulled her handkerchief out of her reticule and handed it to him. It was soft and white and perfumed with some floral scent. Peonies? He resisted the foolish urge to kiss the handkerchief and tucked it into his breast pocket.

"Thank you."

Phoebe darted her eyes to his, and Frederick smiled in return. His feelings toward her were no longer quite so friendly and staid, and he knew he could not relegate Phoebe to the little girl of his youth. She was a woman, with thoughts and feelings that mattered to him, and one with whom he was anxious to share a deeper connection.

Chapter Sixteen

*P*hoebe watched Frederick jog onto the field with his bat as a
gentleman called the players to order. When he arrived at the
center, he glanced back at her, a lock of his hair falling forward as
he gave her another grin. He was acting as though he were smitten
with her, which . . . surely, she must have misread. Phoebe could not
move. She could not even breathe.

"Miss Tunstall, what an unexpected delight. I would not take
you for a fan of the sport." Mr. Conroy glanced at Frederick and
then back at her, frown lines marring his brow. "I see Lord Ingram
is one of the players. Is that why you have come?"

Phoebe had difficulty welcoming Mr. Conroy's presence with
the same contentment she had found before. "Lydia told me her
brother would be playing and that she wished to see him, so we
arranged to come."

The whack of the bat against the ball drew her eyes forward. Frederick was first, and he ran between the wickets, just sliding his bat in
the nick of time to make his ground before the keeper whipped off
the bails. He was a fine athlete, and she could not help the smile that
settled on her lips as she watched Frederick running, the muscles in
his thighs apparent enough in the buckskin breeches he wore.

Mr. Conroy was silent at her side as he watched the game. "I
regret that I am not playing. We had to draw names out of a hat
because there were too many officers who wished to team up. Do
you know much about the game?"

"Nothing at all, other than the oversimplified set of rules Lord Ingram shared with me before getting called onto the field." Phoebe turned to see where Lydia and Fitz were and spotted them at the Marshalls' side. Fitz was still in conversation, but Lydia was now watching the game.

"Allow me to enlighten you," Mr. Conroy said before launching into a muddling description of bowling, fielding, wickets, and throwing the ball from deep cover point versus gully. Phoebe tried to ask intelligent questions, but she honestly had no interest in how the game could technically be played. She only had interest in how Frederick played it and which rules would keep him running back and forth in front of her like that.

Lydia came to stand at her side at last. "Fitz has more to discuss with Brigadier Marshall, so I left him there to do it. Good afternoon, Mr. Conroy."

Mr. Conroy had fallen silent after his long-winded explanation of the rules of cricket, and Phoebe could feel his studied gaze on her. He turned and bowed before Lydia. "Good afternoon, Mrs. Fitzwilliam. Well, I believe I shall leave the two of you. I must sit on the side where the officers are, for that is my team." He gave a tight-lipped smile and bowed before walking around the field to the spectators on the other side.

Lydia swiveled to watch him walk off. "My goodness, I wonder what came over the man. You did not say anything discouraging, did you?" She rounded on Phoebe. "He is your most assiduous suitor, and I had imagined him fixed at your side for the entirety of the match. I left you two alone long enough, but it seemed like he was the only one interested in maintaining the conversation."

Phoebe was helpless against the pull of Frederick's movements on the field, though she tried to hide it. If not even Anna knew how she felt about Frederick, she most certainly could not allow his sister to have any clue. Frederic caught the ball and stretched forward to hurl it to the wicket keeper, who caught it with a snap.

Reluctantly, Phoebe tore her gaze from Frederick's fine figure and turned to face Lydia. "I have no idea. Mr. Conroy was attempting to explain the rules of the game, but I own I did not follow very carefully. Do you know them?"

"Yes." Lydia released Phoebe from her all-too preceptive gaze and turned toward the game. "Frederick played often, so I went to see the games. Did not Stratford play?"

Phoebe shook her head. "Not in my presence. In any case, it looks as though your brother has had much practice. He is a fine player."

"When it comes to sports, there is nothing that Frederick does not excel at, even if his leg sometimes still bothers him from his accident. I almost pity the other team. I cannot see how they can win, because Fred is not the only experienced player. But I also know that Lord Wellington would not suffer his team's loss very easily, so I suppose it is well they will carry the game."

The sun began to beat down, growing stronger than the gentle spring breeze that accompanied it. They were now well into May, and all the chill of the early season was gone. Phoebe opened her parasol and continued watching the movement on the field. Meanwhile, Lydia was making observations that were much more to Phoebe's taste than a rambling discourse on the technicalities of the game. They were soon joined by Lady Turton, who had spotted Lydia, and even the Duchess of Richmond drove up in her barouche near them to watch the match and nodded her head in acknowledgment.

"We have found favor with her," Lydia whispered out of Lady Turton's hearing, appearing more amused than gratified by the fact.

The game was surprisingly entertaining, but Phoebe was glad it was not one of the *several days* variety, for the interest would pall soon enough. Just as she thought she'd had enough, the crowd threw up a loud cheer as Frederick hit the stumps and they went cartwheeling back. He let out a roar and raised his arm in victory as his teammates all ran to him. He turned to look at Phoebe and Lydia, his smile broad, and he waved.

"Huh!" Lydia exclaimed, her voice bright with surprise. "Fred usually ignores me during his matches. But that was very well done."

Phoebe did not dare to look at Lydia for fear her expression would betray the love and admiration that coursed through her for this man who excelled at everything, including capturing her heart.

"Most impressive," she answered with the coolest tone at her disposal. "Shall we rejoin Fitz?"

The next day, Phoebe and Lydia stayed home to receive morning calls. Phoebe hoped that Frederick would come, particularly after the flirtatious way he had spoken with her the day before. He had not returned her handkerchief after the game, and she hoped that it signified the token meant something to him. Then again, he had not been able to do more than greet Lydia and her before getting called away by his teammates to celebrate their victory.

The footman came into the drawing room and announced that Mr. Albert Cummings and Miss Martha Cummings had arrived.

Lydia exchanged a speaking glance with her, and Phoebe once again forced her thoughts to a more charitable turn. Poor Martha. She did not have much going in her favor in terms of beauty and address, but if only she could be made a better listener she would have more friends. Mr. Cummings and Martha entered the room.

"Oh, I am glad to find you at home," Martha began before they had exchanged civilities. "We haven't seen you since last week at the Edgars' rout, and you were so busy speaking with Mr. Conroy—I declare he must be a beau of yours, for I see him always at your side. Have you formed an attachment?"

Fortunately, Martha did not wait for a response, as Phoebe would be unable to answer such a straightforward question. "So, I decided that we simply must come and visit you in your house if we are to have any sort of conversation. And Albert was only too glad to accompany me. He does not often have time for social visits, do you, Albert? Mrs. Fitzwilliam, I rarely see your husband. Is the Lieutenant-Colonel engaged in all manners of preparation? Do you think, as my brother seems to, that Napoleon will march into Brussels?"

At last she paused for breath, and Lydia stood. "For the moment, I am choosing not to think too much about it. It is early days yet. Please have a seat. I shall call for tea," she said and walked into the corridor to speak with the footman. Phoebe suspected that the offer sprang not from a desire to convince Martha and her brother to stay longer, but just for them to have something to do with their hands while they listened to Martha speak.

"Mr. Cummings, do you indeed think Napoleon will march on Brussels?" Phoebe asked. "If so, do you have plans to leave?"

Mr. Cummings sat up straight and pulled at his coat before clasping his hands on his lap. He was not a particularly handsome man, but he appeared to have a degree of common sense that Martha lacked, and it lent a more intelligent air to his features.

"I am no expert in military strategy, of course. But I am following sources who understand the matter because I want to make sure that my business will not be hindered by any invasion. At least not one that comes close to Brussels."

He leaned on the armrest of his chair. "That said, I recognize Boney's ambition because I am an ambitious man myself. I have trouble imagining him waiting docilely in Paris while the Coalition gets organized enough to make an attack. He will be so vastly outnumbered if he does that he cannot possibly win, and he surely knows it. At the same time, does he have the forces needed in order to go on the offensive?"

Mr. Cummings shrugged. "That is a point I cannot answer. The men that I am trading with are both Belgic and Dutch in nature. Half the Belgians long for the former Emperor to come and make the same changes here that he made throughout France. The other half oppose him. But if pressed to choose, my guess is that he is more likely to come here than not."

Lydia re-entered the room with the footman and ordered Sam to set down the tray with the saucers and cakes while they waited for the hot water to arrive.

"So, do you intend to leave, then?" Phoebe asked, her gaze focused on Mr. Cummings. Any signs of flight in their entourage colored the situation with urgency and forced Phoebe to consider whether she should stay put or not. Lydia looked at Mr. Cummings, waiting for his answer as she came to take her seat.

"I will not leave at present, although Martha wishes it."

Martha took this as a sign for her to enter the conversation. "Yes, I do wish it. I cannot be at ease in a place where we might be attacked at any time. If we were on English soil we would be perfectly safe. But here, I cannot but feel that we are in imminent danger."

"Until Napoleon arrives, we are not," her brother corrected. "I told you that I would take care of ensuring both of our safety. Believe me, I have no more desire than you to get caught in the midst of a battle. I am not a soldier and have no means of defending myself. The only thing I have is enough wealth to make sure that we can get out when we need to."

"Well," Martha said, conceding her brother's point, "we do manage to divert ourselves here. If I don't think about it too hard—and I always try not to, for otherwise I will work myself up into quite a fright—I can almost think that there's no danger whatsoever. Brussels is such a gay place to be. Even though I regret that we do not meet as often as I would like, I am able to find many sources of amusement. I suppose that although I fear for our future, I can be content to remain for the moment, especially knowing that we might leave at any time. If we do leave, you must come with us," Martha said, clasping her hands together compulsively. "Both of you. Oh . . . of course, Mrs. Fitzwilliam, you have your husband. So, you will not likely leave, but if he is off fighting the war, then there's absolutely nothing to keep you here. You must leave when we do."

Phoebe glanced at Mr. Cummings, wondering if he supported his sister's offer. Lydia, she knew, would not leave. Phoebe didn't want to leave either, not when Frederick was here. If he went to war, she couldn't bear to go off never knowing if he were injured . . . or worse. "I thank you, but—"

"I assure you, you have a place in our carriage should you wish it," Mr. Cummings said. "You have been a friend to my sister, and there will be two places for you both, should you have need."

"For myself, I could not leave," Lydia said firmly. "Even if my husband were to order me to leave, I believe I must disobey him. I could not go, knowing that my husband was fighting a battle nearby. If I was able to campaign next to him on the Peninsula, I can certainly do so in a comfortable house in the middle of the city. It is not Brussels that is under attack. But I will say, Mr. Cummings," Lydia went on, "that my husband is of the same mind as you. He thinks Napoleon more likely to march northward than he is to stay put. So, I believe we must be ready for all eventualities."

She turned to Phoebe. "And I must add that if there is cause to flee Brussels, I will very much urge you to go. I am afraid Stratford and Anna would never forgive me if I let any harm come to you."

Phoebe did not want to have this discussion in front of near strangers, but she could not help but argue. "You are nearly as important to Stratford and Anna as I am. And whatever is safe enough for you must surely be safe enough for me." *Besides*, she thought, *you are pregnant*. Wishing to turn the conversation, she asked Mr. Cummings, "Why do you not leave now?"

"His business is doing so well," Martha said before her brother could open his mouth. "He finally found a good manufacturing source of men's razors, and he has to finish the negotiations. If he were to leave now, he might lose everything he's been working toward."

"That is the reason," Mr. Cummings admitted. "I will not venture on this course to my detriment or that of my sister's. If I see there is immediate danger, I must cut my losses, and we will leave. However, at the moment there is absolutely no risk attached to us staying here. If I join the few who have already fled to Antwerp, I will be competing with the other merchants and lose my advantage. So, for the present, we remain." He folded his hands on his lap as if to make the point.

The hot water was brought, and Martha almost solely carried the conversation. She stopped only to take a bite of the cake she had put on her plate and would have stayed past the standard time for morning calls if her brother had not pulled out his pocket watch and glanced at it. "Martha, I have a meeting to attend to. We must go."

Martha set her cup and saucer down. "Oh my, is it time already? Yes, you must not be late. Well, Phoebe, Mrs. Fitzwilliam—I hope we will see more of one another soon. Thank you for the tea. It has been delightful."

Phoebe stood, and Lydia called for the footman to show them out. After they bid farewell, the brother and sister left, and Lydia resumed her seat, a slight smile hovering on her lips.

"She means well," Phoebe said. "And she is kind."

"She is both of those things," Lydia agreed and then shut her lips resolutely.

A silence settled over them, and Phoebe wanted to ask if Lydia thought Frederick might come, but she did not allow herself to do so. In any case, they were invited to Lord Wellington's ball the following week, and Phoebe knew she must see him there. The anticipation stole her breath.

Chapter Seventeen

*H*ad it been an ordinary courtship, Frederick would have sent flowers every day to let Phoebe know she was in his thoughts even though he could not visit. The days following the cricket match were filled with busy preparation and social engagements he could not miss. It was not a usual courtship, however, as she lived with his sister. Besides that, he was not even sure if his advances would be welcome. He thought it possible, but it might be difficult for innocent Phoebe to view him as anything other than an elder brother. And then there was that Mr. Conroy, who was glued to her side for much of the match. He hoped she did not look upon his suit with favor.

Frederick removed his hunting coat, which was muddied from spending the day following Lord Uxbridge's hounds on the hunt through the forest of Soigny. His valet had a bath drawn, and Frederick settled into the water, allowing the heat to soothe his weary muscles. It had been hard going these past weeks. The life of one of Wellington's staff was filled with balls, races held by the Prince of Orange, *reading clubs*—which were nothing more than a place for gentlemen to gamble—besides the military reviews and diplomatic meetings, London dispatches, and mobilization of a large number of troops. Every night, Frederick dined with the duke, along with the rest of the staff, and it was usually followed by a social gathering. He considered it ill luck that the invitations lately had not been for the same events that Phoebe attended.

He took the olive-scented soap Caldwell handed him and quickly lathered, scrubbed his hair, and dunked under the water to rinse off. He allowed his valet to dress him for the ball that Wellington was holding that night—the second the duke had organized since he'd come to Brussels. Although the gathering was select, Frederick made sure invitations were sent to Lydia, Fitz, and Phoebe. One benefit of tonight's ball was that Mr. Conroy was not invited.

"My lord, I have had your regimentals cleaned and your boots polished. I took the liberty of cleaning your guns as well. I should not like you to have sudden need of them and not have them in a fit state."

Frederick generally cleaned his own muskets as well as pistols, but at the moment he was too weary to protest and too busy to see to it himself. "You did well. As much as the duke might show an insouciant air to the public, the number of intelligence reports he requests and receives paints a different picture. It is highly unlikely Boney will oblige us by waiting in Paris for the Allies to get mobilized. It is better that we are prepared." Caldwell was experienced in campaigning and could be trusted with these non-specific bits of intelligence.

His valet pursed his lips and nodded. "Just as I thought, milord."

At Wellington's table, only a light dinner was set out, as they would be having a supper later at the ball. Frederick took a seat beside Sutherland and Pinkton, attempting to follow a joke that was already in progress. Although he had not caught enough of it to find the humor, it must have been funny, for the duke gave a bark of laughter.

Anyone who knew Lord Wellington only in these social settings must think him too simple a man to be able to lead an entire campaign against the French. He brushed off the anxious inquiries of those eager for news, saying there was no need to worry. But his staff knew better. In social settings, Wellington was carefree and gay, it seemed, to the point of dissipation. In private, he was sharp and intolerant of failure or laziness. The public façade allowed all of Brussels society to be reassured by his presence, for he laughed off all attempts at alarm. The private one set Frederick and the officers' minds at ease, for they knew that as long as "The Beau" was on hand, he could be relied upon to carry the victory. Even the sight of "Old Nosey"—as his soldiers called him, referring, of course, to his rather prominent beak—inspired his troops with confidence.

Tonight's ball was held in the open rented rooms of the Hôtel du Parc. Frederick's fatigue was forgotten as he kept glancing at the door, waiting for Phoebe's entrance. He hoped tonight they would have a chance to dance together and exchange more than the briefest of words. He would engage her for the waltz before anyone could claim her hand.

He saw Lydia first, walking in on the arm of Fitz, and they stopped to greet Lord Wellington, spending a few minutes in conversation. The duke remembered Fitz from the Peninsula and had spoken to Frederick about him. Frederick was certain that if his brother-in-law distinguished himself in the next battle, he would continue to move up in ranks. Phoebe should have been with them, but next to Fitz and Lydia stood another couple, and Phoebe was nowhere in sight. He knew a moment's panic, wondering if she had been indisposed and unable to come. That would ruin his object for the evening, for he planned to attempt a real courtship, no matter what his sister might say. In the next instant, Phoebe's graceful form edged into his vision, and he moved forward.

After she had curtsied in front of Lord Wellington, she turned to follow Lydia and Fitz, and smiled at Frederick as soon as she caught sight of him.

The smile struck him like a soft blow. His chest had lightened at the sight of her, but it was accompanied by a leaden ball of nerves that had settled in his stomach. *Did she feel for him anything of what he had come to feel for her?* Phoebe was gentle and good, and it seemed to Frederick that she treated everyone the same. He truly could not say whether she was capable of looking upon their relationship in a more intimate light than the one they currently possessed. Until now, it had caused him to behave with the greatest circumspection whenever he interacted with her. He did not dare make any moves that were too bold or displayed too much interest. He could not damage or endanger in any way the friendship they had. But now his desire for more was eroding his common sense.

Frederick greeted his sister and Fitz, then bowed before Phoebe. "Save the two waltzes for me, will you? One of them is before the supper, and that way you might go into the dining room on my arm." He caught Lydia looking at him with a gleam of interest in her eye, and he tried to downplay his particular attention. "We will take a table with Lydia and Fitz and make up a merry party. I have not seen you three often enough for my liking."

Phoebe glanced at Lydia and nodded, smiling. "It would be my pleasure."

The Duchess of Richmond swept up to their circle and acknowledged Lydia and Phoebe with a gracious nod. She looked at Frederick and seemed to be waiting for an introduction, so Lydia provided it. "Lady Richmond, allow me to present my brother, The Viscount Ingram."

Frederick bowed. "I know your husband, my lady. We have dined together and have met on numerous occasions. In fact, I must say I am surprised our paths have not crossed before now."

Lady Richmond accorded this with a nod. "A pleasure. I shall have to introduce you to my daughter, Lady Georgy. Perhaps you might engage her for one of the waltzes."

Frederick gave Phoebe an involuntary glance before training his regard on Lady Richmond. "I would be delighted to dance with your daughter, but I regret to tell you that my waltzes are given out. However, if you would have the goodness to introduce me to her, I will engage her for one of the quadrilles."

Lady Richmond sent a shrewd glance Phoebe's way, which made him wonder how much she also suspected. The idea of attempting a courtship under the eye of Society matrons, which included his sister—without knowing how the lady in question felt—was difficult.

"Very well," the duchess said. "If you will accompany me, I will perform the introductions."

Frederick met Lady Georgy, who was comely with soft brown eyes and curls that sprang out next to her temples. He engaged her for the quadrille, and when they danced she was vivacious and pretty but would have been easily forgotten were it not for the keen understanding she seemed to possess of the military defenses that were forming. She kept up a stream of observations whenever they faced or spun around each other.

"How are you so well acquainted with the regiments?" he asked her as the last notes of music died down and their salutation ended the dance. Her intelligent reflections had made the set most pleasurable.

"Oh, the duke is patient and answers my questions," she said, waving it off as though it were no very great thing that Lord Wellington should take the time to instruct a young woman. Now that Frederick thought about it, he had heard about Lady Georgy and her unusual friendship with the duke. She bid him a friendly farewell and rejoined her mother before being handed off to her next partner.

At last, it was time to lead Phoebe to their dance, and he came to claim her hand. It was everything he had been waiting for these past days—a chance to have her all to himself. Phoebe slipped her hand around his arm, and he pulled her close as he led her to the dance floor. Frederick faced her as they waited for the music to begin. "As you must have guessed, Wellington has been keeping me busy. Otherwise, nothing would have kept me from coming to see you sooner. How have you and Lydia fared since we last spoke?" *Have you thought of me?* It was the question he could not ask.

Phoebe stepped back to look up into his face. "Lydia and I have been nearly as busy as you, I fear." A laugh escaped her. "Of course, not *as* busy. That would be impossible. But we've been doing just about everything! I do not believe I have been this active, even in London."

Her answer didn't quite settle Frederick's doubts. She wasn't exactly pining away with love for him. "What sorts of things have kept you occupied?"

"Well, just this week we have gone riding and attended morning calls. But we've been too busy to receive anyone at our house. We have gone walking in the park and have been invited to dine out no less than three times. One of those was followed by a rout. We've attended a card party and have even gone to see another cricket match—an impromptu game set up between Fitz's regiment and the 22nd."

The music began, cutting Phoebe's speech short. It was unusual for her to say so much at once, and as much as Frederick enjoyed listening to her, this was the moment he had been waiting for. He put his arm around Phoebe and reached up to clasp her hand with his other arm. Frederick had waltzed with Anna in the past, but for some reason this was the first time he had waltzed with Phoebe. He glanced down and saw her throat move as she swallowed, and he thought that just maybe his nearness affected her. He hoped so.

Frederick took a step forward, with Phoebe at his side, and he relished the feeling of holding her in an embrace as he had longed to do that day he saw her in the park. As they were facing forward, he tilted his head toward hers. "I hear there is a *fête champêtre* in the Forest of Soigny in a fortnight. Do you intend to go to that?" As soon as he had learned of it, he became determined to be the one to escort her.

"Yes, we plan to go. Our servants are pleased to no end that they are to enjoy it as well. We will not need them to attend to us once we arrive. I understand there will be people from the Village of Soigny in attendance."

Frederick again leaned down to speak, not so much to be heard as to be *near*. "I believe so. I think there will be a great number of people. I am glad you will go." He saw her cheeks lift in a smile, and he drew her nearer. They did not speak, and although Frederick's ideas for conversation seemed to have fled, their silence was not uncomfortable.

They separated after the first waltz, and Frederick stole glimpses of Phoebe across the room when he was not escorting another young lady to dance. More than once, her eyes were also trained on him when he looked her way, and it gave him hope.

When it came time for the supper waltz, he hurried to her side. "This one is mine."

She lifted her hand to put it on the arm he held out, and her eyes seemed to sparkle with a joy that reflected his. "So it is."

During their second waltz, they spoke little and melded even more closely into each other's arms, despite Frederick's determination to keep his attachment a secret. It exercised all of his self-restraint. Their nearness felt even more right than it had the first waltz. It was everything he had longed to do since the night of his arrival in Brussels, even though it had taken him time to admit it to himself.

When they had finished the dance, Frederick stepped away with regret. She turned and curtsied, her wide-eyed gaze meeting his. He held it for a heartbeat, willing her to know something of what he felt. Finally, he smiled. "Shall we find Lydia and Fitz?"

He led Phoebe into the supper room, where they found the table Lydia and Fitz had reserved. The conversation flowed freely as they ate, with Fitz asking Frederick what the latest intelligence reports were. Frederick glanced at Phoebe before answering. "Only that it appears that uniforms are being made in France at breakneck speed. I cannot believe that Napoleon will wait for us to come to Paris, and I don't think Wellington believes it either."

"It is just as I thought," Fitz said. He clasped Lydia's hand. "Well, let us make merry until we have reason to do otherwise."

Phoebe was silent at Frederick's side. Lydia and Fitz brushed off the heaviness by entering into a spirited debate about what invitations they would be accepting in the coming weeks. Frederick leaned in to murmur to Phoebe, "You see, I have said no more of you going home. Does the talk of an upcoming battle worry you? I should not like to see you upset in any way."

Phoebe looked ahead at some distant point across the room and, without meeting his gaze, leaned in, answering with her soft voice. "I find it difficult to be overly worried when there is such a strength of British troops here. I trust Fitz. I trust *you*." She looked at him and then looked away again, her cheeks growing pink. "Although perhaps we will soon have cause to worry, I am lulled into thinking all will be well."

Frederick reached under the table and gave her hand a discreet squeeze. "You may trust that I will do everything in my power to protect you."

Before long, the small groups at the supper tables began to break up, and the crowds returned to the ballroom, where the musicians were warming up again. Phoebe was immediately claimed for the next dance and the series of dances after that. A number of officers continued to take notice of Phoebe, easily stepping into Conroy's gap, and Frederick wondered if his own interest had been overly apparent. Nothing more would be needed for other officers to throw their hats into the ring than for them to sense competition. He was unable to exchange more words with her until the ball had come to an end, and when he spotted her and Lydia receiving their wraps to go home, he strode over to them.

"If I can stop by this week, I will," he told Lydia and Phoebe. "But as we are scheduled to go to Enghien, I think it unlikely. Expect to see me at the *fête champêtre*, however. We may sit together." Frederick was looking at Phoebe as he said this, but he broke the gaze when he felt Lydia's studied regard.

Lydia was now looking at Phoebe, who smiled at him. "Good night, Frederick."

Frederick bowed and watched them meet Fitz at the door, who had already given orders for the carriage. Phoebe accepted Fitz's other arm as they walked through the entrance and descended the stairs. With the imminent threat of war looming, he was going to take his chances with Phoebe. He would not wait anymore before finding out how she felt.

Chapter Eighteen

At last, the day that held the *fête champêtre* arrived, and Phoebe was strung up with nerves. They were to have breakfast in the forest, but she forced herself to eat something so she wouldn't feel faint. She *was* faint, though, for Frederick had sent a note to her and Lydia reminding them that he would see them today.

After his trip to Enghein, he had been unable to visit. He'd sent word that he needed to travel to Wavre with Wellington to hold discussions with the Prussian general. She could not enjoy the Season's diversions while Frederick was concerned with such weighty matters, and everything felt so empty when he was not there. The days seemed long before Phoebe would see him again, especially now that she held on to some hope of winning his heart. His attention had grown these past weeks—she was certain it was so. Even if they were not often able to meet, he had given her such unmistakable signs of his regard. *Dare I hope?*

Lydia broke her roll in two to apply jam. "It is good news that Frederick promised to join us at the festival. I had feared some duty would hinder him from coming. Although, I must assume that all of Brussels Society will be there today—even Lord Wellington—so he cannot possibly have a reason to miss it. The weather is fine, and the festivities promise to be delightful."

Phoebe responded in the studied, even tone she used whenever Frederick was mentioned—or whenever he was near. "Quite so. I am impatient to discover exactly what this *fête champêtre* will entail.

Do you think it will be like an English *al fresco* picnic, but on a larger scale?" She lifted her cup of coffee and took small sips.

"Do you know," Lydia said suddenly, ignoring Phoebe's line of conversation, "a suspicion dawned upon me when we were at the duke's ball. I did not say anything at the time, as it seemed too extraordinary, but . . . now that we are to see Frederick, it has come to my mind again." She paused and pierced Phoebe with her regard. "I have a suspicion that my brother has developed a *tendre* for you."

Phoebe dropped the cup, and it fell on the saucer with a loud clatter. The cup tipped, spilling dark coffee on the tablecloth and onto her dress. She leapt to her feet. "Oh my," she said, heat rushing to her face. "How clumsy of me. We must ring for the servants."

Lydia was already on her feet, opening the door and calling for one of the servants to come. "You had best go and change your dress, for I have already instructed Sam to bring the carriage around, and it will be at the door soon. Mary, you go assist Phoebe. Good—Sarah, you have come too. Clean this up quickly for we are to leave directly."

Phoebe escaped the room, willing her high color to sink into a more even complexion. She had chosen this particular gown with care for her first meeting with Frederick in a fortnight, thinking it the most becoming one she owned. It was a shame she had ruined it. She would have to wear her second-best dress.

Phoebe hurried into her bedroom. "Mary, quickly if you please—assist me into my dress with green embroidery. And if you can take this one down to soak the stain, perhaps it can be salvaged. But as we are to leave soon, you will have no more time than just to let it soak."

"Never you fear, miss." Mary moved quickly, for the stain had soaked through to Phoebe's shift. She helped her to change the shift and gown and bustled away with both stained items in her arms.

Phoebe stayed behind to compose herself and stared at her reflection in the glass. This dress was not so very inferior, she thought. Its color was not as becoming, but it did give her a nice figure, and the embroidery lent a delicate touch. But oh—she would still have to go down and face Lydia after that embarrassing spill. Lydia had surely read her feelings as openly as if Phoebe had shouted them from the roof. What a *cake* she had made of herself.

Downstairs, Lydia was waiting for Phoebe, her hand on the stair railing. She did not seem inclined to bustle out the door, although Phoebe could hear the clink of the harness outdoors. Instead, Lydia folded her arms and studied her.

"I begin to suspect that my brother is not the only one who has developed a *tendre*. I dare you to tell me I am wrong." She raised an eyebrow, but a smile hovered on her lips.

Phoebe recoiled under such direct questioning. She could trust Lydia, she knew. But there was some obstacle—some *thing* that blocked her from speaking out. She had kept this love for Frederick a secret for so long, it was impossible to admit to it.

"I am sure you cannot be right about his feelings. Frederick and I have known each other all our lives. He views me as only a little sister, nothing more. I am sure you have mistaken the matter."

"Hmm." Lydia raised one eyebrow and kept her arms folded. "Well, I must say that I prefer this gown to your other one. It shows off your bosom quite nicely. Do not blush—I know what I am saying. In that dress, I am not so sure that *any* man will view you as his little sister."

This caused the heat to rise again to Phoebe's cheeks, but she certainly hoped that what Lydia said was true. Lydia added, "Mr. Conroy will gnash his teeth. You will have to let him down gently."

Phoebe frowned at the mention of Mr. Conroy. She had not been kind to him. With Frederick in Brussels and back in her life, and particularly when he paid her such focused attention, she knew she could not consider Mr. Conroy as a suitor. She would have to tell him at the next opportunity.

When their barouche arrived at the Forest of Soigny, Phoebe was enchanted by the row of white tents that lined the edge of the forest. They were set, side by side, under the overhanging branches of large majestic trees, and their open fronts overlooked an oblong body of still water. Many of the crowd had already begun to assemble under the tents, and more continued to arrive in open carriages.

There were tables of food laid out, and people were helping themselves to a selection of the delicacies. Since Phoebe and Lydia had not eaten a full breakfast, Phoebe's stomach began to rumble. There was ham roasting over an open fire, with a servant slicing pieces on a board that sent wafts of steam into the air. Loaves of bread and sweets arranged in a pyramid were placed on other tables, and the light aromas mixed with the spring air carried scents of grass and flowers. The sound of drums and trumpets caught Phoebe's attention, and she turned her head to see a regimental band playing a sprightly tune.

Over the loud music and noise of the crowds, Phoebe leaned into Lydia. "Who are the soldiers playing?"

"I cannot be sure. Fitz should be joining us any minute, and he will be able to enlighten us." Fitz had needed to oversee a military drill that morning and had promised to meet them there.

Sam helped them down from the carriage and held his hand out to assist the maids. Phoebe thought she had detected a growing attachment between Sam and Mary, and the two of them shared a glance as the groom led the horses away. Mary and Sarah took in the sights, their mouths agape. Then the three of them picked up the pillows and blankets, which had been recommended to make the picnic even more enjoyable.

Phoebe looked around and sighed with pleasure. The heat that had grown, at times unbearably so as they entered June, abated in the cool of the nearby forest. The crowd was a motley one, mixing the pink of gentility with the less genteel Belgian people that she assumed came from the village of Soigny. Apart from the few she had met at certain Society events, it was not often that the Belgians mixed with British Society. As Phoebe watched them enjoying themselves and partaking of the refreshments, it dawned on her that she had been looking at them as foreigners. Meanwhile, this was their country, and *she* was a mere visitor here.

The movement of someone approaching caught Phoebe's attention from the corner of her eye. It was Frederick, and her heart gave a leap as she turned to face him. She remembered what Lydia had said and was torn between wanting to show him how much she cared about him in case it was true, and wanting to hide it from everyone else in case it was not. He did not give her a great indication which it was to be, for he greeted his sister casually and kissed Phoebe's fingers, keeping hold of her hand and squeezing it before letting it fall to her side.

"We have reserved a tent over there," Frederick said, nodding his head in the direction of one of the tents, where Fitz was standing. Fitz saw them and came over to his wife. "Wonderful. You've arrived."

"Fitz, who is the band playing?" Lydia asked him.

"It's the 52nd. They make a fine sound, don't they? Come. Let us set up the blankets in the tent. Then we can sample some of the food. There are local dishes as well as English ones." He led Lydia away, and the maids followed him, carrying their bundles.

Frederick held out his arm for Phoebe. He did not seem in any rush to walk quickly, and Phoebe searched for the right thing to say. *I have missed you*, was all that came to mind.

When Sam and the maids came out of the tent empty-handed, Phoebe looked at Lydia, her lips curving upward. "Mary and Sarah are not needed, are they?"

Lydia shook her head. "Just let us know where you will be in case we should need you."

"Yes, ma'am," Sarah said and pointed to a gathering on the lawn of what appeared to be other servants. "We'll be just there." Mary smiled up at Sam shyly before she and Sarah hurried off, arms linked and their best dresses swaying as their legs moved forward.

"You go too, Sam," Fitz said. "You will not be needed." Their footman bowed, his face split with a smile, and he ran after the maids.

"It's a beautiful day," Frederick observed, looking up at the blue sky and the broad wisps of white clouds. His was a general observation, but he seemed to be addressing Phoebe in particular. "Let us see what food there is to be had before we sit."

Lydia and Fitz agreed, and they all went to examine what had been laid out for their consumption. Frederick held a plate for Phoebe and asked her what might tempt her, filling her plate with that and other things he thought she might like. Soon, the four of them were sitting under the tent, away from the sun and listening to the running children and pairs of people that wandered by. The laughter came easily to Phoebe's lips as Frederick and Fitz both teased Lydia, and she retaliated in turn, very well able to hold her ground. Frederick leaned toward Phoebe, and his arm brushed hers.

After they had eaten, Lydia groaned and put her hand on her belly. "Fitz, why don't we go walking? Would you two like to come with us?"

Phoebe sent a questioning glance to Frederick, and he shook his head. "No, I have no wish to move."

Fitz helped Lydia to her feet, and Phoebe settled back on her hands with her legs stretched and feet crossed in front of her, watching the bucolic scene unfold at the entrance to the tent. It seemed they were almost in their own world with the tent giving them privacy on three sides. Only the front was open with a flap hanging down from it against the sun's rays. Although people did occasionally walk by their tent and peer in, they were for the most part alone.

A comfortable silence stretched before Frederick cleared his throat and sat upright, brushing his hands together and leaning back on one hand. He shifted slightly, not away from Phoebe but so that he was better able to catch her gaze. He smiled—a fleeting smile—and it disappeared as he swallowed.

"I have something I wish to tell you."

Phoebe drew in a breath. This did not seem good—or *could* it be good? Perhaps it was what she longed to hear. Perhaps he was finally going to confess that he returned her regard.

"You may say it. I am listening."

At her permission, Frederick nodded once and chewed his lip before speaking. "I wanted to tell you personally that I have developed feelings for someone."

The words echoed hollowly in the small world the tent had provided them, while Phoebe's world crashed to pieces around her. *This is why we have not seen Frederick lately. He is to be engaged!* She had been utterly mistaken in her belief that his regard for her had grown; and what was more—his sister had been deceived as well. The brief flights of fancy Phoebe had allowed herself to entertain this morning died a rapid and cruel death. She swallowed hard.

"*Oh?*" It came out in a tiny voice—the only one she could manage.

Frederick looked down, and he slid his hand close enough to hers so that their little fingers were touching. Neither of them wore gloves. Phoebe's head buzzed, and the touch on her finger made her senses scream so that she almost missed his next words, which he spoke softly. "Yes. But I do not know if she has any feelings for me."

Phoebe's heart had begun to beat in her ears, it seemed, and her mind flew into all sorts of ridiculous suppositions that she could not allow herself to countenance. She desperately tried to rein them in. Hope sprang up again, however, because if he were truly interested in someone else, *surely* he would not confuse her by offering such a small, intimate gesture. She was afraid to speak, but he studied her as though he were waiting for an answer.

"Have you . . . have you told her how you feel?" Phoebe swallowed again, but her mouth was completely dry and her throat would not comply. She peeked at him in time to see his lopsided grin.

"I am trying to."

Phoebe breathed in sharply, and her eyes darted to Frederick. She could not utter a word as she waited to see what came next.

"It has just been difficult," he went on, "because never before have I been so busy. I am at the beck and call of my superior officers, and all in the service of my country. It is such that I barely have a chance to speak to her, much less say what I wish. What's more"—Frederick looked down and she could see his lips curve—"she is someone I have known for some time. And I fear that she does not return my regard or view me in anything but the most brotherly way."

Phoebe could not mistake his meaning. He could not be speaking of anyone else but her. She turned her face fully to look at him, and he locked his gaze with hers and did not release it. Her lips parted to answer, but all thought simply fled. There was no clear way to answer what he said without revealing herself. And what if she was wrong?

"Do you think I should take the risk and tell her?" Frederick's eyes were still on hers, and his lips trembled in a smile.

She was held captive by his gaze, and her answer came out as little more than a breath. "Yes."

"Well then," Frederick said. "It is you."

A breeze entered the tent and cooled Phoebe's cheeks and lifted the curls next to her forehead. Her smile stretched so wide her mouth hurt. "Is it?"

Frederick lifted an eyebrow. "Mm-hmm." His gaze settled on her lips before capturing her eyes once again.

The sound of a horn pierced the general noise of the crowd, and another horn joined the first in its harmony, and then another. They became a chorus, which turned into a swell, and the song of it resonated through the trees behind them. At this novel entertainment, the people made their way toward it *en masse*. Phoebe did not want to move and break the spell. She turned her head to Frederick, and he brought his face close, his eyes flicking up to hers. They sat like that for a moment.

"I want to kiss you," he whispered.

"Frederick, Phoebe!" Lydia poked her head inside the tent. "You must come. You are missing everything!"

Chapter Nineteen

Frederick raised his eyes heavenward and breathed in through his nostrils as Lydia exited the tent as quickly as she had entered it. Phoebe leaned away and brushed her hands together, ducking her head to try to hide a very pretty blush. She could not hide her smile, however, which told Frederick that she had been as seduced as he had been—until Lydia ruined it. Never before had Frederick wanted to shake his sister as he had in that moment. He glanced at Phoebe with a rueful smile.

"Well, I guess that kiss will have to wait for another time." Frederick lifted his head, listening. "It is a rather remarkable sound, don't you think? Let us go see what the fuss is about." He stood and extended his hand so that Phoebe could clasp it, and he helped her to rise.

"It sounds as though there is a musician playing the horn in every tree with the way it fills the forest." Phoebe tucked her hand naturally into his arm without his needing to invite her—without any ceremony. It felt right.

They joined the crowds passing in front of the tent, merging with them and walking toward the edge of the forest. Children in simple pinafores mingled with those whose elegant attire proclaimed a superior station in life, all of them caught up in the curiosity of the sound. Lord Lynedock had spared no expense when he had thought up the entertainment for this picnic.

Phoebe walked on his left, away from the trees and on the side of the crowd. Frederick spotted Mr. Conroy, who, upon catching sight of Phoebe, took a step toward her. Frederick pulled Phoebe closer until their sides were nearly glued together. She glanced up at him in surprise, and the answering smile reached her eyes. Mr. Conroy's gaze followed. He narrowed his eyes at Frederick and abruptly switched direction.

It was possessive and instinctual, and Frederick ought not to have done it, but he found it difficult to regret. *That ought to show him. Phoebe is unavailable.*

Lydia had paused with Fitz at the entrance to the forest, where the circle of horns played in the enclosure. She turned and sent a searching gaze through the crowds until she spotted Frederick and Phoebe. As they drew near, her eyes widened at his close proximity with Phoebe. Her look turned arch as her lips curved up.

"Do you have something you wish to tell me, brother?" She nodded toward his arm which held Phoebe close, and with a feeling of regret, Frederick loosened his hold.

"When I do, you will be the first to know." He knew his vague answer and enigmatic smile was sure to madden her, but he hadn't even had a chance to propose to Phoebe. Lydia leaned in to whisper to Fitz, who nodded and had the courtesy not to gawk.

The canopy of large branches before them was no match for the rays of sun, which broke through and made the brass instruments gleam. The rays lit the carpet of ferns and moss, turning it a brilliant green. The conversation and bustle of the crowds grew still in the appreciative silence. The melody was both mournful and playful, with the notes echoing through the trees. As Frederick listened, the elation of a few moments ago, discovering that the woman he loved returned his regard was replaced by a sort of melancholy, although he knew that was not the point of the music. But he was experienced enough at warfare to know that not everything was the excitement of battle and victory. There would be losses, too. Phoebe seemed to sense his mood as well, for she grew quiet and still at his side.

When the last note rang out, the crowds exhaled in something like a collective sigh of appreciation, and they began to applaud. At last, the conversation picked up as everyone moved about again. Lydia tugged at Fitz to keep step with Frederick and Phoebe. She came abreast and took Phoebe's other arm in her own.

"Did you enjoy the performance? You did seem a bit loth to leave the tent," Lydia said to Phoebe, her face a studied look of nonchalance.

Phoebe laughed and kept her gaze trained forward. "I enjoyed both the comfort of the tent and the musical performance."

Her answer delighted Frederick. As for him, he vastly preferred the comfort of the tent. For the rest of the afternoon, with Lydia and Fitz at their side and others coming into the tent to visit, he and Phoebe had no further chance for an intimate *tête à tête*. However, when the picnic was over, Frederick excused himself to speak to his valet. He had come on horseback from their headquarters and had Caldwell and Joseph come by carriage so he could take Phoebe home. Caldwell would have to ride his horse.

When he arrived back at the group, Fitz was directing Sam to fetch the carriage. Within minutes, their two maids hurried over from wherever they had been enjoying the day. Fitz gave orders for them to gather up the pillows and blankets and bring them to the carriage.

Frederick had reclaimed Phoebe's hand and kept it tucked firmly through his arm. He caught Lydia's attention. "You can return home with Fitz. I had Caldwell drive the carriage, and I will escort Phoebe to your house. I have something I wish to say to her."

At those words, Lydia's smile grew broad. "By all means. Phoebe, we may dine together later, and you can tell me *all* about your day. Do not hurry on my account. I have nothing pressing to attend to."

He heard Phoebe's soft chuckle at his side. "I am quite sure you do not."

Joseph was waiting with the horses harnessed in tandem when Frederick brought Phoebe to his phaeton. "Caldwell has Star Bright and will take her home. Joseph, you may take the leader, for I will not need speed for the journey home. I trust you can find your own way." Frederick did not want a chaperone.

"Aye, milord." Joseph went to retrieve a saddle that was attached to the back of the carriage, and he slipped the harness off the lead horse, holding the reins of both while Frederick assisted Phoebe into the phaeton.

When they were set, Frederick climbed in and flicked the reins, and they moved toward the wide *Chaussée de Bruxelles* in the direction of the city. At first, their carriage was surrounded by other English and some Belgians who returned home from the picnic in a motley array of equipages. By force of adjusting his speed to avoid either lagging behind in someone's company or rushing ahead to join someone new, he managed to be nearly alone with Phoebe. He couldn't decide if he would rather hold her hand or put his arm around her and drive with her tucked close to his side. The latter was perhaps not the wisest. As it was, the spirit of the day—and the longevity of their friendship that made him more comfortable with her than anyone else—had caused him to take risks in showing more affection than was proper.

Then again, it would not be improper if they were engaged.

It dawned on Frederick that he had not said a word as he had been contemplating these things. It was time to speak. "You have given me some indication of your feelings for me, and it allows me to hope. It is . . . perhaps ungentlemanly of me to ask it of you, but I must own that I long to hear from your lips whether or not you return my regard."

Phoebe's laughter was the last thing he expected, and Frederick looked at her in alarm, wondering if he had so wholly misjudged the situation. But when she turned her eyes to him, there was such deep affection there he pushed his doubts aside and waited for her to speak.

"When we were in London, you urged me to do something daring, which in part was what brought me to Brussels. I could not bear to have my fate rest in the hands of someone else any longer. I needed change, and your reminder of the adventure that awaited me if only I was willing to take the first step was the extra push I needed."

Phoebe remained quiet long enough that he glanced at her sideways. She seemed frozen as she stared straight ahead. "But that step pales next to the one I am about to take now."

She took a deep breath, and Frederick heard the sound of a carriage rapidly overtaking them from behind. He uttered a mild curse under his breath, hoping that they were not seeking to join him and Phoebe. In minutes, the carriage barreled past them, with a soldier driving, and two young women squeezed on the seat next to him, laughing and shrieking in an un-genteel way as they held onto their bonnets.

Relieved, Frederick inclined his head toward Phoebe. "A more daring step than coming to Brussels? I am agog with curiosity. Please go on." His eyes were on the road, but he had the sense that she was about to say something significant, and he was breathless with anticipation.

Phoebe bit her lip and looked down at her hands. She tugged at the fingers on her gloves and then tugged them back on tight as she seemed to wrestle with her words. He could not imagine what was so difficult to say.

"Frederick," she said at last, lifting her eyes to his. "You asked if I returned your regard, and it is giving voice to my answer that requires all my daring—terrifyingly so." Their arms were near enough that he could feel it when she began to tremble. "I have loved you from the moment I knew what the feeling was. And I have never breathed a word of it to anyone until now—not to Lydia. Not even to Anna."

Phoebe's words came first as a shock, and Frederick's jaw went slack. Then the meaning of the words settled deep in Frederick's heart until he could not carry on. He pulled the carriage over to the side of the dusty road and pulled the horse to a stop, holding the reins loosely in his lap and turning to face her.

"That *is* daring, Phoebe." He tucked an errant curl away from her cheek. "Even though you are certain of my regard, you still took the risk of telling me. And that, my darling, is a treasure that I shall carry with me." *Into battle* was the thought that came next—unwelcome, but insistent.

He shook it off and put his other arm along the back of the seat, turning to face Phoebe more fully. By some miracle, no sounds of carriages or hoofbeats interrupted their moment. Only the flicker of sunlight as the wind moved through the trees or the movement of a bird taking flight cut through the stillness. He took her hand in his.

"I suppose I have always loved you, almost as one of the family. I saw you as my little sister—as I saw Lydia. But with all my heart, let me assure you that any brotherly feeling I once had has been completely overset. You have taken captive of my heart. I love you."

He lifted her hand to his lips, frustrated at the gloves she wore, which prevented him from feeling the softness of her fingers. Her eyes were clear as she held his gaze, reflecting his form and the trees behind him. The nuances of her emotions seemed to flit through her expressions, and he thought he could read every one as they echoed his own feelings. He held her hand tight.

"Phoebe Tunstall, I beg of you. Do me the honor of becoming my wife."

A smile broke on Phoebe's face like the sun after a rainstorm. "I will," she answered simply.

Frederick bent forward, and with his free hand, he placed his fingers lightly on her chin, tilting it toward him so that she faced him. She came willingly. The rim of her bonnet was daunting but not an impossible obstacle. He leaned down and touched his lips to hers. Phoebe responded with sweet kisses of her own that bore little resemblance to the timid Phoebe he once thought he knew. She rested her hand on his coat and clutched the lapel as she kissed him as desperately as he kissed her. He covered her hand in his own as his other arm went around her and pulled her closer.

The sounds of hoofbeats arriving and wheels skimming the dirt road from behind broke a moment that was as tender as it was agonizing in that he had to end it. Frederick pulled reluctantly away and turned to give a slight nudge to his gelding, who trotted obediently forward. The carriage that had come from behind overtook them, as did the rider on horseback whom Frederick now perceived.

"Lydia tells me you have an announcement to make," Fitz observed in a cheerful, self-satisfied way.

"Everything in its time," Frederick answered, attempting the same calm, though his heart had not slowed. "But yes, I suppose we do have an announcement to make."

Fitz grinned and continued riding forward alongside his carriage as Frederick and Phoebe trailed behind.

"Well, I suppose if anyone were to witness that—and it was not my wisest decision to kiss you on a public road—it was just as well that my sister and Fitz would be the ones to see it. You have made me very happy, Phoebe."

Frederick took her hand and started to bring it to his lips but let it go. "Remove your glove for me, if you please." With the hand holding the reins, he tugged at his other glove. She put her hand in his, and her skin was cool and soft as she laced her fingers through his.

"That is more like it." He lifted her hand to his lips and placed a kiss on it.

As Frederick drove, he peeked at Phoebe, and although she was quiet, he knew from the broad smile that never seemed to leave her face that she shared his elation.

"We shall have to tell Stratford, I suppose."

Frederick groaned and gave her a look of mock fright. "I almost forgot about your brother. I hope he will not call me out. Even if he would not choose pistols at dawn, he is rather handy with his fists."

Phoebe laughed. "He will be much too busy with a newborn to attempt pugilism."

It seemed altogether too soon before they arrived at the Fitzwilliam's house on *rue des Feuilles*. As soon as they pulled up, Lydia opened the door and came onto the street. She walked over to the side of the carriage and peered up, her grin both delighted and mischievous. "There was not a chance I was going to let you leave without telling me all that happened. Fred, alas," she questioned, "am I to have a new sister?"

Frederick could not scold Lydia for her indiscretion, for there was not a soul in sight to overhear her question. But he could tease her, and he sighed loudly.

Phoebe was more generous and responded with a smile. "Shall we tell her, then?"

Fred leaned down to meet his sister's gaze with mock severity. "You have been trouble ever since you made your arrival in my eleventh year—scrawny, red, and shrieking to have your demands met. And since that day you have not given me a moment's peace." His smile was sincere. "But, yes, Lydia, you shall have a sister."

Lydia clasped her hands and bounced up and down on her toes. "Splendid! I expect to see you much more often in our house so that we may plan the wedding. It will have to be in London, of course." Her brow furrowed, as she likely wondered, as he did, how soon such a thing could be arranged with the uncertainty of war looming. "I cannot wait to see what Anna and Stratford think. They will never guess."

She went on in this vein as Phoebe climbed down from the carriage and walked around it. He followed her with his gaze as she began to walk toward the house and then—as he'd hoped—turned back to him. She tilted her face up, her eyes soft. "You will come again soon?"

Frederick smiled and held her gaze. "You have my word on it."

Chapter Twenty

15 June, 1815

Dear Anna,

I know it is an impossibility that I should receive a letter from you in response to my last one, but I find myself eagerly waiting for the post to come all the same. I simply cannot wait to see how you will receive the news of my engagement to Frederick Ingram! If I know you, you will shriek and run into Harry's study, clutching my letter and—in one breath say how divine such a match is in uniting our two families and saving me from spinsterhood— and in another, berate me for not having breathed a word of my attachment all these years. I hope you will forgive me. We share so much, and I needed this one thing for myself.

I did not take the time in my last letter to set your mind at ease concerning my safety. Lord Wellington never displays the slightest alarm when someone questions him about the threat of battle, although Fitz says we must not mistake his insouciance for lack of preparation. Still, Fitz is not quite ready to send off his wife, nor are Lydia and I ready to go even as far as Antwerp. It's hard to imagine that Napoleon is so close with everyone more focused on what they shall wear to the Duchess of Richmond's ball rather than whether to flee. There must be a battle—that much is now sure—but who can say where it shall take place?

In any case, not *Brussels is the opinion generally held.*

I know you will still worry, so allow me to reassure you. Do you remember how I told you Martha Cummings was in Brussels? She and her brother have promised to take me with them should they ever feel the need to flee to England. Lydia will not hear of my staying with her should there be any threat. I, myself, have not decided what I will do, but you may trust in my common sense.

May I borrow the headpiece you wore for your wedding? I think I can replace the silk flowers for white ones since I plan to wear a blue dress, but it would save me time not having to find or make the crown. I expect we will marry in London. Frederick has had so little time for me, but he did say he sent an announcement to the Gazette *all the way from abroad. And, oh! Surely you have had news of a new nephew or niece by now, for you are closer to Stratford and Eleanor. It is hard to be far from home in times such as this . . .*

Phoebe continued in the same vein, jumping from topic to topic and coming back to complete her thoughts so that she filled two pages. Writing about the engagement would have to suffice to fill the emptiness that consumed her from having spent so little time with Frederick. He had had none to spare following their engagement. She did not blame him, but the euphoria had begun to fade in his absence, and the longing for her own family grew more persistent.

Tonight, however, that was about to change. The long-awaited ball hosted by the Duchess of Richmond would ensure that not only would she see Frederick, but she would also have him all to herself and dance the night away with him. It was exactly the sort of diversion she needed, and she looked forward to having him look at her in just *that* way and perhaps even steal a kiss. Phoebe set down her quill and leaned back, smiling as she stared at the tiny shelves on the escritoire. She had set aside hours for her preparation and knew what perfume to put on and just what dress she had in mind.

Frederick had been pulled into a frenzy of preparation that hindered him from keeping his promise to visit Phoebe again soon. The Duchess of Richmond had asked Lord Wellington if she might still hold her ball on the fifteenth of June, and he had replied that she might do so without the slightest worry. Nevertheless, reports arrived, bringing news of sure signs of French mobilization on the frontier.

Frederick knew to be unsurprised by Lord Wellington's confidence when he approved plans for a ball, but the approval seemed to go beyond the dictates of reason. He had been there when Wellington met with the generals and arranged for Blücher to stay positioned to the east near Charleroi, since the duke thought that Napoleon might attempt to cross through the village of Mons. No matter how the French arrived, though, the prospect of battle was now sure. And with the Allied forces trickling in at the pace of a snail— and the English army composed largely of second-line troops—they were not in the best position to be confident. What was more, Frederick had been present when the duke discussed the quantity of armaments with De Lancey, and Frederick had heard for himself that the quartermaster-general did not have good news to deliver. They were distressingly low on guns and round shot.

He was torn by the frustration of not spending time with his betrothed and his concern over the upcoming battle. He longed to truly *know* this woman who had captured his heart and would be his wife, but he needed time for that and it was something he did not have. He appreciated Wellington's air of calm and emulated it along with the other aides. But none of them were deceived. Victory was far from sure until all the Allied nations arrived in Brussels.

He had only been able to snatch a moment for tea at his sister's house and, along with it, a quick kiss from Phoebe when his sister went to oversee the tea tray. And he'd had another brief dance with her at a crowded supper ball, but to his frustration, almost no conversation at all. That was about to change, though, for the duchess's ball promised to be an evening of diversion, free from all military worries. He had been looking forward to it all week, for there he could claim Phoebe's attention for the entirety of the night. He did not care in the least whether it were *quite the thing* to do so.

Lady Richmond's ball arrived at last, but it had not fallen on a day like any other. Along with the preparation for the festivities, news reached Headquarters that the French had crossed over the Sambre river and had engaged with the Prussians at Charleroi.

The Duke and Duchess of Richmond had taken a large red brick house on *rue de la Blanchisserie* in the lower part of Brussels. It was not in the most fashionable of quarters, but this was made up for by the large private garden so coveted in a townhouse. There was a spacious coach house attached to the main building by an ante room. It had been papered with a trellis pattern and intertwining roses and served as a playroom for the children when it rained. It was here that the duchess decided her ball would take place. She decorated the coach house in the most extravagant fashion, with sheer fabrics draped from ceiling to floor, and a perfusion of flowers and artfully arranged chandeliers glowing with the light of candles. As people left the outdoors and entered the coach house, their conversations went from anticipation to enchantment.

Phoebe followed Lydia and Fitz inside, setting one white satin slipper ahead of the other, and allowing the last of the warm outdoor breeze to touch her skin before she crossed the threshold. It was ten o'clock, and the air was scarcely cooler than it had been earlier. They were not among the first to arrive, and the ball would be a squeeze if the number of people pouring into it were any indication.

Phoebe had taken to wearing bolder colors since her arrival in Brussels, as it seemed to match the new person she had become— the kind who took risks and was noticed. *Mr. Conroy had certainly noticed.* Her thoughts took a dip with the guilt that followed. She had not been given a chance to explain her change of heart, and he had given her the closest thing to a cut direct, offering only the barest nod the few times they had crossed paths.

"Why do you look glum?" Lydia had turned on Fitz's arm to examine Phoebe. "That expression does not become you at all. Do not fear. Fred will come. He promised—and even Lord Wellington is to come. Plus, you look divine."

Phoebe smiled at Lydia, shaking off her strange melancholy. She could not please everyone, especially not forsaken suitors. But in marrying Frederick, she would please *him* and their two families besides. And most importantly, she would please herself.

"I am not glum, I assure you. I long only to see Frederick. It has been days."

Lydia tapped Fitz's arm, who had lifted his hand to greet another officer. "Ah, young love. Do you remember?"

"I have some vague memory. But now that we are in our dotage, I find it difficult to recall," Fitz answered, showing that he had at least been partially listening.

Phoebe inhaled and allowed the spirit of the party to lift her mood. Tonight, she had chosen something in a more sedate color than her bold choices of late, and as elegant as she could find. She wore a gray silk gown, whose hem had been pulled in by small tucks with Rose Pompadour thread and whose sleeves fell off her shoulders next to a pleated bodice. Small pink flowers were sewn on top of the sleeves, and her empire waist was adorned with a ribbon in the same pink. She wore her hair up with half of the curls falling down her back in a style that was quite risqué for her, but which Lydia told her would set a new trend. Diamonds sparkled on her ears and a dainty pendant on her neck, and she had confirmed in the glass before leaving that they made her eyes shine in just the way she had hoped. Attired in such a fashion, Phoebe felt like she could do anything.

The crowd was growing thick, and Phoebe turned her head this way and that in an attempt to catch a glimpse of Frederick. She wondered if he would come in his regimentals. If he did, it would be nearly impossible to find him among the scarlet coats that abounded in the ball. True, there were the jet-black uniforms of the Brunswickers, and the Highlanders distinguished themselves with their tartan skirts that had so surprised Phoebe when she had first laid eyes on them. Some men were dressed in evening wear, including Lord Wellington, who had just arrived. But for the moment, the one sight she most wished to see eluded her. Phoebe's breath hitched with excitement. She would not feel calm until Frederick was there to be a steadying rock for her.

Servants brought out iced drinks, followed by platters filled with dishes, extravagant in their variety. From what Phoebe saw, there was fish with herbs, braised goose, sautéed pheasant, turtle with lobster sauce, and cauliflower with Parmesan. She turned and saw another table with poached eggs and truffles, gelatin molds, something she guessed was blood sausage, small breads with baskets of jams, and brioche with cheese. Then there were the pistachio pastries, orange biscuits, and French nougat for dessert. The food was wasted on Phoebe as she could not think of eating.

Where was Frederick? Their last conversation at the supper dance had not satisfied her. Having known his kisses and devotion, she could not settle for a brief squeeze of the hand and polite conversation. Her betrothal gave her hope—gave wings to her heart in a way she had never known. It had only been just over two months since she'd come. That was a short time to travel, on her side from a girlish infatuation to deep admiration—and on his, a near indifference, apart from the most brotherly affection to love. Brussels must be to blame for such a quick development of their feelings. The danger that lurked in the city as a little-spoken undercurrent, combined with their long history, seemed to spark something in them—to force change the way food leapt and sizzled on the pan when a fire was laid to it.

Lydia turned back to murmur something, but Phoebe did not heed it because there in front of her Frederick stood, talking to another of Wellington's aides. She could not go to him, nor could she take her eyes off him. Next to all the scarlet coats of the officers, Frederick wore a dark coat and light breeches, and his appearance outshone every other officer or soldier in the room. She was transfixed.

As if Frederick sensed her regard, he turned and caught sight of her, laid his hand on his friend's arm with a word, and made his way over without allowing his gaze to move from her. His face looked unusually serious, and the crowds moved aside as he strode forward.

"Frederick, you look well," Lydia said, bringing Phoebe back to earth and reminding her that she and Frederick were not the only two people at the ball.

Frederick leaned over and gave his sister a kiss and shook hands with Fitz. "I am sure you two will excuse me. I would like to dance with my future wife." He showed a brief smile as he tucked Phoebe's hand in his elbow and led her toward the dance floor.

"Barely a greeting, and he's off." Phoebe could hear Lydia's teasing voice trail them, but to Phoebe's sensitive ears, it sounded like a focused effort. It was then that the faces of others in the room intruded into her conscience, for some appeared to be more serious than such an occasion should warrant. Although there were many who danced and laughed gaily, others met in groups, and their whispers and frowns made the threat of war loom even greater. Perhaps this would be the last big social event of the Season before their men went off to fight. But that did not bear thinking of at present.

Frederick led Phoebe to the side of the room as the orchestra began to play the tuning notes. He slid his hand up her arm and turned her gently to face him, his eyes roaming from the top of her head to her feet. She felt both petite and beautiful in his regard. And she felt something else—empowered.

"Phoebe," he said. "I will never forget the way you look tonight." He said no more, but his eyes held hers in such an intense gaze, she could almost read the unspoken words underneath. It sounded like a farewell.

No. She rebuked her fears sharply. *I refuse to think of anything but this moment.* Surely something so beautiful could not be torn from her after she had waited for it for so long.

"You look very fine yourself, Frederick." She allowed her gaze to rest on his, unheeding of the stares of others.

Frederick looked at the dance floor, where couples were forming a line instead of a circle, and he furrowed his brows. "I had thought this was the waltz, but it must be the next dance. I find I am not in a mood to dance a reel just now. Shall we have punch instead while we wait?"

Phoebe nodded and followed him to the refreshment table. He accepted two silver cups with slim handles and gave one to her. She sipped at the drink and kept her eyes on the Prince of Orange, who was engaged in a lively conversation with Lord Uxbridge. When the prince saw Lord Wellington, he went up to him and spoke with the same animation. The duke answered him with calm forbearance.

Frederick was watching the discussion, too. However, when he caught Phoebe looking at him, he kissed her on the cheek. Then he smiled at her, reaching up to touch the spot where his lips had been.

There was something tender and almost sad in the gesture, and she studied him for a moment, her feelings of alarm growing. "There is something brewing, isn't there?"

Frederick refrained from answering for a moment, but at last he nodded. "There is. The French are on the move. They have engaged with the Prussians at Charleroi and have broken through their flanks. They must be on their way to Quatre Bras if they are not there already. We will surely engage with them tomorrow."

A buzzing filled Phoebe's ears even as her heart thudded. The room had begun to grow warm and stifled as more people poured into it. Loud conversations and raucous laughter erupted from various corners of the room, but there was a deliberateness to the gaiety. Young women threw off their usual propriety, allowing soldiers to kiss their cheeks and slip their arms around their waists. Older men collected in conversation, as their wives presided over the assembly, drawing their heads together and sharing observations. Only Lord Wellington appeared unaffected, nodding his head in time to the music and allowing his gaze to roam the crowd. He bowed before a matron and her daughters, and when they left, he whispered in the ear of a subordinate. The music played on.

"Frederick," Phoebe said, "I don't see how people can dance at all. I don't see how they can be so light-hearted. They must not know."

Frederick shook his head. "Perhaps it is not commonly known, but that will be remedied soon enough. Word is spreading, and the duke just confirmed it to our hosts before I came to see you. Mark my words. In fifteen minutes the entire assembly will become aware."

Phoebe no longer cared to dance. She watched Lady Georgy approach Lord Wellington, smiling up at him as she engaged him in conversation. As they spoke, her smile fell, and Lord Wellington gave her a small pinch on her chin as though to bolster her mood. Apart from an occasional groove that marred his brow, his affability did not cease as he greeted the guests, almost as though he were completely unmoved by the news.

Phoebe watched the dancing and the conversations in silence. There was nothing worth saying. When the reel ended and people began to form a circle, Frederick turned to her. "Waltz with me."

She looked at him, her brow furrowed, and shook her head slowly. "How can we? I no longer feel like dancing."

"This is precisely why you must dance, my darling. Seize today, and let tomorrow worry about itself. Each day has enough trouble of its own."

The music started up again, and without asking a second time, Frederick swept Phoebe into his arms with one hand around her waist and the other reaching up to clasp hers over their heads. They followed the circle in this way, and as they turned to face each other Phoebe allowed herself to be lulled by the comfort of his closeness. Her heart began to beat more steadily at his side. Dancing with him this way—with his eyes on her, knowing he cherished her above all other women—was something she had dreamed about ever since she had been old enough for love. Now he loved her, but her ability to rejoice was stolen from her.

Frederick was going off to *war*, and why should he be spared? Dread akin to nausea pooled in her belly. A lump formed in her throat, and she had difficulty swallowing over it. When Frederick looked at her in that sweet way, so full of love, it made her want to weep. Why should she be any luckier than any other young woman who hoped for her sweetheart to come home?

They did not speak as they danced, but she found Frederick's eyes increasingly on hers, worried when he saw her eyes bright with tears. When the waltz ended, he led her off the dance floor as others formed for the next set. The soldiers seemed to throw themselves into the gaiety of the moment. Even the Prince of Orange was lounging on a settee entertaining a cluster of young ladies. Lydia was standing with her arm drawn through Fitz's, both of them in quiet conversation with another officer and his wife. Lydia's eyes were tight.

There was a bustle, and the crowds separated to allow Lady Richmond a place in the center of the floor. Her clear voice cut through the din. "I have arranged for the Gordon Highlanders to perform for us. Please join me in welcoming them."

Chapter Twenty-One

*F*rederick led Phoebe to a place on the edge of the crowd where they would be able to see what was being prepared, and she leaned in to ask, "Do you know them?"

"The Highlanders?" Frederick replied, drawing more enjoyment from her closeness than the anticipated performance. "A bit by reputation. They are the 92nd Regiment of Foot, and they're known to be fearless."

Two of the soldiers, wearing dark blue tartan skirts, red coats, and black feathered hats with a red tartan brim brought bagpipes to their lips. There was an expectant silence as four of the officers, similarly dressed, stepped forward and laid down their broadswords in a circle. They put their hands on their hips and bowed. As the plaintive notes of the bagpipe filled the room, the Highlanders began their dance. The officers were surprisingly agile for men, and their skirts flounced as they kicked their powerful legs outwards, then thudded their feet on the ground like the beat of drums. They danced over their swords, one hand lifted in the air as the music picked up and their feet flew in time to the pipes.

Frederick leaned down, Phoebe's curls tickling his cheek. "That one dancing there on the right is Major Alexander Cameron. He is a seasoned soldier and officer." The music was of such a melancholy nature, Frederick swallowed the lump in his throat, despite the energetic dance that was being carried out in front of them.

The Highlanders performed two more dances, and it was after two o'clock in the morning when the performance was over. Frederick's eyes were caught by the movement of an officer weaving through the crowds to hand a message to Lord Wellington, who read it. The duke then walked over to Lord Richmond and conferred with him for a moment before they entered his study and closed the door. Frederick wondered what news it brought but feared it would not be good. Although not many had noticed it, the shift in the atmosphere had grown more pronounced.

Frederick looked down at Phoebe, whose anxious eyes appeared to miss nothing. She surely knew he would not be able to stay much longer. "Let us go see Lydia," he said, and Phoebe nodded.

They walked over to Lydia, who was standing alone. Frederick let go of Phoebe and reached out to hug his sister—an unusual display of affection even at home and highly unusual for public company. No one seemed to care. Tears streamed down Lydia's face. Fitz was no longer to be seen.

"Fitz is gone?"

"He went to order the carriage. We are to join him at the entrance, but"—she glanced at Phoebe—"I wished to give you more time."

Frederick kissed her on the cheek. "You are the best of sisters." He glanced at Phoebe, whose tears had begun to fall, and he pulled her close. "Take care of my fiancée, will you? And take care of yourself. I have only one sister."

"Oh, Freddie." Lydia was sobbing openly now. "How can you say that? You are the one who is in danger. And you are all I have."

As much as he understood and shared the emotions, the excess of sensibility was not helping him to prepare his mind for what was ahead. As soon as he realized it, he cut the farewells short, placing a hand on Lydia's shoulder.

"I will come back, and I'll bring Fitz with me." It was a useless assurance, but it was all he could offer. Lord Wellington had come out of the study, and he called Frederick over.

"Excuse me," he said to both ladies and went to see the duke.

"Ingram, the troops have been ordered to join their regiments and be ready to march at three. You and the other ADCs are to join me at Quatre Bras. I intend to leave Brussels at six and will expect to see you there by ten."

"I will be there," Frederick assured him. He glanced back at Phoebe, who still stood by Lydia but whose gaze was fixed on him. It was time to say goodbye. Frederick returned from Lord Wellington and took Phoebe by the arm.

"Come." There was a spot toward the back of the coach house, whose sparse decorations and rough walls set it apart from the rest of the festivities, and he led her there. The hum of conversation and music was muted in their shelter as he turned to face her. "I must go."

Phoebe cast her gaze downward as the tears streamed freely. She did not speak, although he saw her swallow twice, and he sensed she would not do so until she could control her voice. Frederick absorbed the sight of his beloved. It had taken him too long to realize Phoebe was the one for him. They had shared many treasured moments over the course of their lives, but what good was that if they were not able to spend the rest of it together? What they'd shared had been a mere glimpse; the best—the reality—had not yet come.

Such gloomy foreboding was not in Frederick's nature, and he took a deep breath and shook it off.

He held Phoebe's hands in his, and in their silence his eyes drifted across the room. Wellington bowed over Lady Richmond's hand before taking his leave, and Frederick knew that this was it. It was time to go. The music had stopped, and some soldiers began taking leave of their sweethearts, who were weeping openly, with others bidding a cheerful farewell to their flirts. Unattached soldiers exited together in groups, chattering and jesting in the ebullience of battle as they walked arm in arm toward the door. For them, there could be no other possible outcome than victory.

There was now no time to waste. Phoebe must have sensed it, for she lifted her somber regard to Frederick. What lay before him was too great for words, so he grasped her by the shoulders and leaned down. Once again, he allowed his lips to touch hers. It was just enough to remember the taste of them to tuck away in his memory when he was fighting. *Heavens, but she is beautiful.*

Phoebe grasped the front of his coat and cried out softly, "Don't go!"

Didn't she know it would only break his heart?

Then she drew up her chin. "Forgive me, Frederick. I spoke . . . without reason. Of course, you must go. Of course, you must be brave and fight. I will not hinder you. If only the prayers and pleading of my heart could keep you from harm, I would pray and plead and never sleep."

Frederick slipped one arm around her waist and pulled her close. With his other hand, he touched her cheek. "Sleep, my love. It will give me courage, knowing that you are safe and secure. Just promise me one thing."

She fingered the lapel of his coat, where her eyes had been fixed. She shot her gaze up to his. "Anything."

Frederick was torn between wanting to reassure her and needing to keep her safe. "If there should be any danger . . . that is to say, I do not believe we will lose, but should there be any—" He broke off, knowing he was mauling his words. They would not bring reassurance, but they needed to be said.

He took a breath and continued. "If it does not appear as though we shall win, I want you to promise me that you will flee to England by any means necessary. Do not stay in Brussels. Just go. I could not bear it, knowing that you faced any sort of hardship at the hands of the enemy here. I need you to promise me."

Phoebe's eyes showed her worry. "What of your sister?"

Frederick sighed and glanced over at Lydia before bringing his gaze back to Phoebe. "I do not believe Lydia will leave Brussels, and I don't think I could convince her to do so. She will wait for Fitz to return. But as much as I love my sister with my life, she is not my concern right now. It is for you that I am concerned."

"Why?" Phoebe's brow had furrowed. "Is it because of Stratford—because of some silly obligation you feel to him? Do you think me too weak to stay and wait for you, too?"

When her brows were knit in such a manner, Frederick could only lean down and kiss her forehead. "No, my goose. It is because I love you." He managed a chuckle, though he wished he could weep. "If we are ousted, the invading army will not be kind. I need to know that you, in your innocence, will not fall prey to them. I assure you, by making me this promise, you are removing my last fear. I have already taken the liberty of speaking to Lydia about it, and she agrees with me. She mentioned someone named Martha Cummings and her brother. Said you'd already been offered a place in their carriage?"

Phoebe shook her head. "I do not want to leave you—"

The room was beginning to empty, and the remaining crowds moved past the island he had created with Phoebe. Loth as Frederick was to leave her, at the risk of never seeing her again, he knew he had not long to spare. "If you want to send me off to battle without this worry to weigh me down, you must do as I say. You must leave Brussels at the first sign of danger. Promise me."

Phoebe released his coat and allowed her hand to rest on his arm as she met his gaze. "I promise."

"I must go," he said again. His words were full of the regret he felt, and in hearing them Phoebe looked stricken. She clung to him no more, but just stiffened in his arms and allowed him to step back.

"I understand," she replied softly, the tears beginning to fall again.

Frederick reached into his coat pocket, where he still had her handkerchief tucked. Instead, he pulled out his own to wipe her eyes. He studied her face, measuring the expressions that flitted across it. "I have always loved you, too, you know."

Phoebe shot her head up, and he smiled when he saw the surprise on her face. "You are right. Not in that way. I have always loved you as one who was an irreplaceable part of my life. You were Stratford's little sister, Lydia's friend—the more modest, gentle, and wiser counterpart to Anna. That's how I saw you then."

Phoebe tucked her chin to hide a smile. Frederick had taken hold of her hands, and he caressed her knuckles gently.

"The change I felt for you did not come all at once. Indeed, apart from having always appreciated your good qualities, and noticing back in London that you had grown into a very handsome young woman, I thought of you only as the sister of my friend"—he let out a pained laugh—"and the friend of my sister's. Since I am leaving soon, I want to make sure you hear what I feel now, before I go."

"I can't bear it," Phoebe said. He knew she had been fighting to keep her voice steady, but now it broke. "It is as though you are telling me this because I will never see you again."

"I am telling you because it is something you deserve to hear. I don't know if it was coming out of our usual environment that forced me to see you in a new light, but *that* I did. From my first day in Brussels when I laid eyes on you, well . . ."

Frederick breathed out. The memory and the longing had become too weighty for him to bear. "We are to be married, so I feel it only fair to warn you that ours will not simply be the joining of two families who have long been united in friendship. It will not be a match of convenience, for I have come to feel for you a passionate love that will not be suppressed. And *that* is what I want you to know."

Phoebe lifted her eyes to his, and her smile sent rays of warmth into his heart. "I am glad, for a marriage of convenience would not suit me at all. Besides, the feelings I have for you would make such a thing impossible."

The crowds thinned as more soldiers and officers left, and their wives and families with them—although some soldiers looked as though they would stay until dawn. They ate and drank and put their arms around the young ladies, pulling them into a dance even without the music. The scarlet coats, however, were few, and the gowns were many. What guests remained of Lady Richmond's ball were female by a large proportion.

Knowing time was short, Phoebe drank in the sight of every inch of Frederick's face—his straight nose, the crease on one side of his mouth, his skin that was so smooth it looked as though it were hardly capable of sprouting a beard. After a moment of studying her face in return, Frederick gave a faint smile that looked almost tortured. "I cannot promise that I will come out of this war alive."

Phoebe gave a strangled sob, and he squeezed her hands tight. "However, I will do everything in my power to stay alive, be it only for the purpose of coming back and claiming you as my wife."

"I will pray that you do," she murmured. "Fervent, fervent prayers." She knew he could see her lips move rather than hear her as a group of soldiers walked by them, talking loudly.

Frederick leaned down and kissed her once more on the lips. "It is killing me that I must leave you. So consider this a deposit until something greater may be claimed later on."

Phoebe put her hands on his shoulders. She had to believe he would come back. She had to believe they would marry. Frederick pulled her into his arms and held her close, and Phoebe breathed in a blend of spices that was becoming familiar to her.

Then he pressed a brief kiss on her lips, stepped back, and left without another glance.

Chapter Twenty-Two

*F*rederick slept for two hours. It should have been more as Caldwell had everything prepared, Josef promised to have the horses ready, and there was nothing left for him to do. But he wasted precious time turning in his bed, and there was the ceaseless thrum of a city that did not sleep as it prepared itself for war—drums, pipes, and soldiers beginning to march.

"Did you rest?" he asked his valet, who had brought the shaving kit as soon as Frederick began moving about in his room.

"Here and there," Caldwell answered somewhat vaguely.

Frederick went to the dining room in his suite, where he forced himself to eat something. The coffee was more welcome. He had finished three cups by the time the weak light of dawn gave form to the objects in the room and the candles were no longer necessary. Foot soldiers still marched by his window toward the Namur gate, accompanied by the cavalry and officers on horseback.

He set down his cup at last and opened the door to his rooms. Downstairs, Caldwell was arranging his equipment while the hotel servants stood in a row, waiting, it seemed, to send him off. Josef had gone to bring his favorite Thoroughbred mare Salome and would follow later on with three other horses that would serve as spares. By the time he and Caldwell were saddled and ready, the last of the soldiers marched by to the sound of fifes and the beat of the drums. Frederick urged his horse to a trot and allowed the fresh morning breeze to clear his head as he headed down the road leading from Brussels.

"Ingram," a voice called out behind him, and Frederick reined in and turned around. It was Dalrymple, looking as fresh as a school-boy, although he was still wearing his ball clothes, complete with slippers.

"Got no sleep, did you?"

Dalrymple grinned. "I had a farewell to make."

"Hmm," was Frederick's only reply. He smiled at the ADC's naïveté, despite his own somber mood. Oh, to be young.

Their conversation was light as they rode, and near Quatre Bras, they were joined by Wrotham, who had gotten a late start and had put his horse to a canter to catch up. It was just after ten o'clock when the three of them arrived at Quatre Bras, and Lord Welling-ton was there with most of his aides, including Pinkton, Calloway, Sutherland, and Stewart. The duke had his telescope pulled out and was examining the crucial intersection that connected Brussels to Nivelle—the roads the Allies needed to secure if they hoped to keep their lines of communication open.

Frederick pulled out his own telescope and studied the masses of blue uniforms that could be seen through the trees and tall fields of rye from a mile away. There were no sounds of bugles to indicate enemy troops on the march. No dark blue uniforms crept steadily through the tall fields of rye and corn. There were no drums sound-ing to warn of incoming artillery. He felt only relief that they would not be called to fight at once, particularly since it would be many hours before the rest of their troops arrived.

"Well," the duke observed, "if they are not attacking, I shall not provoke them." He sent four of his aides to inform the officers that he had arrived and that they should be ready for action as soon as the French engaged. As Frederick was not one of the ADCs sent with a message, he seized the opportunity to swing down from the saddle to bring some blood back into his legs. He took a long drink from his flask and wiped his forehead as he peered up at the sky. The morning sun was already beating down hard, causing him to swelter.

"I believe you must be in the best shape of us all." Sutherland pulled up next to him and removed his hat before running his fin-gers through his thin brown hair. "What time did you go to sleep?"

Frederick shielded his eyes from the sun as he stared up at Sutherland. "Three o'clock in the morning. Or rather, I should say I was home at three. Sleep did not come easily."

Dalrymple had begun to slump in the saddle, and his gaze had grown dull from fatigue. Sutherland indicated him with a jerk of the chin. "Sounds like you had it better than Dolly here. That's what he gets for finding himself a Dutch sweetheart. You and I are lucky we are still bachelors."

Frederick hesitated before answering. "I don't intend to be one for long." He spotted the duke turning his horse, and he swung back into the saddle to be ready.

Sutherland rode abreast, his eyes lit with understanding. "Miss Tunstall." Frederick gave a brief nod.

Wrotham was not far and had overheard the remark. "I could see which way the wind blew. I wish you happy."

Frederick smiled. "Thank you." It was not like him to share his heart, even with good friends like Sutherland and Wrotham, but he needed to speak of Phoebe, even if it was only to remind himself of their betrothal. Voicing their attachment made it as tangible as the silk handkerchief of hers he carried in his breast pocket. Besides, speaking of her was an agreeable alternative to thinking of the grim events before them.

"I need to meet with Blücher," Wellington announced, pulling Frederick from his thoughts. "See how things stand at Ligny. Then we shall know how to proceed."

At that, Frederick focused his thoughts. He needed to stay sharp. The duke sent Stewart ahead with a message for Blücher to meet him at the large windmill situated at Bussy, and Frederick and the remaining aides rode with him. The windmill was visible from miles away. It was made of brick and had four long wooden arms that were stationary, at present. A long wooden ladder stretched from the ground to the door of the windmill, and there were presumably stairs on the inside since there was a lookout several stories up that gave a certain degree of visibility over Ligny to the east and Quatre Bras to the west.

They had not long to wait before Blücher arrived with his Prussian aides. The two field marshals unmounted to greet each other, and they spoke as they walked toward the windmill and climbed the ladder. Once inside, they disappeared from view until they reached the top where the lookout was. Frederick saw them take out their telescopes and gesture to landmarks they could see, then to the map that one of the aides had unrolled as they discussed battle tactics. The boom of cannons sounded from the east, causing both military leaders to turn.

Frederick met Dalrymple's inquisitive glance. "The battle for Ligny has just begun," he explained.

The day was already well underway when Phoebe awoke. Lydia was in the drawing room, pacing, and it did not look as though she had slept at all. Phoebe went in and chose a seat, knowing better than to offer some platitude. She, too, now had something to lose. She could lose her entire future with a man she had known and loved her whole life without ever having tasted of its goodness. The thought sent a heavy cloud over Phoebe, threatening to steal all her hope for a happy outcome.

She reminded herself that Lydia had more to lose—the husband and father of her child, as well as her brother—the only two living relatives she possessed. Despite Lydia's agitation that revealed her distress, there was a resoluteness about her mouth, and it steeled Phoebe's nerves.

"Come," Phoebe said gently. "Eat some breakfast." Outside on the street, an eerie silence had fallen as if the entire town was holding its breath, waiting for something to happen that would show the irregularity of the day. With the town this calm, Phoebe could almost wonder if the whole war and threat of war had been a dream.

Lydia met Phoebe's gaze, and the strain showed around her eyes. She shook her head. "I don't think I could."

Phoebe stood and slipped her arm through Lydia's and directed her toward the breakfast room. "Perhaps you will not be able to, but you must try. If you want to be your best for your husband and child, you must do everything within your power to keep up your fortitude. Fitz relies on your strength." She nudged Lydia's arm. "You must not let him down."

The reminder seemed to work. Lydia said nothing further and

allowed Phoebe to bring her into the breakfast room. She filled her plate with a four-minute egg, ham, and an English roll and ate all of it, besides drinking two cups of tea. Phoebe looked on with satisfaction.

The food had brought some life to Lydia, because the eyes she raised to Phoebe when finished were brighter and more hopeful.

"That's better," Phoebe said. "I have been wanting to ask you, but it never seemed like the right time. Did Fitz go off to war, knowing he was to be a father?"

Lydia gave a faint smile in return. "He guessed where things stood last week and chided me for holding it in. I hadn't wanted to distract him, but I should have known he would be able to guess."

Phoebe ran her finger along the smooth silver handle of her spoon. "It will give him more reason to fight like the very devil so he can come home."

"Phoebe!" Lydia laughed. "That is an expression I'd never thought to hear come out of your mouth."

"It was very vulgar of me, wasn't it?" Phoebe's lips curled upward. "I hate sitting back and doing nothing. I wish I could fight, too. Perhaps I would be very afraid, but sitting here is worse."

"I don't think Frederick would agree with your desire to fight, but oh, I *do* understand you. It's insufferable that the men should endure all the danger and get all the glory and we women must simply wait and wring our hands." She flicked an almost playful glance at Phoebe. "You will make a fine officer's wife."

Phoebe blushed with pleasure and glanced through the window, looking up again when Lydia said, "It is so quiet. *Too* quiet. I believe we should go out and see what we might learn, even if it's surely too early to learn anything."

Phoebe placed her napkin on the table and stood. "Have the servants said anything? They are often the first ones to know if there's anything afoot."

"Nothing from our servants," Lydia replied, "but I forgot to tell you. We had early callers this morning. Martha Cummings came by to see you, and she was all in a panic. They had brought no servants with them but one, and she said that their Belgian servants are predicting doom for the Allies. She can hear them in the kitchen speaking French, and the way they talk is that of people celebrating victory. She said she was afraid they would slit her throat as she slept."

"I find her fear reasonable, to be honest," Phoebe said. "It begs the question *whose* victory are the servants celebrating? They must be of the Belgians who favor the Emperor and long for his return so he might restore order in his way." She tried to dampen her fears. How many of the townspeople thought the same? "I hope their support for the Emperor is not so great that they would do harm to their master and mistress."

Lydia gave it serious thought, then dismissed the notion with a shake of her head. "I do not believe they are so bloodthirsty. But I suppose it is unsurprising that some Belgians should worship Napoleon, given the fact that half of their troops had fought for Napoleon as recently as a year ago. Did you know that even their uniforms are French? They just removed the eagles from their shakos!"

Phoebe met Lydia's gaze with wide eyes. "I had not heard that." Eager to throw off these forebodings, she proposed they put on their bonnets. "Let us go and see what may be learned."

Their first stop was to Mrs. Marshall's, whom Lydia knew well enough to arrive at her home unannounced. On their way, they noticed some of the stores had opened for business, although they did not appear to be thronged with people. Phoebe gestured to the English milliner's shop. "I cannot suppose anybody would be in the mood for a hat today."

Lydia glanced inside the shop. "I assume it is more a place to gather information than it is to do business. Look. They are all English. I recognize them. But it's no one we know well enough to approach. Shame."

At Mrs. Marshall's house, they learned nothing more than what they already knew, which was merely that most of the troops had left town before dawn. They did not stay longer than the time it took to drink tea, for even Mrs. Marshall was unable to greet them with her usual equanimity.

"I should have left for Antwerp with Mrs. De Lancey, the quartermaster-general's young wife," Mrs. Marshall said. "They have been married all of three months. Sir William asked me to accompany her there, but I refused him. I found I could not leave my George."

"Whom did she travel with?" Lydia asked.

"I do not know. He said he would manage it, but the poor man looked so harassed by his duties, I thought it odiously selfish of me to have refused him this one request. George told me as much, but he knew I could not leave him and did not press me to go. I must wait here for him to return"—she kneaded her handkerchief between her fingers as she fought to control her voice—"in whatever form that might be."

Phoebe glanced at Lydia to see her reaction. Mrs. Marshall's words could not help but add to her fears. They had certainly not relieved Phoebe's own fears. But Lydia inhaled and laid her hand on Mrs. Marshall's. "As will I. Nothing would induce me to leave Brussels just now."

"Well, that was unfruitful," Lydia said as they exited into the street. She stopped suddenly and lifted her head. Phoebe glanced up at the sky in confusion, searching for storm clouds that were not there. The weather was dreadfully hot and still. What resounded through the air was a doleful *boom, boom, boom.*

"The battle has begun," Lydia said quietly. She slipped her arm through Phoebe's and held her close as she moved forward. Others on the street had stopped to listen as well, and some ran to the stone steps built into the ramparts, which they climbed in a hurry to see if they could gain a view of the battle.

"So close to us?" Phoebe asked her. "It sounds as though they are just outside of Brussels."

"Fitz told me they were marching to Quatre Bras, so I imagine it is there. It's fourteen miles south of here, but cannons can be heard up to fifty miles." She smiled wanly. "It is just something I know from following the drum."

They walked on in silence, occasionally pulling back against the houses to allow people to cross their paths and run to the ramparts. At the next street, Lydia took an abrupt turn toward Lower Brussels. "I believe we should visit Martha Cummings. You may have need of her if you are to flee."

Phoebe shook her head, but Lydia walked with determination and Phoebe had to follow her. "We have been over this," Phoebe said. "How could you think I would leave you—and you with child? If ever you have need of me, it is now, and I must be here with you."

"I will not argue with you just yet," Lydia said, her steps still resolute in the direction of the Cummings' residence. "But please know that I am quite determined that you are to leave if we should learn of any threat. I have a responsibility to my husband to remain. And I made a promise to my brother to get you to safety."

Phoebe did not agree, but hearing Frederick's name spoken reminded her of the promise she had made to him. Still . . . it wasn't fair. "How can he exact a promise from you regarding my safety and have requested none regarding yours?"

"He knows I answer to Fitz, and my husband did not ask me to leave." Lydia set her chin in the obstinate way Phoebe knew well. "I will be going nowhere."

Phoebe sighed, but Lydia was right in saying there was no sense in arguing about it now. At present, *they* were not the ones in danger.

Chapter Twenty-Three

*B*lücher and Wellington remained at their vantage point in the windmill for close to an hour. As Frederick waited for the field marshals to finish their discussion, he spoke to one of the Prussian ADCs. The aide did not have much news to impart, other than that he thought they were evenly matched with the French.

When the two most senior officers parted ways, Frederick and the other aides rode back to Quatre Bras with the duke, arriving mid-afternoon. Before they reached the crossroads, it was clear that the battle for Quatre Bras had begun in their absence, and Wellington wasted no time in springing into action. He sent Sutherland with a note to the English colonel closest to Gémioncourt to try to retake the farm that had gone to French hands. He then turned his attention to the battle for Piraumont—the farm to the east, which had also fallen to the French—sending Wrotham with orders to retake it. On the field in front of them, the French troops deployed to the left and right of the main road in their fight to keep the farms and claim Bossu Woods. The struggle was desperate, and Frederick's every nerve was on edge.

Miles away, the French commander, Maréchal Ney, launched a fierce assault of light calvary on the outnumbered British-Belgian forces. As Frederick saw them charging through the tall stalks of rye, he noticed Dalrymple watching the charge, looking green with fatigue and nerves. Frederick rode over and pulled his horse beside Dalrymple's.

"Watch what they're going to do," he told him. He knew that engaging Dalrymple in conversation would have a steadying influence on the inexperienced aide. "Do you see how our men are forming up? The front rank of each regiment will be three lines deep. You will have the front line on one knee with their bayonets raised, and the troops behind them with their muskets trained. There. They're in place."

As they watched, the soldiers behind the front rows fanned out on either side, creating additional walls of men before dropping into position with their bayonets and muskets, and Frederick explained the strategy. "They're making defensive squares. The rest of the division will line up to the left and right of the front rank, with the rear-guard turning to close the square—swords and muskets trained outwards."

Frederick paused as a wave of French cavalry came thundering across the field. "Watch as the *cuirassiers* charge. Do you see how nearly impossible it is for their cavalry to pierce through our squares? Those soldiers in the middle, there—they'll quickly fill any gap left in the square by taking the place of the wounded soldiers."

Frederick didn't think it necessary to add *or take the place of any soldier who is dead.* Dalrymple was now fully awake, and he already looked frightened enough.

After the *cuirassiers* charged and inflicted what damage they could, they were called back to their line. Frederick next heard the roar of round shot from enemy canons and the pepper of musketry as the Allied defensive squares suffered from a volley of French artillery fire. Frederick saw soldiers fall before fresh troops moved to take their place. The wounded and dead were pulled into the middle of the square, turning it into a makeshift hospital, while reinforcements continued to fill the openings they had left behind.

Frederick stood, agitated and ready for orders, but it was Wellington who jumped into action by riding into the fray when he saw his troops balking under the continued assault. The duke placed himself well in the range of fire to strengthen the defensive squares and encourage the men to hold the position. "Stand fast! We must not be beat! What will they say of this in England?" he called out.

Frederick's horse sensed his agitation, as she sidestepped, and Frederick held the reins firmly. To his right, another defensive square formed, made up of the German Brunswickers in their black uniforms.

They were not operating with their usual efficiency, and Frederick furrowed his brows as the square faltered and began to fall out of position.

What the devil? He soon understood the source of their confusion when he saw the French dragoons chase the Brunswick cavalry toward the road, but he was at a loss to believe that such a disciplined regiment could break ranks. Frederick urged his horse forward, but Wellington had beaten him to it.

The duke galloped forward, calling the confused Brunswickers back to order with the bracing, "Now, gentlemen!" But it was to no avail. The tide of fleeing German cavalry rode past the duke, leaving him vulnerable to the roaming French lancers. Frederick's heart was in his throat as he watched, helpless. If Wellington was killed, their troops would lose all courage.

Lord Wellington wheeled his horse sharply on the open field to avoid the enemy, who pursued him hotly, and rode for his life. He urged his horse toward the closest defensive square, which was that of the 92nd Highlanders.

"Lie down, boys," he called out. The bottom ranks obeyed, pulling their muskets and bayonets down with them, while the duke leapt over the rows of men, muskets, and spears into the safety of the square. The soldiers leapt up again, weapons raised, and fielded off the French lancers.

"The Duke of Brunswick has been killed," Wrotham explained when he rode up to Frederick. "Shot through the heart." The Brunswickers' leader had been young, gallant, and much loved by his soldiers, and without his steadying influence, the troops had lost courage.

It wasn't the only time a square broke ranks.

"Look there, milord." Caldwell pointed to a defensive square of troops on their left, calling Frederick's attention to what appeared to be the 69th regiment. "They'll be struck down for sure."

The regiment had been ordered out of square and into a column, where they were being cut to pieces in the tall rye by incoming French hussars. Once again, Frederick watched, horrified. *Who has given such a disastrous order?*

It was not his place, but he started forward, unable to watch the slaughter without doing anything. Fitz, who was commanding a regiment in the same battalion, rode into Frederick's line of vision before he had had time to go far. Fitz yelled out orders, rallying the men to close ranks. The calamitous order to fall out of ranks had cost them dearly. The French made off with their color, and half of their regiment was slaughtered before they could close up and tighten the square.

Another charge on horseback by the French *cuirassiers* came without respite, and the deterring volley of British artillery on their breastplates sounded like hail on glass. Frederick eyed the desperate struggle, nearly numb by the carnage. Wellington rode back to their position and called out to him. "Ingram. See where we are with reinforcements."

At last! Frederick did not need any further inducement. What he *needed* was something to do. He rode Salome at a gallop back along the *Chaussée de Bruxelles*, only now becoming aware of his thirst. It was late afternoon, but the sun beat down as though it were noon. He ignored his parched throat and continued on toward Brussels. He did not have long to ride when he saw the infantry marching in the distance. They seemed to inch along at a snail's pace, but he knew that what he was seeing was somewhat of an illusion and that they were marching steadily. He arrived at the front of the column and recognized The Honorable Fred Ponsonby leading the 12th Light Dragoons.

"You're a welcome sight," Frederick called out as he slowed his horse and turned, allowing her to rest and walk alongside Ponsonby's gelding.

"Getting hit hard, are you?" Ponsonby asked.

Frederick pulled out his flask and took a deep swallow. He wiped his forehead with his sleeve and nodded. His horse's flanks were heaving. "Ney is sending wave after wave of cavalry, and we're holding the defensive position, but you're needed."

Ponsonby turned and looked at the columns marching behind him. "I'll ride back and tell Alten where things stand. When your horse is recovered, let the duke know we're on our way."

By the time Frederick reached Wellington's position, he gave his estimate that the reinforcements would arrive within the hour. "Good," and a curt nod were his response before the duke turned to relay an order to Wrotham.

Certain members of the duke's staff had returned from their various dispatches, and Frederick spotted Sutherland and rode over to him. "Where're Stewart and the others?" he asked.

"Dead," Sutherland said. "Stewart is, anyway. Hit when he tried to bring the message to the 33rd to take refuge in the Bossu Woods."

Stewart dead! It would not be their only loss, but Frederick turned forward, clenching his teeth in response to the news. He did not have time to think about it before his attention was pulled back into the battle in front of him, and the arrival of reinforcements brought them the welcome relief they needed. With the help of the dragoons, the Allies secured their position at last before evening fell.

Frederick was sent to find a farm where they could camp for the night, and he found one a mile north of their position that would house Wellington and most of his staff. The battle was done for that day, and Frederick, Sutherland, and Wrotham turned toward Gieppe. Dalrymple soon joined them and brought his dappled gelding to ride alongside the others.

"A night's sleep will help," Frederick said. Dalrymple returned a weary nod.

Frederick's shoulders ached with tension. His brain was dull with exhaustion, with the sounds of gunfire echoing in his mind. He could barely stay on his feet for the time it took to eat and prepare for bed. He hoped Fitz was safe. As he lay down, he thought of Phoebe, wishing he could let her know he was still alive. Sleep overcame him before he could form any other thought.

Martha Cummings received them in her drawing room with wide-eyed fright, leaving Phoebe to wonder whether she had blinked even once since leaving their house that morning. It could not be good for her to remain in such a state of anxiety.

Martha reached forward and clasped Phoebe's hands. "I'm so glad you are here. I have been *beside* myself with fright. And did you hear the cannons? There is no doubt now of there being an engagement. Perhaps the battle will be decided today—perhaps even this very hour! I wonder where it is, and how soon we may be rid of those French. But what if the French win? What is to become of us?" Neither Lydia nor Phoebe bothered to say that no one expected the French to be so easily vanquished that the matter could be decided so soon after the battle had begun.

Martha led Phoebe and Lydia to their drawing room and invited them to sit just as her brother entered the room. He was not quite so voluble as his sister, but his agitation was evident. "Someone broke into the stables and stole my carriage horses," he said. Phoebe could hear the mix of quiet fury and fright in his voice. "I specifically held those horses in case we might need to fly to the border. And now I shall have to find a different solution, and one that is likely to cost me dear."

Martha gasped. "Oh, Albert. What shall we do?"

Lydia glanced at Phoebe, her brow furrowed as she turned back to the Cummings. "You are not leaving so soon? You . . . you intend to leave before you learn which side will carry the victory?"

Mr. Cummings puffed his chest in indignation, but he could not quite meet Lydia's gaze. "I have every faith in our troops. But I am a man who likes to be prepared. I will wait to see which way the tide turns, but if there is any doubt, then no, we will not stay put. Some people have already left, and others are refusing to sell their horses in case they need to leave in a hurry. But if there are horses to be had, I will find them."

Martha's pale eyes had grown round again, and her mouth with it. "Oh, yes. Please do find horses for us. I cannot bear the thought of staying here if anything should happen. We are told there is not a canal boat passage to be had, so we cannot rely on that mode of transportation." She extended her hand to Phoebe. "We have room in our carriage for one more person, which will work if Mrs. Fitzwilliam indeed wishes to stay. We will be glad to have you come with us. I know you won't be so foolish as to turn that down."

"I am not so certain—" Phoebe began.

"That is most generous of you," Lydia replied, quelling Phoebe with a look. "We will be sure to stay in communication should such a need arise."

Phoebe did not know how they bore the rest of the day, but repeated cannonades sounded until that evening. They ate little for dinner and went to bed. With each boom, she had feared for Frederick, and the phantom sound did not abate in her mind as she closed her eyes. What if he had been within reach of those deadly shots?

Chapter Twenty-Four

*T*he next morning, Frederick woke, stiff from sleeping on the floor and with the disorienting sensation of not knowing where he was. Some of the other aides were already up and moving about, but Dalrymple was still deep in sleep. When Frederick looked at him, he couldn't help but think of Stewart who was no longer with them.

Outside, the air was heavy with humidity and a lingering smell of gunpowder. Although no morning breeze arrived to bring the relief of fresh air, Frederick judged that the air was heavy enough that it might rain that day. He swallowed two cups of coffee and ate his breakfast, not in the mood to join the conversation that flowed around the table. He wondered what Phoebe was doing and whether she had heard of their close run the day before. Would that be enough to send her to England? He hoped so—and also hoped she had not left quite yet. If only the Allies could join with the Prussians today, together they would have the stronger army, and victory should be theirs. What a thing it would be to finish the battle swiftly and run to Phoebe. To pull her—sweet-smelling and soft—into his arms. He would kiss her more thoroughly than he had allowed himself to do before.

It was just an idle dream at present, however. Without the Prussians, they were outnumbered, so he must not think of victory just yet.

"My lord!" Pinkton entered the farmhouse, followed by a Prussian officer. "This man has news from Blücher."

Wellington read the letter from Blücher in the room that was given for his use, and Calloway invited the Prussian aide to pull up a chair and eat something while he waited.

"How did you fare yesterday?" Frederick asked him.

The Prussian, eating from the plate of food he had been given, stopped to shake his head. "We were badly mauled at Ligny. We had to retreat."

Frederick and Wrotham exchanged glances. The Prussians would not be able to come to their assistance. The Prussian aide said no more but quickly drained his coffee as the duke came out of the room and announced, "Blücher is retreating with his forces intact to just north of Wavre."

Dalrymple was fully awake by now and Frederick, seeing his blank expression, explained, "It's a village across the river, east of here."

By now, all of the staff was fully mobilized, and Caldwell went out to have Joseph ready their horses. He came back, leading his own horse and Salome, and Frederick took the reins and swung his leg over the saddle. Once at Quatre Bras, Wellington pulled out his telescope and assessed the enemy's movements. Frederick did the same. The French troops were lined up, stretching about three miles across the fields, but they did not appear to be actually preparing for battle.

Frederick exchanged a surprised look with Wrotham. "What do you think of that?"

"Don't know *what* to think," Wrotham said. "Can't imagine why he's sitting on his hands unless it's because he's waiting for reinforcements—or because he thinks we have extra troops hidden away and he's afraid to engage."

His brow creased behind the telescope, Wellington continued to examine the enemy across the fields and appeared to come to a decision. He shut his telescope with a snap. "If Blücher retreated to Wavre, we must retreat as well. We cannot allow our lines to be cut off, and if they are not going to engage with us now, we will have the battle on our own terms."

The duke pulled out his notebook and scribbled on one of the sheafs of paper. Ripping it off and folding it in half, he handed it to Calloway before writing another note. "There is a low ridge north of Waterloo at Mont-Saint-Jean that is a good vantage point for us, and we're going to withdraw there. We'll need to keep up a front of cavalry and infantry men to mask the retreat. Calloway, take this to the major-general of the Household Brigade and have them fall back. Sutherland, carry this to Ponsonby. The Union Brigade will fall back as well. The Hanoverians will remain in place. Dalrymple, bring this to Alten to let him know. Ingram, you'll carry this to the 5th Brigade."

Glad once again to be of use, Frederick took the paper and galloped to where the 5th were stationed. He delivered his instructions to Sir Colin, who led the brigade that held Fitz's regiment, then he went to speak with his brother-in-law. Although it was likely mere coincidence that he had been given communication with the brigade containing the 33rd regiment, he was grateful when he rode up to find Fitz unscathed.

Fitz gave a salute from his position on horseback behind his regiment. "Word from the duke?"

"We are to retreat to Mont-Saint-Jean. Your movements will be partially covered, but we are to move immediately to keep our line with Blücher's Army." Frederick glanced up at the dark clouds forming. "Looks like we're to get a bit of rain."

"That might prove to be an understatement," Fitz replied, as he waved his sub-commander over to pass on the orders. "It looks like the heavens are about to educate us on our paltry efforts at power."

The major came over and listened to Fitz's instructions, before darting off. Fitz turned back to Frederick. "Any other orders to carry out?"

"Just stay alive. I'm fond of you," Frederick said. Fitz looked across the field then up at the heavens again, a smile on his lips. He met Frederick's gaze and gave a short nod.

Frederick turned his horse and lifted his hand in farewell. He quickly reached Wellington and the other aides, and they were on the march before noon. The gathering of ominous clouds provided a welcome relief from the heat, but such dark clouds could not promise anything but the most severe storm. It was not long in arriving. Soon, a terrific crack of thunder came, followed by a bolt of lightning from the dark sky, which zigzagged down in front of him. The rain began to fall in sheets. It pounded on Frederick's hat, seeped through his cloak and wet his exposed knees.

The packed dirt road soon turned to mud, and Wrotham rode up alongside Frederick. "The French have managed to shake off their stupor," he said. "They are mobilized behind us and have begun their advance."

"Miss!" Mary was out of breath as she broke into the drawing room where Phoebe and Lydia sat. "The soldiers are wounded. They're coming into the city. Scores of 'em!"

Phoebe and Lydia exchanged a glance and got up, quickly tying on their bonnets as they rushed outside. They hurried to the end of the street, where Phoebe saw the wounded straggling down the busy crossroad. Other Belgians were coming out of their homes as more soldiers poured in through the gate. A few hurried over to them, while others appeared to run back inside for supplies. The clouds were growing black far in the distance, but it was at an odd variance with the beige sky and brutal pounding of the sun where they stood.

There were indeed scores of them. The more ill among the soldiers were carried in wagons, but there were not enough conveyances to carry everyone who needed it. Some of the soldiers could barely walk from their wounds or loss of blood, and many gave themselves permission to sink to the ground as soon as they arrived in the city. Phoebe did not know when she and Lydia parted ways. She could think of nothing but the desperation that engulfed her—the need to examine every man to see if she recognized the face of one.

She refused to fear the worst, but her gaze lingered on those whose faces were covered in blood from a head wound. One man stared at her with such intense recognition that she started toward him. His light hair was darkened with blood and what looked like soot, and it was his pale blue eyes that she recognized at last.

"Mr. Conroy, you have been hurt. Where is your horse?" Phoebe went forward to assist him, realizing only as she reached for him that the sleeve of his coat was charred and empty on one side. His eyes were hollow with pain, and he didn't answer.

She went to his other side and put her arm around his waist, leading him out of the hot sun to a stone square enclosed by trees with a fountain in the middle. She helped him slide down one of the tree trunks until he was seated, leaning against it and shaded from the sun.

"I will get you water," she said and ran to the closest shop that had its doors open to distribute whatever it had that might be needed. She brought a glass of water and helped Mr. Conroy to drink.

"Thank you," he whispered.

"Allow me to clean your wounds." Phoebe brought out the handkerchief from her reticule and dipped it in the fountain, then returned to him. Her hand trembled and she swallowed her nausea as she wiped away the superficial blood and examined the cut on his head. It would be better with some stitches, but she was no surgeon. She looked down at her handkerchief, which was now rust-colored with blood stains. She went to soak it again as her mind escaped to the day she'd handed her handkerchief to Frederick for luck in the cricket match. She wondered if he still had it with him, and whether it was still . . . white.

The dressmaker's shop was bringing out strips of fabric, much of it too fine for its current use of binding wounds. Phoebe grabbed one on the top of the pile, which was a pale pink, and tied Mr. Conroy's head with the cloth. She secured it with a knot to hold it in place, the pink cloth giving him a grotesque, clownish appearance. She frowned, wishing she could do more for him.

He reached out for her with his only remaining hand and held hers. "As I left at the close of the battle, your Lord Ingram was still alive. I saw him myself."

She held his gaze, her eyes filling with tears—with pity for Mr. Conroy and what could not be; with gratitude for his generous gift of bringing her news of Frederick; with wild hope for her beloved. He had made it through the first day. Perhaps he would survive! That optimism did not last and was followed by a second wave of fears. Perhaps he had been killed moments after Mr. Conroy had seen him and was lost to her even now.

Phoebe sat with Mr. Conroy as the storm clouds moved in quickly. A cold breeze brushed her cheek just as the weather broke and the rain began to fall. The storm grew ugly quickly, and she knew she could not leave Mr. Conroy there.

"Come." She tried to help him get to his feet, and a Belgian man ran to assist her. Together, they half-carried Mr. Conroy into the dressmaker's shop, where the compassionate modiste allowed them to lay him on her sofa in the back room.

Once he was safely installed, Phoebe was filled with a strange fear, fueled by the storm, and it made her want to rush home. Everything seemed so uncertain and fearful. "I am sorry, but I must find Lydia."

Mr. Conroy nodded his understanding, and Phoebe escaped into the rain. Thunder cracked the sky, and the street became bright with a flash of lightning as rivulets of water flowed by her on the street. She was now soaked through. Phoebe hurried in the direction of home, and although most of the wounded men had found shelter, some were still sitting on the side of the road in the pounding rain. They looked numb from the wounds, from the shock of battle—numb from the punishing clashes of thunder and bolts of lightning. There were too many of them for her to help all of them, so she helped none. And as Phoebe hurried home, she realized that she was numb, too.

There were no soldiers nearer to home, but at the intersection she saw Lydia arriving at the same time. At that moment, Phoebe was caught up short by the sight of a somber cortege. Eight men carried a body, laid out on a stretcher and covered by a black flag. She recognized the uniforms at once and knew from the ceremony of the procession that they must be carrying the body of the Duke of Brunswick. She stood still. The heavens pelted her bonnet with rain and drenched her gown as the men carried their duke, faces somber as if they had lost their own kin. The sight stole Phoebe's breath. Here was someone who had been alive and dancing only two days before.

Oh, dear God, how fragile we all are. Phoebe's eyes were dry, but she wondered if she would ever smile again. Frederick was in the thick of battle. If this could happen to a duke, would God spare her love?

When Phoebe and Lydia had changed into dry clothes and were waiting for the tea to be brought, there was a knock on the door.

The storm raged, terrific and unabating, and Mary rushed to open the door, allowing Mr. Cummings to enter. He came into the room, shaking the droplets off his umbrella and stamping his feet in the entryway of the drawing room.

"Good evening, Miss Tunstall. Good evening, Mrs. Fitzgerald. I came as promised to tell you that I've acquired horses should the need arise for us to leave. Given the number of wounded soldiers, I should think a flight will end up being necessary, and I encourage you to be ready to leave at a moment's notice."

Phoebe and Lydia exchanged worried glances, and Mr. Cummings raised his hand, adding, "I do not mean to imply there is imminent danger, but it is wise to hold yourself in readiness. I promise to keep you apprised should I receive any further information. I could not forgive myself if I brought my sister back to safety but did nothing for the women who have been so kind to us. Mrs. Fitzwilliam, should you change your mind, we will make room for you in the carriage. Our maid can sit next to the groom. We will not leave you behind."

"You are kindness itself," Lydia replied.

Phoebe summoned a smile but said nothing further. It was generous of Mr. Cummings to think of her, but how could she leave? How could she allow Lydia to stay on her own—and not be here to welcome Frederick when he returned? Or if anything should happen to Fitz . . . She could not bear to think that anything might happen to either man. She would have to be here to sustain Lydia through it.

Besides, if something did happen, she would learn about it right away in Brussels. If she left for London, it would be weeks before she knew anything, and that would be agony beyond what she could bear.

"I beg you will understand. I cannot stay." Mr. Cummings tipped his hat, and with another glance at Phoebe, bid them farewell before exiting into the storm.

"Phoebe," Lydia said when he had gone. "You must see that it is impossible to refuse his offer. If he leaves, you must be in the carriage with him. It is the kindest thing I can do for my brother."

Phoebe stared at the furniture in the room, darkened without the light of day. Neither had enough energy to call for candles. "Did you notice how quiet it was today?" she asked. "I don't think we heard a single cannon fired. Do you think . . . could it be that the battle is over?"

Lydia shook her head. "If the battle were over, Fitz and my brother would be home. I fear that the worst is yet to come. We must gather our strength and prepare for it. While our men are out there fighting, let there be nothing wanting in our own courage."

Chapter Twenty-Five

$\mathscr{I}$t was dark by the time the staff officers set up headquarters in the inn, located in the center of Waterloo. The rain continued to fall, and although the Allied troops had reached their destination and were allowed to set up camp, Frederick did not envy them having to bivouac in a thundering rain that would not cease. His horse was well trained and did not flinch at the storm, but the rumbling thunder and sharp cracks of lightning left even Frederick, an experienced campaigner, ill at ease. It was as though the heavens were weeping.

From his vantage point on the higher ground, Frederick turned and caught sight of the French advance. They were following the British, but he knew from experience that it would be slow going. Their guns could not possibly roll in this sort of mud, and even the most devoted soldiers would be hard-pressed to find enthusiasm to fight for their emperor in such conditions. He was never more grateful than when he handed Salome over to Joseph, and he joined the other aides in the farmhouse.

The rain did not let up at all during the night, and Frederick truly pitied the soldiers who would not have in their possession a single dry article of clothing the next morning. As dawn broke, a different ADC from the Prussian Army entered the inn, carrying word from Blücher. Pinkton led him to the room where the duke ate his breakfast.

Sutherland arrived shortly afterward from his errand to deliver

Wellington's orders to the officers. He shook out his cloak and lay it over a chair, although the rain was abating. "Is that coffee? Pour me a cup."

Frederick poured him some coffee, and Sutherland drank it as Calloway was called in to Wellington and came out again holding a dispatch. "What's the news?" Frederick asked him.

"Blücher said he would march with his troops at daybreak, then join us as soon as he can. The duke has engaged to hold our position until he arrives."

Frederick pulled a chair over to the window and set up his shaving kit on the window ledge. He opened his shaving knife and scraped at the bristles while looking in the small portable glass. When Calloway left with the missive, Frederick said, "Stewart would not have been sorry to miss the storm. He hated the rain. Said it curled his hair like a poodle."

Sutherland gave a wistful smile. "He would have liked to have seen more action, though. At least the soldiers are in good spirits."

"Are they?" Frederick looked at him in surprise. He couldn't imagine how they could be when drenched to the core.

"Said the rain's a good omen. It always rained before one of Wellington's victories, and this was such a prodigious rainfall."

The thought that the troops viewed the rain as a good thing cheered Frederick, and as they set out that morning, he saw a number of soldiers gathered around campfires that they had somehow managed to light. They drank tea, talked and joked, as they dried out their clothes and waited for marching orders.

It was just after daybreak when Frederick and the rest of the staff accompanied the duke to the extensive Hougoumont farm on their right. The château and outlying buildings, along with the orchard, were all enclosed with a thick wall made of brick. Wellington conferred with Lieutenant-Colonel MacDonnell of the Coldstream Guards and recommended some changes to its fortification. The duke impressed upon him the importance of safeguarding Hougoumont as a strategic point at all costs, and MacDonnell promised to hold it.

After Hougoumont, Frederick and the staff officers trailed the duke as he took up his position for the day, which was near a lone elm tree on the ridge. There they had an excellent vantage point on the enemy troops. The air was still fresh, but the ground was muddy, and at times his horse's hooves sank deep into the mud, even on higher ground. Located in the valley in front of them was La Haye Sainte, another farm that Wellington said they must keep as an important stronghold. A smaller farm named Papelotte lay to their left, and they had orders to safeguard that as well.

A deep valley stretched between the two opposing ridges—the English on the side that defended Brussels and the road leading to the coast, and the French closer to Quatre Bras and the French border farther south. In the central valley lay tall fields of rye and corn. Through his telescope, Frederick saw masses of French gathering across the valley, but for the moment there was a surprising calm. He spotted Napoleon and his traveling carriage on the opposite ridge, with soldiers occasionally stopping to kiss his horse who grazed nearby, but the French did not seem to be assembling for battle.

The duke observed the movement as well, and when there appeared to be nothing of interest, he took to reading the society pages of a newspaper someone had brought. When he came to some more interesting bits of gossip, he read them out loud and laughed.

Frederick shared a smile with Wrotham as he jerked his chin in Wellington's direction. "Cool as you please," Frederick said of The Beau. Then he stared across the valley again. "What do you make of Boney? You'd think we'd hear the cannons signaling the start of battle. I cannot understand the delay."

"Can't say. But anything that gives us time for the Prussians to join us can only be a good thing." Wrotham dismounted and led his horse to where the grass was less trampled down in the mud.

De Lancey had arrived and was in conference with the duke regarding the status of the Royal Wagon Train and where they stood in terms of supplies and ammunition. Wellington sent Pinkton to check on the state of the roads to Ostend to see how things stood for getting reinforcements, including the expected arrival of more troops.

As Frederick sat in the saddle and waited, he experienced a wave of fatigue that had him longing to curl up on the ground no matter the mud. He had had little sleep these last few nights. But he steeled his nerves by sheer will. He knew this battle could decide all, and there was much at stake. His sister and Phoebe were in the city, and if the Allies did not hold their own, Brussels was at great risk of being overrun by the enemy. That could not happen.

A single French cannon sent out three shots, signaling the start of battle. Frederick pulled out his pocket watch. It was eleven-thirty.

In the valley that spread out in front of Frederick, the Allies formed their defensive squares in preparation for the battle, but the French instead concentrated their efforts to the right and began their assault on Hougoumont. Wellington quickly led his staff to the road that circled around to the entrance of the château to assess their movements. From there, French troops were visible as they crept around from the southern side of the walled enclosure and launched a fierce volley of artillery into the buildings and courtyard of the farm. The men inside returned the fire.

Satisfied that the Scots were holding their ground, Wellington turned to Frederick. "Ingram, you and Dalrymple, keep on the lookout here. Bring me word if there's a breach." He then signaled to his other aides to regain their position in the center, and they rode off.

Dalrymple had begun to look to Frederick when he wanted something clarified, and Frederick explained the Allied strategy. "The Highlander's defense of the château will have to do. The duke will not concentrate our troops there, leaving our center exposed. It would weaken his link with Blücher's Army, you know, which will be arriving on our left flank. We can't let the French separate our armies or all is lost."

Dalrymple licked his lips and turned to watch as French troops spilled out of the woods and began launching round shot and artillery fire on the walls, courtyard, and rooftops of the château and its outlying buildings.

For Phoebe, the morning of June 18 was a trial of agony—of both longing for news and fearing the worst. The thundering storm from the night before had given way to a temperamental sun that brought none of the intense heat that had accompanied the last couple of days. However, the rain had turned the dusty streets into a perfect quagmire of mud.

Lydia entered the house and made her way directly to the drawing room. The hem of her dress had not escaped the muck, which marred its pristine condition, though the Devonshire brown dress had been chosen precisely to avoid showing dirt. She sat and allowed her arms to drape over the sides of the chair. "I have been unable to learn anything further than that the duke has withdrawn his troops to the village of Waterloo."

At the news, a wave of panic seized Phoebe. She drew in a sharp breath and squeezed her hands together. "The English are retreating? That is very bad news, is it not?"

"Not necessarily." The corner of Lydia's lips tilted in a wry, weary smile. "Lord Wellington is known for strategic retreats. I had not witnessed one when I followed Fitz on the Peninsula, but he has taken part in them. Wellington will not waste time holding ground that is not advantageous. He will retreat to a stronger position."

"Do you think that is what he is doing now?" Phoebe was desperate for any good news that could be gleaned, but Lydia only shrugged.

There was a knock on the door, and Phoebe heard Sam go to open it. He, Mary, and Sarah had remained a reassuring presence ever since the soldiers had gone off to fight. If the servants were afraid, they hid it well and continued to carry out their duties with calm assurance. Phoebe heard the voice of Martha answering Sam in the entrance, and she got to her feet. Perhaps there was news.

Martha was pulling at a knot in her bonnet strings as she walked into the drawing room, her uneasiness causing her words to tumble out more quickly than usual. "I am *so* relieved you are here. I am still all astonishment that you were out helping the wounded men yesterday. I could never do such a thing. I would be afraid they would expire right on the spot while I was giving them something to drink—or worse! That they'd put their hands on me." She finally succeeded in removing her bonnet, and her blond corkscrew curls fell forward into her flushed face.

"Where is your brother?" Phoebe asked.

"Albert is seeing to our last-minute affairs. He is far from being confident of our carrying the victory. Have you packed your trunk in case you should need to come with us?"

Phoebe perfectly read the look Lydia shot her. She was to be compliant. "I have. But I must hold on to the hope that such a thing will not be necessary. We must have faith in our troops."

"Of *course*, I have faith in them. Our troops are the best in the world. But they might not be able to withstand that tyrant. It seems nothing can stand in his way. What if the French kill everyone and there is no one left to defend us?"

Lydia returned no answer but looked out the window, and Phoebe could not think of a single thing to say. Silence reigned in the drawing room, and ordinary sounds of townspeople going about their business could be heard outside. As the Fitzwilliam's house was not situated where most of the wounded men were, Phoebe could almost imagine, looking at the leafy branches outside their window, that it was an ordinary summer day. The silence was broken by a *boom* of a cannon, followed by another, and then another. Lydia sat up straight.

"Oh, it's happening again," Martha said. "I simply cannot bear it. The noise is fearful."

"It is closer this time," Phoebe said quietly, and Lydia nodded.

Martha put on her bonnet and began to tie the strings. "My goodness, I had better be going," she said, breathlessly. "Albert is sure to wonder where I have been, and I want to see if there's any news. Perhaps he is having the horses harnessed even as we speak." Martha came over and clutched Phoebe's hand. "I give you my word that we will not leave Brussels without you."

"Thank you," was all Phoebe could manage. In truth, the sound of cannons that much closer did frighten her, and Martha's obvious fretfulness did not aid her composure in any way. Then there was the promise she had made to Frederick to think of. She had promised him that she would flee Brussels if ever there was any need. Her mind knew no rest from that promise but turned around and around ever since the men had left. For her to leave now would mean leaving Lydia behind, and that seemed like such a want of courage. More than that, it seemed like betrayal.

After Martha left, Lydia turned to face her. "I know what you are thinking, Phoebe. But I must tell you that I am quite determined that you shall go if there is any cause for it. I am going to faithfully discharge the promise I made to my brother if it's the last thing I do. Besides, you are not a military wife—at the very least, not yet. Truly, I will feel much more at ease when you are safely on your way to England."

Phoebe was much less firm in her denial than she had been even the day before and returned a placating reply. "Very well. We shall see. There may never be cause for us to go after all."

Chapter Twenty-Six

The battle for the château had been raging for nearly an hour. Frederick set his face like flint as he watched, despite his dismay in seeing the Allied forces being driven out of the Bossu woods near Hougoumont. The French were concentrating all their forces on England's right, it seemed, and the Allies were too outnumbered to hold off the assault.

"I don't see how they can bear it," Dalrymple said, his eyes on the mass of enemy soldiers focusing their efforts on the entry point.

Frederick returned no answer. By now, several of the smaller buildings had caught fire from the cannon shot, and the French were climbing the walls and struggling against the gates of the enclosure. When the gates burst inward, Frederick hid all signs of emotion as he ordered Dalrymple, "Go let the duke know that Hougoumont has been breached. I will stay to see the outcome and will come with a second report."

Dalrymple galloped off toward Mont-Saint-Jean, and Frederick kept his eyes trained on the château as the fierce struggle continued. He could not see inside the walls from his vantage point and could only judge what was happening by the mass of soldiers outside of it. They did not appear to be streaming in, which meant the fight continued and the Coldstream Guards were holding ground, just as they had promised. Black smoke poured upward as soldiers extinguished some of the fires inside the courtyard.

Frederick heard the first wave of cannon shot coming from the center and knew that it would be followed by a cavalry charge in the valley. Fitz, he knew, had his division situated in the front closest to the French, and he sent up a disjointed prayer that he would be spared. Frederick kept up his watch for another hour and interrogated some of the Allied soldiers in retreat, but they only reported that the woods were swarming with the French.

At first he was uncertain, but the longer Frederick watched, the more he became sure that the French had been cut off from their access to the château, which meant that the British had managed to bolt the gates again. Outside of the walls, the enemy troops were being picked off by sharpshooters from the windows of the château and were forced to retreat into the woods.

"By George!" Frederick yelled. He could not contain himself. They had regained the farm against all odds. There would surely be another attempt, as Hougoumont was too important to give up without a fight, but Frederick had already been away too long from the command center and did not dare remain any longer. He wheeled his mare and rode toward Wellington to deliver the news.

He arrived at Mont-Saint-Jean a short time later and gave his report just as the enemy guns began sending out another thunderous cannonade. The valley, peaceful and untouched as it had been early in the morning, was now steeped in mud so thick it made it difficult to distinguish one regiment—or even one side—from another. Horses and soldiers alike were covered in it.

Wrotham saw Frederick's arrested gaze as he tried to make sense of the confusion in the valley below them. "The fields have become so waterlogged from the torrential rains, most of the round shot is falling in the mud and bouncing instead of exploding." He laughed. "Just as well for us. We don't have enough shot to give it back to 'em."

"Have the French not charged our center?" Frederick asked.

"They have, but La Haye Sainte is still ours."

The sound of a horse riding toward them at a clipped pace brought Frederick's face around. It was Pinkton, returning from an errand. "I have a message for the duke."

Wellington had ridden down into the valley to encourage the troops to hold their squares against the punishing artillery fire and was riding back to their rendezvous spot. When he returned, Pinkton told him he'd passed by Hougoumont and that they were in desperate need of artillery. *I need to help*, Frederick thought as he moved his horse forward. He had left his post too soon before victory had been assured.

De Lancey overheard the request and rode up to Wellington to respond to the need, but he was struck in the back by round shot. He flew forward off his horse, landed on his back, and got up again. Immediately, he fell backward and stayed there.

"Get a surgeon here and tell him my quartermaster-general is down," Wellington ordered Sutherland, who sped off.

De Lancey's assistant dismounted and gripped him by the arm. Frederick did not know the quartermaster-general well, but he hoped that his young bride would not be the recipient of bad news. His attention was pulled by a messenger, who rode up and handed the duke a letter. He read it, then scribbled a quick note and handed it to Frederick.

"See what you can do to get more ammunition to Hougoumont."

Frederick knew roughly where to find the Royal Wagon Train, which was partway between the center and the headquarters at Hougoumont on his right, and he rode toward it. As he pulled up in front of the supply wagon and turned to call out orders, a musket ball struck him on the side of his chest at a deflected angle, knocking him back in the saddle. He sat up and waited for the pain that was sure to come, along with the blood, but felt only a dull ache as though he had been through the worst boxing match of his career.

When he looked down, no blood marred his coat, though there was a hole. Puzzled, Frederick swung down from his mount and felt his coat. Inside was the musket ball still intact, wedged in the silk handkerchief that Phoebe had given him before the cricket match, which he had kept folded in a tight square in his inside pocket. He opened the handkerchief, which was now shredded, but had managed to stop a musket ball that was probably close to being spent from lodging in his flesh.

The commanding officer of the Wagon Train caught sight of Frederick. "Did you get hit?"

Frederick felt his chest again, where a welt was beginning to form. It was tender and would be bruised, but he had been lucky. He shook his head rather than explain and held out the note from Wellington. "Hougoumont needs ammunition urgently."

A young private stepped forward. "Allow me, Colonel. I'll see that it's done."

The colonel yelled for the soldiers standing nearby. "Private Brewster has volunteered to get the ammunition to Hougoumont, so let's waste no time in sending him off."

It was a dangerous endeavor because it would mean riding along an unprotected road all the way to the château. Frederick stopped to watch with no small degree of anxiety as the private drove a tumbril of ammunition, at breakneck speed and under heavy fire, the entire way to the château. He made it to the gates, and they opened to receive his precious charge. A breathless laugh of relief escaped Frederick, and he shook his head in admiration, tipped his hat to the colonel, and rode back to their rendezvous spot near the elm tree.

With a broad view over the valley, Frederick estimated about 17,000 infantrymen of their own lined up between the center farm of La Haye Sainte and the smallest farm of Papelotte on their left flank. So far, they had been lucky, and they had not lost any of their strategic farms. However, mid-afternoon, it looked like the French were determined to change that as they began their heavy offensive on the center. It began with thunderous volleys of fire taking out soldiers in the front ranks. Replacements would pull them back into the center of the square and bravely fill in the holes of men, musket, and sword.

The artillery would cease only for the Allies to brave a second wave of charging *cuirassiers* riding through and around the squared-off formations. The short swords of the British were no match for the lances held by the incoming cavalry.

"Give orders to fire at the horses, not at the men," Wellington called out. "And when they are in between charges, have the troops lie down to minimize the casualties from the artillery."

Frederick and the other aides sped off to relay Wellington's command. Frederick rode first to the Prince of Wales Own Volunteers—one of the regiments receiving the brunt of the attack—and they opened the square to allow him to enter just as the *cuirassiers* flooded the ground in between the islands of red soldiers. After Frederick had passed on the message to the major-general there, he dismounted and put his hand on Salome's saddle, taking in the sight of the square's center, which had become a morass of wounded and dead.

Black smoke from artillery mingled with a fog from the humidity rising off the ground and covered every inch of the men where mud had not reached. The moans and cries of the wounded mixed with the sound of musketry fire, and Frederick saw how quickly the ground was being filled with fallen soldiers. Soon there would be barely a yard to spare.

He rubbed his face and waited for the cavalry charge to withdraw before leaving the safety of the square. Artillery fire whizzed by him as he galloped behind the formations to the joint battalion that included the 33rd regiment where Fitz was. Frederick entered the square just as the next round of artillery ceased and the new *cuirassiers* charge began.

"For heaven's sake, get down, Ingram!" Fitz shouted from one of the sides of the square, where he was helping to haul a dead man from the flank and gesturing for another soldier to take his place and close ranks.

Frederick waved his acknowledgment and slid down from his horse. He led his mare over to Fitz, the Thoroughbred stepping gingerly through the field to avoid the wounded soldiers. "Where's the colonel?"

"Dead," Fitz replied. "I'm acting commander."

Frederick shook his head in sympathy. "This is rough work." He relayed the instructions from Wellington, and Fitz replied that he had already given similar orders but that he would reinforce them.

A movement on Frederick's left had him turning as the Belgian cavalry sped down the hill to counter the attack from the French *cuirassiers*. They rode in hard; and with a roar, the French cavalry charged just as fast. At the last possible minute, the Belgians reined their horses in, wheeled about in terror, and fled the scene of battle. Their commander yelled for them to regroup, but they ignored him as they continued onward; the mud flew from the hooves of their horses as they thundered down the road toward Brussels.

"What the—" Frederick could have screamed in frustration. Could they not have held their ground? They would cause other inexperienced troops to lose heart. And not only were they fleeing the scene of battle, they were heading straight toward the city, where they would frighten Phoebe and Lydia to death.

Tight-lipped, Fitz met his gaze and Frederick could see his own fury reflected in his brother-in-law's face.

Phoebe's wish that there might be no cause to think about flight proved in vain. In mid-afternoon, after enduring the first sound of violent cannonade, followed by a stretch of silence in the distance, then followed again by another wave of cannonade with the pattern repeating, their anxious peace was disturbed. A cavalcade of thundering hooves and shouts poured into the city, coming from the Namur Gate in the direction of Waterloo.

"Good heavens!" Lydia cried, her composure gone. Deeply alarmed, Phoebe followed her out of the house and into the street, where they hurried toward the commotion on *rue Haute*. There a small crowd was gathered, gaping after what appeared to be a troop of fleeing soldiers in blue uniform.

Phoebe touched the arm of the woman beside her and asked, "What is it? What is happening?"

The woman was Belgian and replied in French. "*Les Alliés battent en retraite. C'est une déroute complète!*"

Phoebe turned to Lydia to see her reaction. The Allied Army had been fully routed and were now retreating. Lydia's eyes were round with terror, but her face was resolute.

"Come," Lydia said, linking her arm through Phoebe's. "It is time. The Cummings will be here for you shortly, and we must have your trunk brought down."

"You must come too!" Phoebe insisted as she hurried alongside Lydia. Then she gasped. "And the servants! We cannot leave them behind. We shall have to find another way."

"Nothing will induce me to leave. I will not go without Fitz, and Sarah has said they are resolved not to leave without me."

Phoebe was swept along by Lydia's determination even as she wrestled within herself. On one hand, she was truly afraid, and she *had* made a promise to Frederick. On the other hand, she feared that she would despise herself for the rest of her days if she fled the country with thoughts only for herself. But she was not strong enough against Lydia's resolution, nor against the insistence from the Cummings who arrived within the half hour.

Even Mary seemed to have no thought for herself as she assisted Sam in bringing down Phoebe's trunk. Her smile was tremulous, but her words were bracing. "That'll do, miss. You'll be off."

"We have no time to waste," Mr. Cummings shouted. "Miss Tunstall, please, allow me to assist you into the carriage. Mrs. Fitzwilliam, are you sure you will not come with us?"

"I am quite resolved to stay," Lydia said, urging Phoebe into the carriage. "I shall do very well here. If need be, the servants and I will go to Mrs. Marshall's house, where we shall contrive together."

Phoebe had her hand on the open window of the carriage and she leaned out. She had not even bid a proper farewell to Lydia, and she lifted her arm as the carriage sped away—her friend a lonely figure on the street, becoming smaller and smaller as the carriage sped away. She had left Lydia behind. Phoebe's fate was sealed.

"Well," Martha said, playing with the strings of her reticule. "At the very least, we did manage to procure horses, unlike so many of the other English who could not find one. Brother, I applaud your industry. You may very well have saved our lives."

"Well, I was quite determined," he replied with a glance at Phoebe. He clutched his portmanteau in his hands. "But we are not out of all danger yet. We will break our journey at Ghent and be off early tomorrow. I shall be at ease when we have booked passage on the boat and are safely on our way to England. Let us just hope that Corsican monster does not follow us to England and attempt something on our own soil. We shall show him."

Phoebe remained silent. She could not bring herself to felicitate Mr. Cummings or even to thank him, so disgusted was she with herself for accepting his offer. She turned her face to look through the carriage window and knew that for the rest of her life she would despise herself for this moment—for her unforgivable lack of courage and resolve. All that had been required of her was loyalty enough to remain and support Lydia in her distress, and she had been unable to do even that.

Chapter Twenty-Seven

*F*rederick turned his attention from the fleeing cavalry back to their troops. Fitz's square held, despite the cavalry charge, and Frederick left his horse to graze in the middle of it on a patch that was not matted down with mud. He walked with Fitz to the front defensive line and stood watching the action outside of their square. Raw recruits had been placed next to hardened veterans, and the sangfroid of the older soldiers seemed to have a strengthening effect on the younger boys. In the vast space in front of their square, bodies of horses and men piled up from wave after wave of *cuirassiers* charges.

The sound of the horn blared from behind Frederick, ordering the Allies to meet the cavalry charge, and this time it was the Union and Household Brigades that charged, their horses trained to ignore the chaos. Frederick went back to his mare and held the bridle as he watched the brigades thunder past the defensive squares. The sheer volume of Allied cavalry bearing down on the enemy was enough to deter them, and they wheeled about, mid-charge, and made for the safety of their lines. Fueled by success, the Allied brigades continued to gallop well into the enemy lines, though their officers saw the danger and yelled for their men to halt and regroup. The trumpets sounded the call for retreat in vain, however. The thrill of the chase was too much for their cavalry, and the brigades rode all the way up the slope to take out the soldiers at the enemy guns.

By the time they were ready to retreat, it was too late. The French lancers had snaked around from the left and cut off their access to the Allied front. The horses were now spent and, slowed down by the mud, the troops were easy prey for the French cavalry. The British tried to break through enemy lines and flee but were mowed down before they could do so, and only those with the best horses were able to escape. Although three-hundred Scotts rode out, only a few dozen returned.

Frederick watched in dismay the massacre of their horsemen. Inside their defensive square, one of the young soldiers was kneeling at Frederick's feet, holding his musket, his mouth slack with horror. "They're fleeing like the terror is on 'em."

The wizened soldier next to him recharged his musket with sure strokes, replying, "We must blow the froth off before we come to the porter."

Fitz left his position and came over to Frederick. "Still here?" His face was blackened with soot, and with the air dense with smoke, Frederick imagined he must not look much better.

"Just going," he replied.

A shot whizzed by the air, and Frederick saw Fitz flinch at the same time that he heard the thud of ball hitting flesh. A crimson stain spread on Fitz's arm, and his frown lines grew pronounced.

Fitz! Frederick ran the two steps toward him. He couldn't tell if the ball had just hit the arm or if it had gone through and perhaps hit something vital. "Does your brigade have a surgeon?"

Fitz shook his head. "Don't bother him. Just . . . just cut my sleeve here and see if you can bind it up. It's nothing more than a flesh wound."

Frederick took his knife out of his boot and cut the cloth of Fitz's jacket. He put his knife in his teeth as he examined the wound. It was more than just a flesh wound, but it didn't appear to have touched the bone, and it had not angled into his chest.

Fitz's ensign ran up. "Here, sir. We have a few strips of linen for this use." He handed one to Frederick, who tied the wound to staunch the bleeding. Fitz gritted his teeth when Frederick pulled the cloth tight, but then pushed his hat more firmly on his head and turned to look at the front flank.

"The bullet is still in there. Get that looked at as soon as you can so it doesn't infect," Frederick said. Fitz gave a curt nod before running to the front flank where the replacements were too slow to fill the gaps made by the wounded. Frederick was reluctant to leave him but had to trust his brother-in-law was capable of doing what he was trained to do.

Frederick waited for the cavalry charge to abate, then rode out of the square to rejoin Wellington. It was late afternoon, and they were hard-pressed as the valley began to fill with chaos and death. The Prussians had not yet arrived to relieve them, and the men on the field were beginning to lose heart. He hoped that evening would arrive before they must declare defeat.

The carriage ride began well in the confines of the city, despite the confusion, and they made it through the Anderlecht Gate with little to hinder them. However, as they ambled along the road to-ward Ghent, their travel became more difficult. It was impossible to keep to a steady trot, due to the mud from the heavy rains the day before.

"It is most irritating that we must move slowly," Mr. Cummings said, "but we might still achieve our destination this evening." They were not the only ones on their way to Ghent. Occasionally, other carriages would bypass them that carried less of a load. And their carriage also overtook other, heavier coaches.

Phoebe continued to stare through the window, disinclined to make conversation. *Please, God, spare Frederick,* was her thought over and over again. She began to notice English foot soldiers trav-eling in the opposite direction toward Brussels. She almost wanted to call out to them to say to turn around for all was lost. If she could spare their lives, at least, there would be one blessing to this regretful decision to have fled.

But of course, she could do no such thing, and even Phoebe knew that a soldier would follow his colonel's orders and not the orders of some miss who happened to be fleeing in the opposite direction. She sat back against the squabs and had a perfect view of the side of the road, where she was able to witness cavalry ac-companying the foot soldiers. Soon, it appeared to be an entire regiment of cavalry heading east. The sight only served to increase

Phoebe's discomfort at the idea of leaving. Her return to England could be nothing other than unpatriotic when she was leaving loved ones behind.

Mr. Cummings pulled out his pocket watch and glanced at it. He leaned over to his side and looked out the window, snapping his watch shut. He gave other signs of agitation but said nothing further to break up their journey. Martha made up for his lapse, alternating between commonplaces and pointing out the things she spotted on the side of the road, then repeating her worries that they would not be able to leave on the boat and that something would happen to deter them.

At last, their pace slowed to a crawl. Mr. Cummings tapped on the ceiling, and the carriage came to a halt while the footman swung down to receive his orders. "We are going so slowly. See if you can make out what is keeping us."

"*That* I can answer for meself. Coaches is stuck in the mud and we've to find a ways around them."

Mr. Cummings sighed in frustration. "Very well. Do what you must, but do not be one of the carriages that gets stuck in the mud."

"Aye, sir." The footman resumed his seat next to the groom, and the carriage lurched forward.

Much of the day had gone by now, and it was late in the afternoon as the road dipped into a valley. Mr. Cummings leaned far outside of the window to see what was ahead as the carriage slowed again.

He tsked. "There are two carriages stuck in the mud, blocking our path." He leaned out the window to shout, "You will need to go around them!" Phoebe felt the carriage tilt as it moved off the side of the road, rolled several feet, and came to a complete standstill.

"I'll be d—" Mr. Cummings broke off. "I beg your pardon, Miss Tunstall." He leapt out of the carriage, and his boots immediately sank into the mud.

"Deuce take it!" He wrenched his foot loose, and Phoebe could hear him conferring with the footman and groom about the best way to get the carriage unstuck. He climbed back on the road and went to the occupants of the other carriages to speak to them. The parade of troops and cavalry heading toward Brussels seemed to have ceased, and Phoebe wondered if there would be more. She leaned out of the window to look.

Martha sighed loudly. "It is just as I feared. It was entirely too easy to leave Brussels. Now we shall remain here stuck overnight, prey to brigands and wild animals, and the enemy will be upon us before we can get away." She continued this fretful monologue without waiting for an answer, and Phoebe was not obliged to give one.

Instead, Phoebe looked to the side of her carriage, idly studying her surroundings, when a movement caught her attention. It was the blond head of a child, almost imperceptible against the color of wheat on the field opposite the road. Phoebe leaned out of the window and searched for an adult but could see none. The boy appeared to be entirely alone. She opened the door to the carriage.

"Phoebe, what are you doing?" Martha cried out. "If you leave the carriage, you will become all muddy."

"There is a child there. I cannot imagine why he is all alone, but I must see that he is unharmed."

On the side of the road, the groom and footman had begun searching for branches that they could place under the carriage wheels to allow them to roll out of the mud, while Mr. Cummings stood with the horses. The occupants of the other carriages had begun to do the same. Phoebe crossed the road and went over to the boy. His face had been burnt in the sun, and his trousers appeared to be soiled with something other than mud. He couldn't have been more than three, and his lips trembled when she went over to him.

"Good afternoon, young man. Where is your mother?"

The child looked at her in apprehension and did not answer. *Of course—he must be Belgian,* she reminded herself. She repeated the question but in French, and his look of confusion did not alter.

"*Koeien*," he said.

Phoebe scrunched her brow. How unfortunate. He spoke Dutch, which she did not. Poor boy. It was unthinkable that she should leave him here with no one to care for him. She stretched her hands out to him, and he came willingly. She picked him up, despite his soiled trousers, and held him close. His arms hung at his side, and Phoebe supported his full weight as she walked over to the carriage. "We must find this little boy's family, for he is quite lost. There is not a house in sight."

Mr. Cummings was in the process of supervising the extrication of the carriage. "That child is not my concern right now," he said shortly.

Their maid glanced at the boy then looked away, and Martha moved over to the side of the carriage to see. "Oh, but he is so dirty. I am sorry, Phoebe, but we cannot possibly take him into our carriage. What would we *do* with him? Besides, we have not a moment to waste. We must make it to Ghent tonight as soon as our carriage is unstuck. Set him down. Surely his parents will come."

Phoebe looked at the little boy, whose nose had begun to run, and a fierce determination coursed through her, giving her strength. "I shall not abandon you," she murmured to the boy. Returning her gaze to the Cummings, she said, "If you will not help this boy, I am afraid you shall have to go on without me."

"But, Phoebe, that is madness," Martha cried. "You are endangering yourself for nothing. The child is not even *English*!"

"Nevertheless, my mind is quite made up. Have my trunk left at the inn in Ostend, and I will retrieve it before boarding a boat to England—*after* I've found out where this child comes from and have reunited him with his family."

"Miss Tunstall, I urge you to reconsider. You are placing yourself in grave danger." Mr. Cummings, still holding the reins, turned back to speak to her. "We do not know when the French will descend upon this part of the country. You will not be safe here."

Phoebe could not understand how they could leave this poor child to fend for himself and was tempted to give a curt reply. But she owed them a gracious response after they had gone to so much trouble for her.

"I understand, and I thank you for all you have done for me. But I cannot in good conscience leave this child here. Good day, Mr. Cummings." Phoebe turned and went in the direction the child had been walking along the side of the road. It seemed the most logical direction to look first, but even if she were wrong, perhaps someone local would recognize him or assist her in bringing the boy to his family.

The child grew heavy, but Phoebe's protective instinct gave her a strength she did not know she had. Eventually, the child stuck his fingers in his mouth and lay his head against her breast. Phoebe was touched by the gesture and forged on, though her arms and back had begun to ache and her legs shook slightly from fatigue. When a small dirt path snaked off the side of the road into the trees, she followed it, thinking she was more likely to find a house here than on the road. And as she trudged onward through the quiet path, with only the sound of an occasional breeze stirring the leaves, she found she could not regret her decision at all. All doubt had fled. She had perhaps behaved in a cowardly manner when she fled Brussels and Lydia—*and Frederick*—against her better judgment. But she had been given a chance to redeem herself.

Frederick retraced his path up the slope of the valley, changing course to where Wellington bolstered the troops. With unshakable calm, the duke corrected formations and called out orders for them to tighten up. To the divisions receiving the worst of it, he called out his encouragement.

"Hard pounding this, gentlemen. Try who can pound the longest."

The duke seemed to have been born under a lucky star. No matter how many shots flew by him, not one met their mark. Frederick fell alongside Wellington and Dalrymple as they rode back to the reconnaissance point on the ridge. Once on higher ground, Frederick spotted from a distance the line of Prussians moving toward them from the east. Blücher's troops must have had skirmishes with the French for him to delay so long, but all that mattered now was that they had at last managed to repel the French and come to Wellington's aid. Frederick trained his telescope to the farm in the center, La Haye Sainte, which must be even more critical now. Napoleon would have seen their reinforcements arriving, and he would be keen to take the center stronghold and divide the Prussian and British Armies before it was too late.

It therefore did not surprise him that Wellington sent Dalrymple with orders not to lose La Haye Sainte. The young aide rode down the incline toward the formations. It was in between cavalry charges, and Frederick silently urged him to weave in between the defensive squares to be less of a target for the artillery, but Dalrymple headed instead for the main road that led directly to the farm. He had not made it past the Allied troops before he was shot. Frederick froze when he saw the boy fall. It was a bullet to the temple—fatal.

He didn't have time to grieve with the enemy assault intensifying both on the center farm and their troops in the valley. The French sent wave after wave of cavalry charges, and the fighting grew too fierce for the British to hold. In under an hour, La Haye Sainte fell to the French.

Wellington trained his telescope at the Prussians, who were arriving at a steady pace but were still too far away to be an impediment for the enemy. "We're pulling back," he called out. "Send orders for a retreat while we wait for help to come."

Nearly every available aide now rode down into the valley to deliver the orders to the commanding officers, and the squares of infantry pulled back and scrambled up the incline. The effect was impressive. Even to Frederick, who knew what they were doing, it looked like a full retreat.

Wellington waited on top of the ridge, and he ushered the men over it and on to the reverse slope, where he gave orders for them to crouch down out of sight. He called for his remaining cavalry to take position on the ridge as a thin line of defense. They looked like an easily vanquished foe—almost like canaries for a cat. Frederick was in a position to see everything, and although he knew there was a force of troops behind the calvary to rise up and fight, he felt like a canary himself, ready to be plucked.

There was no artillery fire this time, only a rush of enemy cavalry. Once the Allied troops had scrambled over the ridge and out of sight, Napoleon launched his *Immortels*—the Imperial Guard—in a heavy push to cut through the thin line of British resistance that was visible on the center line and divide the Allied strength.

The French Guard rode with the wind down the valley into the muddy battlefield, then up the slope toward the ridge where the Allies waited. Wellington called down to the reserves lying in wait. "Steady now. Not yet."

Frederick held his breath, willing the enemy toward them—for it simply must end; the battle had been too much—and willing the Allies to show themselves and fight. The enemy came within a hundred yards, then a hundred feet, their horses at full charge.

At sixty feet, Wellington yelled, "Maitland, now!"

The line of Allied soldiers stood at once with a shout and rushed up the incline. They launched a direct assault against the Imperial Guard, who could not withstand the surprise attack or the superior numbers. The *Immortels* cried out, turning their horses in a panicked retreat.

Frederick heard cries of "*Trahison!*" as the French guard fled into the valley toward their camp. Within minutes, the Prussian cavalry arrived at Mont-Saint-Jean at last. They were tired from their march, but nothing like what the British had endured that day on the battlefield. The Prussians calvary poured into the field on a gallop, spreading out across the valley as they pursued the French. Lord Wellington stood in his stirrups, lifted his hat high in the air and swept it forward, signaling the general advance.

It took a stunned moment for Frederick to make sense of what was happening. The enemy was fleeing by the masses on the other side of the valley with the Allies in hot pursuit. Napoleon had not managed to break through the Allied defense, and now that the Prussians had joined up with the British in the center, there was no hope for the enemy to make a comeback. This retreat was final.

Those who had fought all day in Waterloo, and who were still standing, lowered their weapons. Some gave a weary but heartfelt cheer. Riderless horses grazed on whatever untrammeled ground they could find or bolted after a herd that ran aimlessly. Groans came from all quarters, and it was hard to distinguish the men from the mud. The dead horses and soldiers were strewn across the field, as though they had been carelessly tossed aside. And amidst the dead were some of Frederick's close friends. He would have to face that at some point.

Soon, the last of the Prussians thundered across the field to escort the vanquished army back to Paris, and the Allies had a reprieve from Napoleon's murderous assault. Frederick could hardly believe that the war was over after three days of tragic losses, culminating with seven hours of brutal, relentless fighting. But it was over.

He was too numb to think clearly about what he must do now. Even if he could have, he was not sure his limbs would obey him. Only one thought repeated itself in his mind: *We have won!*

Chapter Twenty-Eight

The small boy was heavy, and the burden was becoming almost too much for Phoebe by the time she reached the sunny hamlet that held five modest houses, plus another building that—from the sounds that came from within—constituted a stable. She hoisted the boy, who was now sleeping, more firmly in her grasp and walked over to the side of the closest house where there was a low shelter for firewood that was covered by some sort of worktable. The area happened to be in the shade and was slightly out of view from the main area, which made it a suitable place for the boy to continue his nap while she sought help.

Phoebe laid him down gently, frowning at the thought of his tender head on the rough wood. But she had only her reticule to serve as a pillow, and there were too many valuables inside for her to consider leaving it unattended. In it was all she had to get her back to England. In the end, she kept it on her wrist and went to look for help.

Her arms now free, Phoebe circled around the first house and went to knock on the front door. Her heart was in her throat at the thought of approaching strangers who would not likely be able to speak English. There was no answer. Phoebe walked to the second house closest to it and knocked again, but there was no answer. It was then that she noticed that the hamlet was unusually calm. It could not be deserted, for she could hear the sound of chickens and horses in the stable, but there were no noises of the women and children that should ordinarily populate a rural hamlet. Even if the men were off to work, surely the women would not leave their homes as well. No, someone must be here.

She crossed over to the third house on the opposite side, then the fourth house that was next to it but met with no success in either place. By the time she walked to the last house in the hamlet that served as the end to the row of houses, she noticed clothes hanging on a line next to it, swaying gently in the breeze and was now reassured that wherever the people were, they could not be far. Despite that assurance, Phoebe could not figure out why there was no one in the hamlet in the middle of the day.

She knocked on the last house. This time, when there was no answer, she turned the handle and stepped over the threshold. The room was darkened without windows visible except for the ones that faced the center of the hamlet. But her eyes lit on bowls of food set on the table, with clean spoons next to them, indicating that no one had begun eating. One of the chairs was overturned as though people had left in a rush. A sense of disquiet began to grow in Phoebe's breast.

What could've caused such an alarm that someone would not take time to put the chair upright? What would cause these people to abandon their homes, their possessions, and even their meals? The answer came to her at once. *The French have overrun the Allies at last. They have spread out into the countryside.*

Phoebe swallowed in fright, but her throat was dry. She was at their mercy. Who would defend her from them? Shouts from the woods surrounding the hamlet reached her ears, and it could only mean one thing. French soldiers were coming, and they would not treat her kindly when they found her. Phoebe suffered a strong temptation to stay sheltered in the house and find someplace to hide, but she clamped her jaw and reached for the door handle. That poor boy was outside sleeping on the work table, and *he* had no one to protect him. She would not leave him to his fate.

Phoebe ran outside into the sun-filled enclosure where the men's shouts appeared louder. But it was not soldiers that came into her view. To her astonishment, a woman ran between the end house and one of the two that made up part of the enclosure.

When she spotted Phoebe, she gasped and rushed over to her, speaking to her in a panicked language that Phoebe could not understand. She grasped Phoebe by both arms, but Phoebe frowned and shook her head.

"I don't understand. *Je ne comprends pas.*" She tried it again in French, but no comprehension dawned on the woman's face. Her panic reinforced Phoebe's fear. She was certain the woman was trying to let her know that the soldiers were hot on her heels and that Phoebe needed to hide.

She followed her into the house to see what she was doing, but before she could fully enter, the woman pushed past Phoebe on her way out, carrying a piece of cloth.

Now, truly perplexed, Phoebe returned to the hamlet's center. Her sense of alarm had not lessened, but she had no clear idea of what she was supposed to do and knew only that she needed to watch over the boy that Providence had placed in her care. She started back toward the first house, where she could make out the bare foot of his sleeping form, which reassured her insensibly. She had just made the decision to stay with him until she could make sense of what was happening when a hound came tearing into the clearing, causing her to spin around. A crowd of people followed hard on the dog's heels as they rushed into the enclosure.

Phoebe was terrified by the hound's behavior. At no time did she feel perfectly at ease with dogs, although she liked them well enough. But she did not always understand animals, and this one was sniffing at her dress, pulling on it with its teeth, and encircling her and barking. Phoebe remained paralyzed as the crowd of people advanced upon her, their faces a mix of wariness and fear. There were children crowding in with the men and women.

Wholly bewildered, she met their gazes. "I beg your pardon, but I am English. Does anyone here speak English?"

"Yes, miss." One of the young women with a neat appearance came forward and bobbed a curtsy. "Good afternoon, miss. You must forgive us, but we are quite troubled at the moment. My sister's child is missing, and our dog has led us to you. Do you have knowledge of where the child has gone? Have you seen him?"

All of the tension in Phoebe's muscles relaxed at once. Now it all made sense. "Yes," she said, smiling in relief. "I found him, and I have brought him to you." She gestured to the table nearly out of sight. "He is just there."

"*Hier zit'em!*" the woman shouted.

The other woman, who had come to fetch the article of clothing earlier, uttered a strangled cry and ran toward the table. She gathered the boy into her arms and fell weeping over him as he came awake and rubbed his eyes. The crowd gathered around them, and a woman put her hand on the mother's shoulder. The men relaxed their stance, and one of them leaned down to pet the dog's head.

"You are a God-send, miss. I am Tinneke, and my sister is Trees." She came to stand at Phoebe's side as the conversation flew back and forth in a language Phoebe could not follow. "Please tell us how you happened to find my nephew?"

By now, the boy had fully woken up, and he put his arms around his mother, tucking his head into her neck at all the commotion. Phoebe was unable to answer because Trees brought the boy to Phoebe, expressing words that Phoebe thought she could understand even without translation.

"My sister thanks you from the bottom of her heart," Tinneke said. "She also wants to know how you found Jos and where. She thought my cousin's wife was watching him, so he must have been gone for some time before we realized it."

"Well," Phoebe answered, "I was in a coach on my way to Ghent, then Ostend, to book a packet bound for London when our carriage became stuck in the mud. I looked through the window and saw the boy. I could see almost at a glance that he was all alone, and it was just something I could not ignore. My companions were unwilling to help me find his mother, so I bid them farewell and carried him in the direction where I thought he might have come from. I had no idea if I would have any luck, but I thought it the most likely way to go."

The boy repeated what he'd had said earlier, and Phoebe turned to Tinneke. "He said the same word when I found him, but I don't speak Dutch, so I could not tell what he was saying."

She and her sister were talking earnestly, and Tinneke said in a voice of mild exasperation. "He went to see the *cows*. We should have thought of that. He loves cows, but he must've lost his way, for the cows' pasture is in an entirely different direction than the road that leads to Ghent. The road is so busy, I shudder to think what could have happened to him. I do not know what we would've done had you not cared for him."

"It was an easy decision for me." Phoebe reached up to pat the boy's back in his mother's arms. "I could not leave him alone."

The two women spoke again, and Tinneke said, "My sister insists that you come inside with us so we might find a way to assist you and repay you for your goodness."

"You are very kind. How is it that you speak English so well?" The families dispersed to go into their houses, and Phoebe followed Tinneke's sister into her home.

"I was a lady's maid to an English family in Brussels, but they fled the city two days ago when they heard that the French had engaged." She looked up as one of the men came to speak to her, darting a glance at Phoebe. "My cousin is asking how you intend to get back to London."

That was the question. Would she still go to London? It took only a moment's hesitation for her to decide she probably should. After having used up all her resolution to help the boy, Phoebe found she no longer had the courage to return to Brussels, especially without knowing what awaited her there. Besides, she had told the Cummings to leave her trunk in Ostend, and although there was nothing irreplaceable in it, it would be useful to have her things.

"This is just the dilemma I am trying to work out in my mind. I suppose I shall walk back to the road and see if my friends are still there. Perhaps the carriage is stuck yet, and I will be able to join them in continuing our way to Ostend."

Tinneke translated this to her cousin, who responded. He left the house, and Tinneke turned to Phoebe. "He will take you in his wagon."

Phoebe's shoulders sank with relief. If she was lucky enough to rejoin the Cummings, she could change out of her soiled dress. "That is most gracious of him."

"It is the least we can do," Tinneke assured her as she accompanied Phoebe to the wagon.

The cousin, whose name she learned was Lorre, hitched a horse to the wagon, and they rode through the forest path. Even when riding, the journey seemed to take forever, and Phoebe could not believe she had walked for so long carrying such a heavy boy. She indicated where the carriage was, but by the time they reached the main road and had traveled to where it dipped into a valley, the Cummings' carriage was gone. A sense of despair at being left behind threatened Phoebe's courage, but she refused to give in to it. She had done the right thing, and God would take care of the rest.

Tinneke and her cousin spoke back and forth in Flemish, and Phoebe prayed for strength and courage. She had no countrymen of her own to depend upon.

Finally, Tinneke turned to Phoebe and announced, "We have decided to take you to Ostend. It is a long journey with the wagon such as we have, and therefore we think it best to begin soon and even travel overnight. It is not the comfort that you are accustomed to, but we will return home first to eat supper and fetch blankets for the back of the wagon where you may rest on the way. We also have friends about halfway to Ostend, who will surely allow us to stop and borrow their horse for the rest of the journey. With our slow pace and rests, we will arrive by tomorrow afternoon."

Phoebe had not expected this silver thread of mercy, and she clasped her hands together. Still, she hesitated. "I cannot trouble you to undertake such a journey on my account."

The carriage hit a rut, and they both bounced forward before Tinneke could reply. "It is no worry, but I am afraid we do not have enough money to pay for your passage."

Phoebe sat back again and shook her head. "I have what I need. If I am lucky, I will find my trunk waiting for me at the inn at Ostend. Otherwise, I shall have to leave it behind. But I do have money for passage."

"We will return to my sister's house to let her know, and I believe we should eat first. I see your dress is soiled, and if you are willing to wear one of mine for part of the journey, I can wash it before we leave and let it dry overnight."

"You are so very gracious," Phoebe replied, squeezing Tinneke's hand. It was a spontaneous gesture for someone she had only just met, but Tinneke returned the squeeze as Lorre drove back to the hamlet.

When the last of the Prussian Army had disappeared in pursuit of the French, all that was left on the two opposing ridges and the valley in between was a scene of carnage—mud, abandoned guns and ammunition, wounded horses and men, and an inestimable number of dead. This would require a medical and mortuary service beyond the capacity of the Allied Army, and not even the quartermaster-general had been spared from the punishing cannonade to see to it.

As evening fell, Frederick turned his flagging horse northward and accompanied the duke back to the inn at Waterloo, where Caldwell had gone ahead, and where Joseph kept the other horses. The staff that returned with Lord Wellington was greatly reduced. Dalrymple and Wrotham were gone, along with Stewart. Calloway had lost an arm. De Lancy, from the last Frederick had heard, was not long for this world.

A supper was set in front of Frederick, and he ate it mechanically. He was weary to the bone, but his nerves remained tightly wound from the fear, energy, and the devastation of the day. It would take time to deal with the loss, and he was almost calloused to the victory. As he swallowed his food and drank from the tankard that had been given to him, Phoebe's face flitted through Frederick's mind. He could not summon emotion, but the thought of her was a promise of better things to come.

Blücher would lead the Prussian Army back to Paris after the vanquished French, and Wellington would join him there in a couple of days. Frederick would doubtless be required to go to Paris, too, and it was most likely that his reunion with Phoebe would have to begin by correspondence. He would write to both Fitz's house in Brussels and Stratford's house in England, because Frederick could not be sure whether or not Phoebe had fled the country as he had urged her. He refused to wonder whether she might still be close. In any case, he did not anticipate being permitted to see her, as he would surely accompany the duke to Paris to restore order and see to Napoleon's surrender.

Wellington called him into his room, where the remains of a

dinner sat on a nearby table. He shook sand off a letter he had written and gestured for Frederick to come in. "Mighty glad to see you alive, Ingram. Too many were not so lucky." Frederick nodded, and they shared a somber look before the duke folded his letter and melted wax to seal it.

"It was the nearest run thing you ever saw in your life," Wellington said. "I told Bathurst that myself in the letter. If the Prussians hadn't come when they did . . ." He shook his head. "I will be accompanying the Army to Paris in two days' time, and I need you to carry this letter to Headquarters in London—and two of the captured eagles along with it. Do you still have good cattle that can carry you there?"

Frederick's brain had trouble deciphering the information he had just received. He would not need to leave for Paris but would actually be going home. He answered numbly. "Yes, sir."

Wellington stood and walked over to the captured Golden Eagles which leaned against the wall. He grasped the tall blue staffs underneath the flags and brought them to Frederick. "I imagine the sight of these will be cause for celebration, so do not delay in bringing them, along with this letter. Start out tomorrow morning first thing."

Frederick took the letter and looked up at the Eagles perched at the top of the rods, feeling their weight as he nodded. "You may count on me. My bâtman and I will make haste. This is a task he will relish as much as me."

"Well then, I recommend you get some sleep." The duke turned to the bedroom, which adjoined his private sitting room. "I plan to do the same."

The exhaustion that had been kept at bay by sheer will came over Frederick suddenly. He went into the room that he shared with Caldwell, an arrangement they were accustomed to when campaigning. His valet was putting things in order.

"Caldwell, we leave for London tomorrow." He brought the eagles over to his portmanteau, but kept the letter in his hand. He would sleep with it. "I need not tell you that we must guard these with our life."

"No need, milord. Nothing shall happen to these beauties." His valet took the eagles with the fierce look of the patriot that he was and brought them over to his billet on the floor. Frederick was too tired to do more than wash his face and hands with the water that Caldwell had provided, remove his soiled clothes from the day and climb into bed. The letter went under the pillow. He told himself that he must wake with the dawn and trusted that he would do so, despite the fatigue.

Chapter Twenty-Nine

The trip to Ostend in their humble conveyance was indeed rough. It was the most uncomfortable journey Phoebe had ever made. On the back of the wagon with its thick wooden wheels, she was jolted back and forth until she was sure she would see bruises the next time she undressed. However, never had she appreciated a journey more. The friend they had spoken of was eager to help and, after a stop that allowed Phoebe to walk off some of the stiffness and change her dress, they served the travelers a hearty breakfast. They even offered an old barouche that was an improvement on the wagon, even if it was pulled by a hag that could not be urged into a trot.

By the time they reached Ostend, it was growing late in the afternoon. Phoebe's every muscle ached, and the bustling activity and sight of so many people overwhelmed her. She swallowed nervously, knowing herself to be quite unprotected. Tinneke insisted upon coming with her to purchase the passage, so she would not be taken advantage of or harassed in any way. Although Phoebe figured it was unlikely, she checked at the inn for her trunk but there was none waiting for her. Her dress and few possessions would have to see her back to London.

As she neared the packet boat, the occasional conversation in English that flitted across her hearing reassured her. *She was going home!* Phoebe had been able to secure a small private cabin, and she stood in front of the boat to bid farewell to Tinneke and her cousin. "I cannot thank you both enough," she said, clasping Tinneke's hands and nodding her thanks to her cousin.

"We could do no less to the one who saved my nephew." Tinneke smiled and stepped back, waving as Phoebe turned and boarded the gangplank.

A sailor looked askance at Phoebe as she stepped onto the boat, and she knew she was quite a sight. In a rumpled dress that was not entirely stain-free, unaccompanied, and with no trunk. It was then that the reality of the situation hit her. Avoiding further scrutiny, she took refuge in her cabin and found great comfort in the fact that there was a lock. She could hide there and be safe for the time it would take to reach the English coast. As the boat dipped in the waves, she sank onto the bed and prepared herself for the hours to come. The trip itself was not long, but they had to wait for the tide in order to set sail, and Phoebe had not thought to ask how long that would be.

She would face difficulties when she arrived—that she knew. If it were shocking to be dirty and unaccompanied in the Lower Countries, such a thing would be even worse in England. She would need God's favor to bring her home safely, and she did trust in His care.

She clasped her hands together tightly. *Do I trust Frederick in His care?*

The next day Frederick woke before dawn without the help of his valet, although Caldwell was already up and about, preparing the shaving kit and seeing that there was coffee coming from the hob. Every muscle ached in Frederick's body, but his mind had shaken off the fog of sleep with the monumental day that lay ahead of him. Today he would leave Brussels and return to England to announce their victory!

Today—provided she had not already left Brussels—he would tell Phoebe that he was alive and would marry her. Despite the astounding shock of the day before, this glimmer of hope was enough to bring a smile to his face.

A knock came at the entrance to the inn, and Frederick heard the door open and the voice of someone entering and announcing, "A letter for Lord Ingram."

He came out of his room, and a first-line soldier of the 33rd regiment bowed. "My lord, this letter is from Colonel Fitzwilliam."

Alive! And he has moved up in the ranks, Frederick thought. His brother-in-law well deserved it, though it was sad that it had come about because Fitz's superior officer had been killed in battle.

"Thank you." Frederick broke the seal and quickly skimmed its contents.

Ingram,

> *I am well. I am sending Ensign Kirkland to Brussels to fetch my wife so she might join me in Paris. I do not know if Phoebe is still there with her, but she will wish to go back to London if she is. Kirkland is carrying a letter to Lydia with instructions to see that Phoebe is safely on her way to London, if that is not already the case and if you are unable to see to it. I wished to apprise you of this fact since you have some interest in the matter.*

> *If you are reading this, well—then I am heartily glad of it. I am fond of you, too.*

> *Fitz*

A smile crept on Frederick's face as he folded the letter and stuck it in his coat pocket next to Lord Wellington's. He faced Ensign Kirkland.

"You may accompany Caldwell and me, for our first stop is at Colonel Fitzwilliam's house. The matter is much simpler than he knew when he penned the letter, for I intend to take Miss Tunstall back to London should she still be in Brussels, and Mrs. Fitzwilliam will be ready to go with you. We will leave in fifteen minutes."

"Yes, my lord." Ensign Kirkland stepped outside of the inn to wait for them to set out.

Frederick leaned in to Caldwell. "Go bring the man coffee and some breakfast, will you?"

They left a short while later and going at a brisk canter, it took them a little more than an hour to reach Brussels. They arrived to find the city in chaos, with wounded men pouring into the streets from the gate, and townspeople dividing their time between celebrating the news of the victory and stopping to do what they could to attend to the overwhelming needs. Frederick hoped Lydia had been wise enough to stay home and wait for news, for he could not delay his departure.

At their house on *rue des Feuilles*, he left Caldwell and the ensign with the horses and ran to the door. He opened it and stepped in the corridor, calling out, "Lydia!"

"Fred!" He heard the shriek from upstairs.

"We had the news late last night!" His sister ran down the stairs and would have fallen had she not held onto the railing. At the bottom, she leapt onto his chest and threw her arms around his neck, sobbing. "And Fitz?"

"He is alive and well. A flesh wound on his arm that I trust he is smart enough to tend to." He turned her to the door that was open to the street and gestured. "This soldier is to accompany you back to the camp, for Fitz is to march with his troops to Paris. He sent a letter to explain it all. Are you ready to go?"

"Oh yes," Lydia said, inhaling with a shuddered breath and wiping her tears. "I will need an hour at most. And the servants—"

Frederick cut her off. He had no time to listen to her preparations. "Where's Phoebe?"

"She left yesterday with Martha Cummings and her brother. She should already be on her way to Ostend. I believe they were to stay overnight at Ghent."

"Very good," Frederick said, unable to identify in himself any clear reaction to the news. Of course, he was relieved that she had made it out of the city, for should there have been a defeat he would not for the world want her in danger. But with the knowledge that she was gone came an empty disappointment from not being able to hold her as soon as he would've liked. "I trust you will know what to do with the servants and the house and everything else."

"Yes, of course. Why are you not going to Paris as well?"

"I'm carrying the news," he said.

Lydia peered outside and finally noticed Caldwell holding the

Eagles along the side of his horse, and she gasped. "Yes, you must go. Send the soldier in. I have prepared for all eventualities and he shall see how quickly I might be made ready. It shall not be said of my sex that we are slow."

Frederick squeezed his sister's hand and laughed. Never could he have imagined in their youth what strength resided in a seemingly superficial exterior. It was entirely deceiving. Their father had always been proud of her, but Frederick wished he could have seen his daughter now.

He started to leave the house but turned back. "Lydia, if you have some rough cloth, give it to me now that we might wrap the Eagles. I do not want people to know what I'm carrying."

His sister turned back to Frederick and thought for a second before darting toward the kitchen. She returned with tweed bags that were generally used to carry bread. With the help of Caldwell, Frederick wrapped the cloth around the two Eagles and tied them together, covering all but the blue staff on the bottom of the rods. That was much better.

After bidding Lydia farewell, Frederick mounted his gelding, and he and Caldwell started forward at a brisk trot, heading to the gate that led to Ghent. They would have to break their journey if they could not find a change of horses there, but he would do all in his power to be on a packet going to London by tonight. Both of them rode mounts that were fresh and that had not participated in the battle the day before. As for Salome and Caldwell's brave horse, Frederick left them in Josef's hands, who would see that they were safely brought back to England. They deserved a peaceful end to their days, grazing on the pasture at his country seat.

The road to the coast was, by stretches, in as much turmoil as the city of Brussels had been. Carriages were stuck at intervals in the mud—some with occupants still in them and others that were wholly abandoned. Occasionally, a regiment would march by them toward the city, their process slowed by the abandoned supplies. Whenever they saw Frederick, the troops would lift their hands in a greeting and salute, but they did not stop. The soldiers would still be needed in Brussels to bring everything to order.

Early in the afternoon, Frederick and Caldwell arrived at

a posting inn at Ghent. There, Frederick was able to procure a Thoroughbred stallion, negotiated at a fair rate by a Belgian patriot who was overjoyed to hear the news of their victory. It was an excellent stroke of luck; however, there was only one horse.

"Well, I guess this is it," he said to Caldwell as he drained the contents of the tankard the inn's servant had brought him. "You will have to stay with these horses and bring them back on the first boat you are able to book going to England. I will carry on with the Eagles and will meet you back in London."

"Yes, milord." Caldwell had dismounted, and he took the reins of both horses and started toward the stable inn.

Frederick had left him with more than enough coin to care for the horses' needs and his own. Now he needed to leave at once. He had to be on the first boat to England—today, if possible. He was struck by a happy thought. Perhaps he would be lucky enough to be on the same boat as Phoebe, since she had left Brussels the day before and had stopped to break her journey. He swung onto the saddle of his new mount, cheered by the possibility, and was about to urge the horse forward.

"Lord Ingram! Oh, my lord, what a happy sight you are for sore eyes. If you are here, does that mean what I think it does? Have the Allies won after all?"

Frederick had turned in his saddle and gave a curt nod. He vaguely recognized the young woman, but he did not have time to waste on idle chatter. "If you'll excuse me, I must make haste."

"Of course. It is only that Phoebe—"

Frederick had started to move forward, but at the sound of Phoebe's name he reined in. "You know Miss Tunstall? Where is she?" Caldwell also paused in his steps and turned to look.

"I don't know, my lord." This answer came from a fair-skinned gentleman, who exited the inn and stood beside the young woman. These people had to be the Cummings that Lydia told him about. "She was traveling to England with my sister and me, but she got out of the carriage on the road—against all our protests, I might add—before we arrived at Ghent. We have not seen her since."

Fear settled in Frederick's stomach like a stone. "Why did she get out of the carriage?" He could not imagine any reason strong enough for Phoebe to leave the safety of an escort and wander through the Belgian countryside alone.

"We tried with all our might to warn her," the man said.

"It was the most nonsensical thing," Miss Cummings cried out. "She saw some child, wandering on the side of the road and insisted upon helping him. She said she had to find the child's mother. We could not make her see reason."

"Why did you not bring the child into the carriage with you and assist her in finding the mother?" Frederick asked, anger pulling his mouth downward.

"We could not risk missing the packet boat—" Mr. Cummings began, but his speech died down and his skin grew mottled with embarrassment under the withering glare that Frederick shot him.

"You left a young woman to wander about a foreign country, unescorted, in your haste to save your own skin?" He let his severe gaze rest on them until the woman flushed and they both looked away.

"Caldwell," he called out. "Make inquiries. Attempt to find Miss Tunstall. Send word to my house in London if you do, and stay here until you receive word from me."

"Aye, milord."

"There's still her trunk," Mr. Cummings said. He cleared his throat. "I thought you might like to know we have her trunk."

An impotent fury seized Frederick. Phoebe had not even the sanctuary of her belongings. "Caldwell, do all that is needed."

"Aye, milord."

Frederick wheeled his horse about and urged him to a canter. As much as he would like to gallop, he knew he had to save his horse's strength if he was going to make it to Ostend today.

As he rode, Frederick ground his teeth under the constraints placed upon him. He could not abandon his mission to save Phoebe. For all he knew, she might have come to grief, but what could he do? He had no choice but to bring the Eagles and the letter to Lord Bathurst—to do his duty as a patriot. That came first. Once that duty was just discharged, nothing in all creation would stop him from returning to find her.

If only he might not be too late.

Chapter Thirty

*F*rederick arrived in Ostend as evening set in. He found the stables attached to the posting inn near the docks and brought his newly-acquired horse there. He made arrangements to have the Thoroughbred stabled at the inn until Caldwell could come and reclaim him. The packet boat was still attached to the dock, which was a stroke of luck as he hadn't been sure when it would set sail. When Frederick went to book a passage there were no more cabins to be had, but that was of little importance. All that mattered was that when the boat set sail, he would be on it—and that once they docked in England—he would continue his journey to London with all possible speed. Lord Bathurst would be waiting in daily expectation for news, and how fortunate it was that Frederick brought something *better* than news. He had the Eagles and the letter detailing their victory.

It was not until after midnight that the boat set sail, allowing Frederick more time than he would have liked to sit and think. He was glad for his foresight to drape burlap over the Eagles and conceal what they were. Although the sight of them was more likely to bring cheers, he did not trust unscrupulous men who might try to steal them for their own advantage. Now that Frederick was on his own without his bâtman, he had to be even more careful.

The tide was in their favor, but there was little breeze, and it almost seemed as though the boat was suspended on the waves rather than rushing him closer to England. Frederick chose a spot on the deck, leaning up against the rails, with the Eagles set behind him. As the wind picked up, it lifted the locks of hair from his damp brow.

He could not afford to let his guard down, but the absence of activity made it hard for Frederick to stay awake. He was thankful when someone came and offered him something to drink and eat, and he handed over a few coins in exchange. It would pass the time and keep him awake—and he *was* hungry.

Having eaten, Frederick felt his strength renewed, but his thoughts remained somber. It ought to be an unalloyed victory. He would go down in history, perhaps, as the man who had brought back the news of victory. But with Phoebe missing it could be no victory at all. What good was it for him to have kept his country safe if he could not even protect the woman he loved? These reflections oppressed him like a band around his skull, as though he were wearing a hat that was too tight. One benefit of being in motion—of riding like the wind on his Thoroughbred—was that these thoughts did not harass him. When he was still, the worry over her safety nipped and snarled at him, oversetting his peace.

The sky had turned pink by the time the welcome shouts came signaling that the boat had neared land. Frederick reached down and grasped the Eagles and stood, his hand on the railing. He watched the port of Ramsgate grow nearer, finally making his way to the spot on the boat where the gangplank would be extended to shore. All he knew was that he had to be the first one to disembark. Nothing must hinder him from hiring the best horse he could find and hurrying to London.

The boat angled toward the dock, and someone on the deck threw a rope to pull the boat in. Frederick shifted on his feet, his eyes fixated ahead on the street where he knew a reliable stable could be found. The minute the gate was opened, he hurried down the gangplank and leapt onto English soil. He strode to the posting inn, and as he walked into the stable yard, gave orders for the swiftest horse they had. Servants from the inn approached to offer him meat pastries and ale, but he shook his head.

"You there," he shouted to the stable hand, who was still not moving fast enough for Frederick's liking. The lad was still in the courtyard, instead of rushing into the stable to harness a horse. "There is a reward for you if you hurry."

At this, the boy did rush into the stable, and Frederick turned his head, attempting to garner his patience. His gaze was caught by the passengers disembarking from the boat. There was an English family, who had likely fled Brussels, if the thankful look on the woman's face could be read correctly. An older gentleman assisted his wife down the gangplank. Behind them, was a young woman of unkempt but genteel appearance, whose face was down as she crossed the gangplank. It was not easy to make her out in the dim light of dawn, but . . .

Surely his eyes deceived him. Frederick took two steps forward, his heart beating in his throat.

"Milord, your horse."

Without removing his gaze from the woman, Frederick called over his shoulder, "In a minute!"

It could not be! Such a thing was *impossible*, but—as surely as he lived—it was Phoebe. She stepped off the gangplank and took a minute to steady herself. Her face was as white as a sheet, and her dress was soiled. Her hair was disheveled underneath her bonnet.

"Phoebe!" he shouted.

She looked up in surprise, then shock. Frederick dropped what he was holding and darted past the people in his path as he ran to her. She cried out, "Fred!"

He reached Phoebe, just as she seemed about to fall into a faint, and he circled his arms around her, lifting her up. Phoebe did not faint but threw her arms around his neck and held on. Frederick did not look at her—he could not. His eyes were closed, and tears leaked from their corners. And he could feel Phoebe shaking in his arms. The unexpectedness of seeing her, coupled with her closeness deprived him of all rational thought. Neither spoke for several moments. At last, he pulled back just enough to look at her.

Her white face now had two spots of red in her cheeks, and her eyes were shining as she absorbed the sight of his face. She reached up to touch his bristled cheeks. "You're alive." Phoebe's voice was faint. "You must forgive me. I believe . . . I believe I am in a state of shock."

At that moment, Frederick was incapable of speech. He leaned down and kissed her, not caring one whit who saw them or that they were in the middle of a crowd of people milling by. He cradled Phoebe's face in his hands, cherishing the gift that God had brought back to him, and she returned his kisses with as much passion, her arms now around his chest, holding him tight.

It was not propriety that yanked them apart but the bolt of reality—and panic. Frederick had let the Eagles fall to the ground in his haste to see Phoebe, and he was in danger of failing his country by losing them. As quickly as he could, and without letting go of Phoebe, he raced with her back into the stable yard. She asked no questions but seemed to sense his urgency and went with him readily.

"Forgive me," he said. When he entered the courtyard to the inn, he nearly sank to his knees with relief. There they were. The Eagles rested on the ground, the cloth bag still wrapped around them, not far from where the stable hand was standing with the horse. No one had thought to see what they were.

Not wishing to release Phoebe, Frederick briefly slipped his hand from her waist and reached down to pick up the Eagles, then turned to face her.

"My love." He leaned his forehead against hers and whispered. "We have won. I am to bring the Eagles back to London, along with a note from Wellington to the Secretary at War. I've had the fastest horse in the stable harnessed, and I must go. I cannot accompany you back to London, and it tears my heart to leave you behind—"

He was not able to finish from the sudden lump in this throat, but Phoebe shook her head earnestly, her forehead still pressed to his. "You must go without me. Of course, you must. I shall be fine."

Frederick pulled back to look at her face, and his heart nearly burst at her bravery—at the beauty of Phoebe's soul. He glanced at the stable hand, holding the horse, then made a quick decision. "You there. Keep the horse for me. I will be but a moment." Frederick strode forward, his arm still around Phoebe as he led her to the inn. "You *shall* be fine, and I will see to it."

When they were in the public dining area, he called to the innkeeper, who was just coming from the kitchen. "I am Lord Ingram," he announced. "Do you have a private parlor to let?"

"Yes, my lord. Shall I prepare one for you and your . . ." His voice trailed away as he took in Phoebe's appearance.

"This is my fiancée, Miss Tunstall. We have just arrived on the boat from the Lower Countries, where the Allies have been engaged in war, as I am sure you must have heard. Miss Tunstall has endured much in her journey back to England." Frederick looked around at the interested faces. "But I think I might better explain it all to you in the privacy of your parlor."

"Of course, my lord." He led the way to one of the doors on the other side of the dining area and opened it, ushering them into a pleasant room with rose bushes visible, climbing up the wall outside the window. The innkeeper gestured to the room with a proud flourish. "I trust this will be suitable. How may I assist you, my lord?"

Frederick kept his arm around Phoebe, pulling her tight. "Do you have a wife? If so, I would like to meet her."

The innkeeper bowed and left at once, returning with a woman who satisfied Frederick with her air of neatness and capability. She curtsied to Frederick. "Good morning, my lord." Without batting an eye at Phoebe's appearance, she curtsied to her as well. "Good afternoon, miss."

"I am unable to escort Miss Tunstall back to London, for I have an urgent duty to discharge. However, I want no expense spared for her comfort. She will need a maid who can accompany her the entire way to London, as well as a suitable change of clothing. I must have a note sent to my valet on the Continent as well. May I leave all this in your hands?"

The innkeeper's wife curtsied. "I will see that no harm befalls your fiancée, my lord. I know who I might trust to accompany her to London."

"Very good." Frederick said. "If Miss Tunstall's journey to London is peaceful and unhindered by any worries thanks to your care, I will send an additional expression of my gratitude by post."

The innkeeper exchanged a glance with his wife. "Yes, my lord," he said with another bow.

His wife drew herself upright. "It is very kind of you, my lord. But even without that, I will see to it that Miss is not plagued by any worries."

The couple left them alone, shutting the door behind them, and Frederick knew he had only a moment to spare. He went to lean the

Eagles against the wall and came over to hold Phoebe in his arms, looking at her gravely.

"I saw Mr. and Miss Cummings in Ghent. They said you had gone off without an escort. I cannot tell you what torture it was to not know whether any harm had come to you—to be unable to go in search of you."

"I could not leave that boy alone," Phoebe replied. "I did find his family, and they were the ones who brought me to Ostend. We traveled overnight in the wagon."

He brought his fingers up to graze her cheeks. He could not get enough of her soft skin and the sight of her face. "Of course you could not leave him. That is not who you are. You, Phoebe, are a most courageous, intrepid, beautiful"—he placed a soft kiss on her lips—"kind-hearted woman. And I cannot wait to claim you as my bride."

She had tilted her face up to his in such a charming way, he could not resist giving her another kiss to which she responded most adorably.

She broke off with a sharp breath. "Fitz! I almost forgot. Have you seen him?"

Frederick nodded. "He is well. I returned to Brussels with a soldier who was to accompany Lydia to meet her husband. Fitz must go with his regiment to Paris."

Phoebe smiled and breathed out a sigh of relief. "Ah, that is good news indeed. They will be reunited. It was all that Lydia wished for—even if it means she is not yet to return to London. I don't believe she will care for that, however." As if inspired by Lydia and Fitz's reunion, she tucked herself more closely into Frederick's grasp.

"Is it still good news, though it means our wedding must certainly be delayed until they return from Paris?" Frederick added, his eyebrow raised.

"I am willing to wait as long as we need just to have your sister at our wedding," Phoebe said. She had finally stopped trembling and seemed to grow comfortable in his arms, just as he needed to leave her.

"I am not so generous," Frederick retorted and kissed her once more. This kiss had to be the last one for today. He had to fulfill the mission that had been given to him.

He forced himself to break away and put his hands on her shoulders. "When you arrive in London, if I know Stratford, he will be at his townhouse, waiting for you. If for some reason he is not there, come to me. *I* will be waiting for you. But now—" Frederick tucked a strand of hair that had fallen into her face back behind her ears—"I must go."

"You must." Phoebe smiled and stepped away. "There are people waiting in great suspense to hear the news. They will need to know we have been victorious. Go and give it to them."

"And you, my darling—my *daring* Phoebe," he said. "I will be waiting in great suspense until you are safely with me in London."

"Oh, someone as daring as I could hardly fear something so ordinary as a journey to London," she teased.

"Then I will wait in great suspense until you are safely in my arms." As though in anticipation, he wrapped his arms around her, kissed her forehead, then her lips, then strode out of the room.

Chapter Thirty-One

Mary put a final pin in the wreath of tiny white flowers that formed a crown in Phoebe's hair then stepped back. "You look a picture, miss." She had been Phoebe's maid in the months since the Battle of Waterloo, ever since she had arrived with Sam, Sarah, and whatever possessions Lydia had not brought with her to Paris.

Phoebe smiled at her maid in the reflection of the glass, then stood. She turned to face Anna who sat on the bed, holding their baby girl, Jane. Her sister's eyes filled with tears, which was not entirely unexpected. After all, Anna had just presented Harry Aston with his second child and was—as she termed it—a regular watering pot.

Laying the sleeping baby gently on the bed, Anna came over and made a few minor adjustments to Phoebe's gown, which was in the palest blue and trimmed with Belgian white lace. "I predict that Ingram will be too speechless at the sight of you to pronounce his vows."

"That will not be very practical, will it?" Phoebe chuckled. She took a deep breath, tugged her gloves on more securely and smoothed the front of her gown. "I suppose we must go, or we will be late."

Anna went over to take Jane in her arms. "If Ingram is not already accustomed to having to wait with Lydia for a sister, then he shall learn quickly enough."

Phoebe smiled, though it seemed as though her nerves had sprouted wings and fluttered in her stomach. "I am sure Frederick is the most patient man alive—except for your saintly rector," she added with wry humor. However, I am not sure it is fair to ask the same of St. Helen's vicar."

"Very true. Not every man of the cloth is granted the saintly patience of my husband," Anna said with mock pride, although Phoebe knew deep down she meant it. "Lydia and Eleanor are waiting downstairs, and Stratford has gone to see about the carriage."

"Where is Fitz?" Phoebe asked, turning and taking the tiny reticule Mary handed her which contained the barest essentials.

"I believe he is already at the church. I saw him patting the pocket of his waistcoat to make sure he had the rings." Mary opened the door, and Anna followed Phoebe into the corridor. "That was after Lydia called out the reminder, of course."

When Phoebe entered the drawing room, Eleanor stood and came over to her. "Oh, Phoebe." She let out a soft laugh as tears filled her eyes. "You look magnificent."

Her child, Sophie, was sitting on a blanket next to the couch, sucking on a wooden toy, then banging it on the floor. Chubby legs poked out from under her dress. Anna's son Peter lay on his stomach at her feet and handed Sophie a different toy, attempting to attract her notice. He was attached to his little cousin, who laughed at him, whereas his sister he barely deigned to notice. "All she does is eat and sleep," he informed his father in disgust.

Lydia got to her feet, which was not an easy matter as she was growing close to her confinement. Her expression was lit with the deep joy that had seemed to infuse her since their recent arrival in London, what with her impending confinement and the happy event of seeing her brother married at last. Fitz had accompanied his regiment to Paris, and although he was not the first to be allowed to come home, they had finally been granted leave. The Fitzwilliams had arrived in London just a week earlier, and as Frederick had wasted no time in posting the banns upon his own arrival, he wasted no time in seeing that they were wed.

"It was much to my relief that I learned the news that Fitz was being sent back to London," Lydia had said, when in the company of women. "As much as I am confident of the skills of French midwives, I prefer not to have to communicate in a foreign tongue while writhing in the agonies of labor."

"I don't think it will matter very much what language you speak," Anna had responded wryly. "Shrieks are a language universal to women." Eleanor had only chuckled and bounced Sophie on her lap.

"You look very fine, Phoebe," Harry said as he entered the drawing room. He took his daughter in his arms and held out his hand to Peter. "How would you like to ride on the box seat with me and John-Coachman?"

"Oh, would I!" Their son forgot his baby cousin and took his father's hand.

There were two carriages. One of them belonged to Stratford, and he helped Lydia into it and then Eleanor, who had Sophie in her arms. Phoebe would be riding with her sister's family. Only Anna and the baby sat inside the carriage with Phoebe, as Harry and Peter had gone to sit on the box seat with the coachman. They did not say much, but Anna held out her hand and Phoebe put hers into it.

"I am glad we have these few minutes to ourselves. You really are the dearest sister to me. It did not require the fear of you coming to harm in Brussels for me to realize that." Anna squeezed Phoebe's hand.

Phoebe leaned over and kissed Anna's cheek, then planted another kiss on top of Jane's head, who squirmed and let out a small cry before falling asleep again. "You are lucky she still sleeps," Anna murmured. "We do not want our dearest baby to wail throughout the ceremony."

In a short while, their carriage pulled up in front of the old church. Frederick and Phoebe had decided this was to be a family wedding. No guests who were not immediate family would be invited. For one thing, it had been arranged rather suddenly since they did not know when Lydia and Fitz would return from Paris. For another, despite the satisfaction of the war coming to an end, there were enough sober post-war issues that required Frederick's attention. He found he was not in the mood for a wedding on a large scale. Phoebe assured him she did not mind in the least.

Frederick had not been idle since his arrival from Brussels. There were soldiers returning from the war, many of them wounded and unable to find work other than soldiering which was no longer needed. Frederick had been doing what he could to bring up the issue in Parliament and have provisions made for them. No one knew more strongly than he how much they deserved it. But since Fitz's return, he had put that aside for a time in his eagerness to be married.

When they entered the quiet church, Phoebe could see Frederick waiting for her in the front. He stood with the vicar, with Fitz at his side, and even from far away, she could see the smile that lit his face at the sight of her. Her heart leapt. She wanted to run to him, but Stratford restrained her steps with a gentle touch on her arm. She looked up at him.

"Mother and Father would have been happy today. I am sure of it. They would be content in the knowledge that each one of us had found someone truly worthy—someone we loved with all our hearts. They were willing to put aside the opinion of the ton so they might be wed, and their marriage was a happy one. We each have found all of the passion and endured none of the sacrifice." Stratford smiled down at her and patted her arm. "I believe that is all they would have wanted for us."

Phoebe blinked away the tears that were a mix of nostalgia and joy and grasped the small bouquet she held in her free hand. Its fragrance and colors seemed to breathe life into the antique stones of the church. Stratford's daughter banged her toy on the wooden pew before Eleanor could stop her, and the vicar smiled benevolently at the child, despite the noise. Life was so rich—so tender and complex—so abundantly full of mercies and grace.

"I see Ingram beginning to look anxious," Stratford said. "Let us put him out of his misery, shall we?"

Phoebe met Frederick's gaze from afar and nodded. Stratford led her up the long aisle, their slippered feet noiseless on the stone floor. Frederick waited for her, his hands clasped in front of him. He did not take his eyes off his bride as she approached, nor did he remove his gaze when she came to stand at his side. The significance of the moment was reflected in his eyes, and she saw him swallow. It reassured her. *He is as nervous as I am.*

The ceremony was short, filled with noble instructions and sweet oaths, before the vicar pronounced them man and wife. Phoebe peeked up at Frederick, and he kissed her soundly on the lips to the loud cheers of their family members. The young vicar seemed to appreciate the exuberance because he made no sounds of reproach but smiled broadly and bent down to speak to Peter.

"Lady Ingram," Frederick murmured, smiling down at her. "How well it suits you."

"I find that I am of the same mind," Phoebe replied.

They walked toward the entrance of the church, where Ingram had arranged for a private carriage to carry just the two of them. It would take them to the wedding breakfast at Stratford's house, where they would celebrate with those who were dearest to them. After the breakfast, the carriage would bring them to Frederick's London house before they set out to spend the holidays at his country seat.

Christmas was only one month away, and the longing to be reunited was universal and strong enough that all four couples were arguing about which of them would host the others for this first holiday as a true, extended family. Frederick had been determined to win this bout and said he thought that Lydia should be confined in the place where she had grown up—and with the nurse who had cared for her as a child, despite the fact that Nurse was getting on in years. This argument had seemed to win everyone over.

The happy thoughts of the day ahead of them, and the weeks ahead—even the years—crowded in Phoebe's brain until she had no room for anything else. She was fully occupied with being happy and was determined to drink in every last ounce of it.

Frederick closed the door to the carriage, and they were alone at last. He tapped on the roof for the coachman to move forward.

As the carriage jolted into motion, he looked over at Phoebe and gave her a private smile. "I find you are much too far away."

She returned his look, fighting to keep an innocent expression. "But I am sitting right next to you."

"You are still too far, wife." Frederick reached over and, in one movement, pulled Phoebe so that she was sitting sideways in his lap, her legs dangling on the edge of the seat, and it only made sense for her to put her arms around his neck. She knew her face must be scarlet with embarrassment, but she could not help but laugh with pleasure.

"I shall be all mussed when we arrive. People will wonder what happened."

"I promise to be very careful. I shall only muss your lips." Frederick kissed her. "And since they are already as red as a ripe fruit, no one shall be the wiser."

"Well," Phoebe said, sighing deeply. "I suppose I cannot argue with that."

Acknowledgments

Dear Reader,

I've read about the Battle of Waterloo in the past, and even stayed with Belgian friends who live across from the hill where the battle was fought. I wish I had known then that I would one day write about it. I would have insisted on a tour. I've been told that the Château of Hougoumont, riddled with shot, is still standing.

For these past five months, I've been plunged into the stories surrounding Waterloo and the city of Brussels in the months leading up to it. I go to bed and wake up thinking about the stories. Since I live in France and am a citizen by marriage, the French are not my enemy. It's not the Allies vanquishing Napoleon that excites me so much as the stories of humans conquering their foes, whether it be a physical enemy on the ridge across from them, or simply the fear to step outside one's comfort zone, as was the case for Phoebe.

Fans of William Thackeray and Georgette Heyer—particularly Heyer—will recognize the influence of those greats in my book, although I fought to tell my own story. I felt my book needed the trip by canal boat, the picnic lunch overlooking the valley, and the wounded soldiers returning to Brussels in order for it to be properly told. My hero needed to be a member of Wellington's staff so he would have a bird's eye view on the battles. I present my apologies to those who might feel even those scenes trespassed upon the novels that came before me.

Many of Lord Wellington's quotes came from my research, as did the seasoned veteran's quote to the raw recruit when the British cavalry fled from the cuirassiers. Most of the events that you read about during the battles of Quatre Bras and Waterloo happened in a similar manner to how I've told them. Private Brewster really did drive a tumbril of ammunition to Hougoumont, and a man really did get saved from a bullet by a silk handkerchief in his coat. (My son really did wander off on a French country road to see the cows). However, apart from a few direct quotes, the historical figures I included in my book were molded to suit my purposes. This remains a work of fiction.

My knowledge was derived—along with countless pages of online reading and historical maps of Brussels and Waterloo—from the following books:

The Sharpe Companion, Mark Adkin
Redcoat, Richard Holmes
The Regency Years, Robert Morrison
Our Tempestuous Day, Carolly Erickson
High Society in the Regency Period, Venetia Murray
Dancing Into Battle, a download from The Goodwood Estate

(And to a lesser degree, or for world building):

An Infamous Army, Georgette Heyer
Vanity Fair, William Makepeace Thackeray
Regency London, Stella Margetson
Le Grognard Putigny, Bob Putigny

The latter book tells of an illiterate peasant who went off to fight for Napoleon for twenty-three years. He lived through the beheading of Louis XVI, fought against the royalists, campaigned on the Peninsula, escaped Russia with his life barely intact, and ended his career at Wavre against the Prussians the day before Waterloo. He learned to read and write, was made Baron of the Empire by Napoleon himself, and left a memoir of his life for us to read two hundred years later.

A very special thanks to my dear friends and critique partners: Jess Heileman, Arlem Hawks, Julie Christianson, and Emma Le Noan. This book would not be what it is without you. Thank you to Christophe and Geneviève Lépinois for your tour of Brussels all those years ago, including the visit to the one remaining canal there, and for your recent help in better understanding Belgian history. Thank you, Tinne De Beckker—Tinneke, in honor of your dad—for all the Dutch help. Your collective advice, critiques, and information was invaluable. A special thanks to my editors: Rachel Hathcock and Heather Holm. I also want to thank Cedar Fort for being so amazing to work with. You've been patient with all my requests and have gone the extra mile to create gorgeous covers, audiobooks, and do everything to make this series a success.

A Daring Proposal seems a fitting end to the Tunstall, Ingram, Aston, and Fitzwilliam families, even if it's hard to say goodbye. As the sweetness of life is often tempered by its sorrows, these families would grapple with the sight of soldiers returning from Belgium by the thousands. With many missing limbs and no prospects for employment, they would be forced to beg on the London streets. Our heroes and heroines would witness the injustices brought about by those fixing the prices of grain in Parliament (which Jack Blythefield fought against in *Philippa Holds Court*), and would be horrified by news of the Peterloo Massacre, where people rose up to protest the high price of bread and were run down by British cavalry.

But the Tunstalls, the Astons, the Ingrams, and the Fitzwilliams are a compassionate crew, and they would bring all the relief in their power to those in distress, while celebrating the blessings of marriage and children—the sweet pleasures that are theirs—and enjoying life to the full.

They seldom reflect on the days of their life, because God keeps them occupied with gladness of heart.

—Ecclesiastes 5:20

About the Author

Photo by Caroline Aoustin

Jennie Goutet is an American-born Anglophile who lives with her French husband and their three children in a small town outside Paris. Her imagination resides in Regency England, where her romance *A Regrettable Proposal* is set. Jennie is author of the award-winning memoir *Stars Upside Down* and the modern romance *A Noble Affair*. A Christian, a cook, and an inveterate klutz, Jennie writes about faith, food, and life—even the clumsy moments—on her blog, aladyinfrance.com. You can learn more about Jennie and her books on her author website, jenniegoutet.com.

Scan to visit

jenniegoutet.com   aladyinfrance.com